Holidays mark the passage of time in a way that synchronizes the calendar kept by the heart with the one kept by the head. More than just dates, holidays are intersections of memory and emotion, annual snapshots of who we are as we travel through life—and who we're travelling with. Holidays remind us of who we want to share special moments with, and of those without whom the moments aren't quite as special.

Julian Keys shows us how the quest to discover a secret love restores a cynic's hope, how a moment of compassion turns a thief into a hero, how sympathy for the Devil can lead to a happy ending, and how a multicultural celebration opens the way for even the most unlikely unions.

Cold Days, Hot Nights shares four tales of holidays that become turning points in life and love for people who have lost faith inthemselves, in each other, and in romance. From Halloween to Christmas to Valentine's Day, Keys' stories show how not simply the feeling of love, but the willingness to risk pain to be open to the possibilities love offers, can change a person's life in wonderful ways.

Also recommended...

The Keys to Romance, by Julian Keys

In this volume, award-winning author Julian Keys gives us seven love stories where sharing is caring, truth is daring, and a one night stand might last forever. Witness the evolution of the human heart, students on the market for romance, lovers cooking up something special, and a beautiful photographer realizing his big dreams. Take up the Keys to Romance, and unlock worlds of love.

Liquid Longing, by Annabeth Leong

From Annabeth Leong's penetrating view of the sensual, the sacred, and the profane comes an anthology of erotic tales of wonder. Passion flows, mercurial, through these eleven tales of sex, death, and rebirth. For every dark soul pining for something beyond their grasp, there is a moment of ecstasy to tantalize the heart and mind. Come, immerse yourself in Liquid Longing.

Cold Days, Hot Nights

A Romantic Anthology for the Holidays

Julian Keys

ForbiddenFiction
www.forbiddenfiction.com

an imprint of

Fantastic Fiction Publishing
www.fantasticfictionpublishing.com

COLD DAYS, HOT NIGHTS

A ForbiddenFiction book

Fantastic Fiction Publishing Hayward, California

© Julian Keys, 2017

CREDITS
Editors: D.M. Atkins and Lon Sarver
Cover Designer: Siolnatine
Inside Cover Designer: Siolnatine
Cover Photo: Adapted from photos by solominviktor at Shutterstock.
Inside Cover Art: Photos by Fcscafeine and Konstantynov and Martinmark at Dreamstime. Photos by Kiselev Andrey Valerevich and Yuricazac and kiuikson at Shutterstock.
Production Editor: Kaye O'Malley
Proofreading: Erika L Firanc and Evron Malaika Teig
Font: Wellrock Slab, by Manfred Klein

SKU: -T13-1.100017-1 FFP
ISBN: 978-1-62234-340-9

Published in the United States of America

DISCLAIMER

Contents

Preface
Love Among the Holidays

My romance with holiday tales began, appropriately enough, with a Valentine's Day story contest. I decided to enter, and at first, all I focused on was making sure there were plenty of references to poetry and paper hearts. I soon realized, however, that the paraphernalia of the holiday wasn't going to make this a Valentine's Day story. If I wanted to achieve that, I had to make sure that this romance could not have happened on any other day.

I changed the story around, giving the holiday the respect it deserved. The results were a prize for the story, and an addiction to holiday romances, particularly widely celebrated holidays where cities and towns put up special decorations, stores sell special items, and neighborhoods plan special events. Holidays, as it turns out, are incredibly romantic and that's not just the romance writer in me talking. In the United States more marriage proposals happen during the winter holidays of Christmas, New Year's and Valentine's.

Why? Because lovers want to declare their devotion at a singular, memorable moment and holidays are exactly that. Coming but once a year, each holiday is dressed up in a unequaled way and offers a lover not only an extraordinary setting for a proposal, but rare treats and traditions. The magic of a holiday, in short, mirrors the magic of love.

This is certainly why I love holidays and have written upwards of five romances celebrating them—four of them in this anthology. But wait, there's more! In the days before and during a big holiday, it's that much easier for complete strangers to meet, connect, and engage. Normally, a woman would never invite a man she'd just met to join her for dinner at her parent's house, but, as in *The Many-Colored Lantern*, she'll feel it safe to do just that during the Yuletide holidays. It being the season of welcome and gift-giving, she might even think it right. Similarly, in *By Traveler's Moon*, Halloween events allow strangers to meet and flirt in ways that wouldn't have been possible if not for the costumed carnival atmosphere.

And if the lovers are not strangers? Holidays, with their heightened feelings often reveal the truth about relationships. In *An Act of Charity* a woman's romance with Christmastime has her questioning her romantic feelings for the men in her life. In *Valentine Prayers*, that first holiday story I wrote, the cautious hero is wooed into re-examining Valentine's Day and his conflicted feelings about love. In both of these stories, finding the true meaning of the holiday helps the characters to discover true love. Which, I suppose, is the heart and soul of such stories. Our feelings about a holiday are often as complicated and powerful as our feelings for someone we love, or have loved, or want to love.

In the day-to-day of the year, it's hard to believe in love. During those brief, magical times of the year, however, it's easy. That's what makes the holidays so very special, and so very romantic, and why I'm certain that you'll find renewed "love" for the holidays in these romances.

Julian Keys

Valentine Prayers

Chapter 1
A Blue Heart

Wade found it hard to do what his heart told him to do. It was pastel blue and floating on the thick foam of his latte. It said: "Be True."

"Hokey, I know," Nora said from the other side of the counter. "But it is Valentine's Day."

"It certainly is," Wade sighed, fishing the candy heart out and onto a paper napkin.

"My brother's brilliant idea to put candy hearts in every drink," Nora smirked fondly at her sibling, Eddie, who was on a ladder fiddling with the coffee house speakers. "He's a romantic."

Wade, who was taking a sip of the latte, twitched at the word, getting foam all over his beard. "Fuck."

Nora laughed and handed him more paper napkins. She was cute as a button this morning, as always. Wade had a long running crush on Nora. Today, however, he found it painful to look at her. From her strawberry sweater with its decoupage of fabric hearts to her clever bow-and-arrow earrings to the heart-shaped rhinestone clip holding back her honey brown bangs, she was too much of a reminder of the day.

He could no more gaze on her than he could take in the valentines and cupids decorating the coffee house walls. He kept his eyes, instead, on the plaque behind the counter, which quoted the aria from Bach's Kaffee-Kantate: *Lovelier than a thousand kisses, sweeter far than muscatel wine! I must have my coffee.* Now that was romantic.

"At least candy hearts are short and sweet," Nora relentlessly went on. "I hate it when guys drag out all that wine and roses stuff, like they're laying bait for a trap."

He winced. "You don't have a sweetheart for the evening, then?"

"Hell, yes. But there's no reason he should have to read me *poetry* if he wants to get laid." She loudly emphasized the word "poetry" while gazing up at her brother. Eddie paused in his fiddling to give her the finger.

1

"His idea." Nora touched on the stack of fliers announcing tonight's "Romantic Poetry" evening featuring classic as well as original love poems. She rolled her pretty brown eyes. "He's promised to take care of everything and he'd better."

"I'm not into poetry," Wade lied. "Have a good morning," he added, clipping a plastic lid onto his latte.

"Happy Valentine's Day," she wished him.

He didn't wish it back. Any other holiday he could give as good as he got, but not this one. Leaving the warmth and light of the coffee house he pushed out into February's cold shadow. The old town mall was sugared over from last night's storm; virgin snow piled up before storefronts and on benches. It was still dark and the streetlamps glowed. Wade's breath clouded out before him along with the steam rising from the little slot in the lid of his coffee cup. He glanced at the display windows as he passed, seeing cupids, roses and heart decorations, as well as his own reflection.

His ghostly image showed a solidly built man with straight, maple brown hair and a close trimmed beard. In his sheepskin coat and heavy boots, he gave off a mountain-man vibe. Ironic because he was far from being a macho man.

That was the whole problem, he mused, as he made his way to the small bookstore occupying the second-to-last space on the three-block mall. In the bay window was a pyramid display of new and used books: Books on relationships. Books on chocolate desserts. Romance novels. Sonnets. The door was unlocked. Wade's assistant, Linda, who had created the window display, had gotten there before him.

The local public radio station was on and Frank Sinatra, singing of love, wafted between the shelves, but the heat hadn't been turned up yet and the little fireplace hadn't been lit. The store was icy cold. Even so, Wade sighed with relief as he shut the door behind him. The bookstore with its cozy furniture, Indian rugs and dark wood cases was more home to him than his empty apartment.

"Meow!" Ralph, the bookstore cat, came trotting up to greet him. Ralph was a hefty, black and white with a loud purr and an endearing way of rolling at customers' feet. Wade bent to give that fluffy tummy a rub.

"Good morning, Ralph," he murmured then, to the room at large. "Morning! Did those signed copies arrive?"

"All put away," Linda appeared from the stacks. Her Rubenesque curves were outlined by a scarlet sweater and pink jeans. As she flipped back her dark, shiny hair, Wade found himself swallowing in a dry throat. He'd been two years without a woman and lately he'd begun to really feel it. Linda loved books as much as he did and she'd broken up with her last boyfriend some three months ago. Granted, they were boss and employee, but maybe it was time to change that relationship? See if they could be more? He ought to offer, at least. No woman should have to be alone on Valentine's Day.

"Can I leave work early," Linda asked, even as Wade opened his mouth. "I've a date tonight."

Wade felt his heart pause. "Really?" his emotions sunk. "Good for you. Um. Sure."

"Thanks." She snatched up the glass teakettle from its hot plate. "Paperwork for those books is on your desk."

So much for that. Wade stepped over Ralph, got off his gloves, scarf, and jacket. Sipping at his cooling latte, he scanned his desk. The paperwork was there, right under his desktop screen, and something else as well.

"What the fuck is this?" He didn't mean to snap, but it came out that way.

"What's what?" Linda shouted from the bathroom.

"This, Goddamnit!"

Linda reappeared, the water-filled pot in hand. "What?"

"This," he said in a quieter tone and pointed to an envelope. It was petal pink and sealed with a green heart sticker.

Linda shrugged, set the pot on the hot plate and flicked it on. "I didn't put that there."

"Well who did?"

Another shrug as she got out the box of teas. "I've been shelving books for half-an-hour. Someone must have snuck in." She held up two different packets. "Which is more romantic? Roses and jasmine green or strawberry black?"

"Neither," he said, dropping into his chair. "If you lift up the false bottom on the box, you'll find a stash of white chocolate herbal chai."

"Really? Yum. That *is* romantic."

"Hmm," Wade was still glowering at the envelope. He thought about chucking it into the trash. "Fuck."

"I don't see what the big deal is." Linda opened the packet and, as the water started to steam, brewed up the tea. Its spicy-sweet fragrance filled the store. "So someone left you a valentine. You can't expect the world to know you don't want one."

"Doesn't mean I have to like it," Wade grumbled. He didn't think he'd get any sympathy. He'd told Linda why, but she hadn't known him before, so she couldn't really understand. Valentine's Day was the day that he'd lost his heart. The day he'd lost his faith. The day he'd lost himself.

Three years ago, Wade would have described himself as a born romantic. His working class background notwithstanding, he'd always been a sensitive male and by high school he'd earned the nickname, "Romeo." He was the type who would bring a thermos of hot cocoa to share with his girlfriend, or leave her mushy messages in a bottle. He gave girls silver pendants engraved with quotes from love songs and, as if that wasn't enough, he liked to read classic tales of the heart: *Wuthering Heights, Cyrano de Bergerac, Doctor Zhivago*. He devoured D.H. Lawrence. Then he discovered poetry and completely lost his soul, from Solomon's *Song of Songs* to Omar Khayyam and beyond. He was especially fond of sonnet sequences, those series of poems about love found and won and lost again. He read Sidney's *Astrophel and Stella*, Daniels's *Delia* and, of course, *Sonnets from the Portuguese*.

Other guys razzed him, but come Valentine's Day, they always asked him for amorous ideas, and a good poem to write up in a card for their girl. Valentine's, of course, was Wade's holy day. Especially when he got to college and realized that modern ladies had a cynical bent. They might yearn for romance, sigh over its portrayal in novels and films, but when faced with it for real, they often balked. A man on his knees embarrassed them. Poetry bored them, and too many were allergic to flowers.

On Valentine's Day, however, Wade could get away with just about anything—balloons, string quartets, decadent desserts. It was the one day when he could go over-the-top, be as theatrically demonstrative as he yearned to be. It wasn't only accepted, it was expected.

Or so he'd naively assumed. And then he'd met Joyce. Joyce was a serious, blond accountant with a mind sharp as a tack. It was hard now to remember exactly what he'd seen in her, but there'd certainly been the attraction of opposites: she cool, he warm, she fierce in bed, he gentle. She'd lived in the present, aware and sure. For a man like Wade, lost in time, that had been irresistible, like finding a loadstone.

The only problem: Joyce was a pragmatist, every hour of every day, no exceptions. Wade's first try at Valentine's Day had been a disaster. When she'd found out they were dining in a snowy park, she'd been horrified.

"You're joking," is all she'd managed, staring at the picnic supper, candles, wine and flowers. She'd eaten the meal, but she'd huddled in her goose down jacket, her expression sour the whole time.

His attempt to go low-key on their second Valentine's by reading her poetry in bed hadn't fared much better. Wade had never given up hope, however, that romance would win out. Maybe that's what had kept him infatuated with Joyce, the challenge she posed. Why, for their third Valentine's he'd gone so far as to buy a ring with the intention of asking her to marry him.

To this day he could still feel the butterflies of anticipation that he'd experienced planning for that Valentine's Day, as well as the disappointment because he knew he wasn't going to be able to go down on one knee as he'd always romantically dreamed. That wouldn't fly with Joyce. Before February 14th even came around, however, she informed him that she'd been offered a new job.

"It's in Manhattan," she'd said over a cup of coffee in the lunchroom. It was the first week of February and he could still recall the paper heart decorations on the white cabinets and the box of chocolates someone had left out by the coffee maker.

"Joyce, that's fantastic!" Wade had grinned. "We can finally move in together. And to live in New York City! All those hidden bookstores and museums. And carriage rides. I've always wanted to take you on a carriage ride—" He'd reached out to take her hand.

"No," she'd said flatly, pulling back. "This isn't a vacation. Can you even understand that I'm going there for a job? For a *life*? That means a career, a future. Neither of which you seem interested in."

"I'm interested in anything that involves you. Whatever is important to you is important to me, too."

"You know that's not true. At least, it hasn't been true in the three years we've been together. I value frugality, yet you waste your money on things I don't want or need: trips to the country, jewelry, perfumes. You know I'm not into public displays of affection, but you keep urging kisses and hugs on me. And frankly... I don't want a housemate who cooks me dinner and cuddles me at night. I want a partner who's as ambitious and goal oriented as I am."

"What are you saying?" he'd asked with a sinking soul. She couldn't mean what he feared she meant.

Joyce had shaken her head. "I can't give you what you want. And you can't give me what I need. It's not working. I don't know if it ever did."

Months afterwards he'd still find himself going over that last conversation, amazed that he hadn't seen it coming. Oddly, or maybe not, the one thing that would linger, hurting him the most was that she'd left him bereft for Valentine's. But then, for Joyce, Valentine's had always been just another day.

Wade had gone home and spent the evening throwing back shots of Jack Daniels, staring now and again at the engagement ring. Rage and anger had filled him. Fury, like a hammer that wanted to punch through doors. Grief as well. Dark enough to make him dream of driving his car off a cliff. In the end, however, he hadn't been able to blame Joyce. She'd been absolutely right. What did he really have to offer a woman? Even a romantically inclined lady didn't want a guy who wasted his money on flowers and trinkets instead of investing in a house. He understood now why Joyce had always resisted his suggestions that they share an apartment, because she didn't take him seriously. He was just an indulgence, like a romance novel a woman might read before bed. There was no place for him in her moving boxes.

What he couldn't forgive, however, was how she'd killed his faith, like some negative Cupid remorselessly shooting him through the heart with an arrow of ice-cold reality. In Elizabethan sonnet sequences, the story told by the poems was usually that of a cynical man becoming a believer in Love. Wade had been jolted in the opposite direction. Never again would he listen to *Le Boheme* or *Tristan und Isolde*, read the "The Lady of Shalott" or watch *Camille*. He could no longer afford to be a romantic. There was no future in it.

Chapter 2
The Garden of Venus

Joyce left for New York, and Wade, after returning the engagement ring, looked to moving as far in the other direction as he could go. It occurred to him that the one thing he might actually want to do was run a bookstore, uncertain as that was in this day and age. Reading had always been his other great love. His apartment overflowed with books.

He started searching and settled on a remote town in the Rockies. Some years back, a big chain bookstore had killed off the independents in the area. Now, ironically, digital books had put that chain—and the town's one large outlet—out of business. Meaning there was no place to get books anymore; there wasn't even a local library. Quaint and snowed in for half the year, Wade figured he could make this work if he was careful about what he stocked for the residents and those staying at the nearby ski lodges.

With a modest bank loan, he'd traveled halfway across the country and started up his little place using his own books as stock. He called it "The Bookkeeper," an ironic tip of the hat to his last job. That first year, the store lost money and Wade, lonely and alone, had drunk or wept himself to sleep every other night. He'd also jerked off while pathetically reliving his time with Joyce. He couldn't seem to blot their passion from his mind.

That was last year. This year he'd gotten things under control by creating an online site. It helped that he could sell his used and out-of-print books globally, while buying up other such libraries to maintain his supply. That solved the cash-flow problem. Meanwhile, he'd taken to featuring unique editions and rarities like coffee table tomes and special children's books. These lured in customers wanting gifts or amusements, and often got them curious about the old fashioned paperbacks lining the walls. More often than not, they came back to browse and buy one.

The change had been dramatic. Other shopkeepers began dropping in to ask about books for their stores, making him feel a part of the community. And Wade got regulars who stopped by weekly. The town grew on him, as did his new profession, fitting itself around him like a favored pair of jeans, broken in and comfortable. Valentine's Day, however, remained his bane.

"NO!" he'd barked at Linda, that first Valentine's, when she'd tried to decorate the store with shiny red hearts. "No valentines."

"Why not?" she'd asked, blinking down from a stepladder.

He'd debated, then told her the story as briefly and dryly as possible.

"But that was a year ago," she'd tried. "I mean, I know it's still going to hurt—"

"Linda. No. You don't understand. It wasn't just getting dumped, it was... a loss of faith."

"A loss of faith?" Her face had gone utterly blank and he'd known there was no explaining it.

"In Cupid," he'd said. "Just do as I ask. We don't celebrate Valentine's Day."

Now Wade's eyes flickered to the envelope on his desk. That damn, pink envelope. Some good-hearted regular must have left it. Sighing, he nabbed the damn thing and used his letter opener to rip off the top seam.

It was a valentine, a reprinted, old-fashioned valentine, as a matter of fact. The image featured a golden heart resting on a painted red rose. Inscribed on the gold heart were the words: *With this rose, I offer love divine/I beg of thee, be thou my valentine*. He opened up the card. There was a short note inside that had been typed up, printed out, and pasted in: *Have faith in Venus. Go to the flower shop*. Wade frowned. What the—? He turned it over looking for more. There was nothing else.

I don't have time for this! he thought. But that was a lie. He didn't have that much to do today. He also couldn't lie about the fact that he was suddenly intrigued. Before Roman Venus had ever taken on Greek Aphrodite's attributes of love, she'd been a goddess of gardens. It was very apt to connect Venus to flowers. Coincidence? Or did the sender know their romantic deities? More to the point: did the sender know that Wade would get it?

He debated with himself for several minutes. Finally, he sighed, tossed his latte into the trash, and fetched his jacket. "Linda, watch the store."

"Don't I always?" she murmured from behind her book.

The sky was a bit lighter and the snow-covered mountains that cupped the town were now visible, looming all around. The chill air smelled of spruce and fir trees. Wade passed by mothers holding to the mittened hands of children in puffy jackets, and ladies with bags dangling from gloved hands. Down he traveled to the second block.

The Gentle Rose was bustling, even though it hadn't any customers. Carla, the owner, had hired two young delivery men for the holiday season and they bumped into Wade as they hustled arrangements out from the front area through a back door and into a van. Wade stepped around buckets overflowing with bright sunflowers, merry daisies and timid violets. The chilly shop reeked of flora.

"Hey, Wade." Carla, slipping bright pink snapdragons into a heart-shaped vase, smiled up at him. She was an older woman with skin brown as hazelnuts and a lush figure. Cream ski pants hugged her round ass and a tight, v-necked sweater displayed her ample cleavage.

"Hey, Carla. Um...." He shifted foot-to-foot and considered turning around and just walking out. He was beginning to wonder, however, who this secret valentine might be. He'd made no overtures to any ladies, not since Joyce. A few, however, had flirted with him. Like Carla.

"Um..." He tried again. "Were you expecting me?"

"I sure was," she said. "Just pick out what you want."

He blinked. "What? I mean... what am I picking out?"

She raised a sassy brow. "What do you think? Curtains? I've been paid for a standard bouquet."

"I... don't understand. Someone bought me flowers?"

"No," Carla said, all patience and amusement. "The flowers aren't for you. You just get to pick them out."

Wade frowned. Now he was really confused. Were the flowers going to the one who had sent him the card? Or someone else entirely?

"God, I love this day, don't you?" Carla leaned on the counter, flashing her stunning cleavage. "I mean there's another six weeks of winter out there, but in here..." She waved at the riot of petals and leaves. "In here it's already spring. It's like Valentine's Day has brought all these flowers into bloom."

She sighed with wonder, and it occurred to Wade that if Carla was the one who'd sent him the card... well, he wouldn't mind. For a moment, he indulged himself with the fantasy of nuzzling and licking those heavy breasts, feeling those dark nipples harden as his lips brushed over them.... Would she taste like hazelnuts? Toasted hazelnuts? He felt his blood stir.

"*Love is the flower of life,*" he quoted aloud, "*and blossoms unexpectedly...*"

Carla raised her brows at that.

"D.H. Lawrence," he quickly explained. "I used to read a lot of D.H. Lawrence. In *Lady Chatterly*, the lovers adorn each other's naked bodies with flowers symbolizing the marriage of their souls and sexual passion. I always think of that chapter when I see flowers on... this particular day."

Carla tilted her head. "Now I'm gonna have to read that book."

"I'll set aside a copy for you," he murmured, but inside he was wondering what had just come over him. He didn't mention things like that anymore, didn't even think them if he could help it. Somehow, the flowers and Carla had slipped under his skin, like water feeding a thirsty plant. And what had been woken up scared him. He could not, absolutely could not, have such ideas floating like pollen through his head. Not again.

"Well?" Carla said, hands going to her hips. "What'll it be? Not to rush you, but I've gotta get back to work. I've a lot of orders to fill."

"But—" Wade tried. How could he create a bouquet if he didn't know who it was for? Of course, if it was for Carla he'd know exactly what to get: roses so blood red they were almost black with, perhaps, one cream blossom. That's what she'd like. He instinctively knew that. It didn't make much sense, however. Why would a flower lady want him to create a bouquet for her?

Perhaps he ought to look for inspiration in the card he'd been sent? Venus, the goddess of gardens. And a rose. *A rose garden?*

"A dozen roses," he abruptly told Carla. "Two lavender, two red, two yellow, two orange, two pink and two white."

Carla's brows went up again, impressed. "A rainbow."

"A... rose garden, actually."

"How romantic!" Carla's eyes glowed. "Didn't know you had it in you, Wade."

He outright blushed. Didn't have it in him? Fuck. He'd had way too much of it, that had been the problem. "Well, yeah," he muttered. "Umm... Should I wait for them?"

"No, no. On your way." She smirked. "They'll be sent to the right place."

He wondered where the "right place" was as he stepped out of the flower shop.

Chapter 3
Gold and Chocolate

When he got back to the bookstore he found it mildly busy. Linda was gift-wrapping a volume of romantic stories for one man, while another waited with a chocolate dessert book in hand. Rebecca Cho was on the sofa reading a murder mystery, and Miranda Kraft was there with her two young children picking out new, interactive picture books.

Wade didn't even bother getting his jacket off as he hurried over to light the neglected fire. Armchairs and a cozy loveseat surrounded the little hearth, creating an intimate reading-room. Wade considered that area to be the heart and soul of the store. When the fire was lit, customers stayed, sometimes for hours, sipping at complementary tea and reading books.

"Hey, Wade," Rebecca greeted him. She'd cut her raven hair boyishly short; a sexy look that enhanced her almond-shaped eyes.

"Hey, Rebecca," Wade got a good blaze going under the logs and pulled the screen closed. "Is it a good one?"

"A whodunit for Valentine's," she said, showing him the cover of the used paperback. It was wonderfully old school with colorful hearts, a gun, and a sexy femme fatale in the background. "Back when I was sixteen, I discovered this series and totally binged out on it. Read every one I could find. I'd forgotten about them, until I saw this one in your window."

"Is it as good as you remember?" he asked, dusting his hands and rising to his feet.

"Amazingly enough, yes. What's really surprising is how romantic it is. I mean, this was authored by a guy writing back when men were men and women were sex kittens." She offered Wade a dimpled smile. "I always forget men can be romantic. You're such perverts."

"We are," Wade said, "But that doesn't mean we can't also be romantic, some of us, I mean. The rest are just perverts."

She laughed and went back to her reading. Wade crossed over to his desk. Ralph was there, nosing around the blotter for a good spot to curl up and sleep. He pawed at a stack of invoices and... another envelope. A gold one.

"Linda?" Wade said, picking it up and stepping over to the register. His assistant was giving change to the man buying the book on desserts.

"Did you see who left this?"

"Hmm?" Linda glanced up at him harried. "Wade, I've been handling the register since you left. I didn't see anything. One of the kids maybe?"

This was ridiculous, Wade thought, impatiently breaking the seal (a red sticker heart this time). He felt like he was back in elementary school and some giggling girl was playing a prank on him. It was another old-fashioned valentine. This one featured an Edwardian gentleman handing off a heart-shaped box of chocolates to a shy female. It read, not too surprisingly: *Candy is sweet, and so are you.*

On the inside of the card was pasted yet another printed note: *Tribute is owed to Kama. Go to the candy store.* Wade read the words, then re-read them. He felt suddenly quite cold. Whoever this secret card-giver was, they really *did* know their mythology! Kama was the Hindu god of sexual desire. The original Cupid, he carried a bow made of sugar cane and shot flower arrows to induce desire in his victims. Who in this town, Wade had to wonder, outside of himself would know that?

"I'm... heading out again for a minute, Linda."

"Uh-huh," his assistant responded as he left.

A light flurry of snow had started coming down from the gray sky, along with a cold wind. Wade pulled up his collar, ducked his head and hurried down to the other end of his block. Bells jangled as he stepped into the warmth and cocoa fragrance of the candy store. A trio of coeds in striped blouses were busily filling up gold, red and black beribboned boxes with confections. A line of impatient men waited. Ah, thought Wade, the last minute panic of Valentine's Day.

"Wade, howdy!" The owner, Jess, smiled at him from behind the cash register. A master chocolatier, Jess had strawberry hair and a winsome smile. He was also gay.

Christ. Wade froze. Could the card-giver be a man? He suddenly found it hard to return the smile. He felt a superstitious prickle at the back of his neck. Having read many a sonnet sequence, he knew that such ironies happened to those who disrespected Cupid. And Wade had just spent two years ignoring the mischievous god.

I'm sorry, he found himself praying with sudden desperation. *Don't fuck with me, please. Being broken by Joyce was hard enough. I don't deserve to be jerked around more. Do I?*

"I sold all the special edition *Water for Chocolate* books you got me." Jess passed the register off to one of the girls. "Created a package deal. Box of sweets and a book. They went like hotcakes."

"Glad to hear it."

"So. What kind of box do you want?"

Wade shifted. "Um. Jess, man, be honest here. I was expected, right?"

The candy man grinned. "A medium sized box has already been paid for, and the person who arranged for it—also known as the recipient—has no food allergies. You're to pick out said box and what goes in it. That's all I can tell you. You look a little shell-shocked. Are you that surprised to have a secret admirer?"

Is that what they were? This mysterious card-giver who used cryptic, mythological references to send him on shopping trips?

"Surprised?" he answered, "Fuck yes. I was always the one who romanced the girls, not vice versa." Assuming, he reminded himself, that the card-giver was a girl. "I've never thought of myself as someone who might be... admired in secret."

"You got that idea in high school, didn't you?"

"Well, yeah, I guess."

"That's where we all get screwed," the chocolatier observed. "See, most of us are at our very worst during those years, pimpled and growing all out of proportion. Meanwhile, a rare few are at their best. You know: Skin, hair, teeth, figure. All perfect. If they're of the gender we're after—guys for me, girls for you—well, they seem unearthly, right? In fact, they'll probably never look that gorgeous again."

"True enough. But we sure do want them at the time," Wade reflected ruefully.

"Yep. And when they reject us, we end up thinking we're monsters. But it's not true. We graduate and turn into human beings. Become as differently desirable as the chocolates in this store."

"I... never thought about it that way."

"Don't let your self-image be trapped in high school," Jess said. "You've got that rugged, solid guy look going for you. Trust me, it's very, very desirable."

Wade swallowed hard. "Thanks for the encouragement. Um." He glanced nervously at the boxes. "Give me a gold box."

"Heart-shaped?"

"No," he decided. He was getting an idea. Among the tribes of South America cocoa beans had been traded like money and chocolate elixirs had been drunk from golden cups. So why not emphasize that eternal connection between riches and chocolate? "I want any candies you've got that are decorated with gold leaf."

"White, dark or milk chocolate?" Jess asked.

"All three. I'm going to make up a treasure box."

Jess dramatically slapped his hand to his chest. "Be still my heart. That is *so* romantic!"

"Um, yeah," Wade said dubiously. *I do not want to experiment with my sexuality*, he thought earnestly, *I really don't*. Jess slipped nine different chocolates into the box, each of them decorated with a glitter of gold.

"And the chocolate dipped fruit that's golden in color," Wade added. "White chocolate and dark."

Jess added in dried pineapple, papaya and apricot. "That does it," he said, showing Wade the contrasting shades. They glowed and glittered like a cache of rare coins.

"Um. Do I take it?"

"Nope." Jess winked at him. "I know where to send it. Oh, and this is for you." From a back shelf he presented Wade with a little white Cupid statue. It was made of plaster and contained a small candleholder at its feet. A pink tea candle was there.

"And here's a free chocolate," Jess added, handing him a caramel.

Tribute is due to Kama, Wade remembered. "Thanks."

He set the Cupid on his desk, dutifully lit the candle and placed the caramel before it as an offering. "I don't know what this is all about," he said softly to the statue. "Just... please, don't let it hurt too much."

The rest of the morning passed quietly, the music on the public radio station moving through sexy jazz to classical. Rebecca read her mystery, Linda her western. A few folk came and went, buying last minute books as presents.

"Happy Valentine's," Rebecca wished Wade, as she finally left the loveseat and shrugged on her coat.

"Yeah, thanks," he said. He saw her dimpled smile and his heart skipped a beat. *Could she be the one?* Rebecca had a wicked sense of humor and a sharp mind. She read mysteries and something like this, secret cards, enigmatic instructions, would be right up her alley. In Wade's mind flashed an image of Rebecca, warm and naked in his arms, grinding her hips against his while smiling that dimpled smile. He wouldn't object to finding out she was his secret valentine. Wouldn't object at all.

"Mail," Linda said unnecessarily. Wade had seen their mailman handing her a pack of letters. She tossed them down on his desk. And there it was: A purple envelope. No stamp, no return address. Not even his name on the front. The seal on the back was of a white lace heart. He didn't even try to ask Linda about it. He just broke it open.

This valentine featured a champagne bottle and two clinking flutes. *Your love is of a vintage sublime*, it announced, *Promise me that you will always be mine!* Clearly, not every Edwardian had been Yeats. He opened the card up. *Bacchus is waiting for us. Join me at the wine shop.*

Us? *US?* He hadn't expected that. He was going to meet her... or him? Already?

"Heading out again, Linda," he said, getting back into his jacket and gloves. His assistant didn't even glance up this time.

Wade was half way there when it occurred to him that he didn't need to be doing any of this. Why was he encouraging this card-sender? Because, he answered himself, what this person was doing was exactly the sort of thing he would have done back in the day. Old-fashioned valentines, references to gods of love. This secret admirer was romancing him into romancing them. Which was... incredibly romantic. And heaven help him, he couldn't find it in him to crush such notions. Besides, he was curious.

Chapter 4
Sweeter than Wine

"Dude!" Todd greeted Wade as he stepped through the wine store door. The owner was a blond, ex-surfer now snow-boarder.

"Todd," Wade returned, making his way about the displayed bottles and cases. There was yet another last-minute line of would-be-lovers at the counter buying merlots and chardonnays to go with tonight's candle-lit suppers. Todd worked the register by himself, rolling bottles up in tissue paper.

"Busy day," Wade sympathized.

"Passion is the most intoxicating vintage there is," Todd acknowledged. "Loved that book of Persian wine poems you sold me. I may print up a few and post them on the walls. Oh, and hey, can you repeat what you said to me a few weeks back? To him?" He pointed to one of the men examining the Pinots.

"What I said? About—?"

"That girl I was interested in who didn't think she was attractive. I asked you how to deal, remember? What to say when she complains that her ass is too big or her face isn't pretty enough?"

Several men in the line groaned sympathetically, and the one looking at bottles turned round. "I think you should ignore 'em," he announced. "Women all hate something about themselves, and there's no convincing them they're wrong."

"You can convince them if you do it right," Wade sighed. Criminy! It was always a wonder to him that women wasted their wonderful selves on bozos like this.

"Oh, really? Okay, smart guy, what do you recommend?"

The men were all looking his way now, and in spite of what Jess had said, Wade didn't feel that far from high school and the days when all the clueless boys wanted to know how to sweet-talk their girlfriends.

"You get them to see themselves through *your* eyes, that's what you do. So if she says she's too fat, you say, 'You're all woman and I love every inch

16

of you. Don't change a thing.' If she hates her ass, you tell her not to disrespect her yummy behind, which is one of your favorite features."

"Yeah!" one of the guys agreed and the men laughed.

"And if she doesn't think herself pretty, you go over everything you find magical about her: the sparkle in her eyes, her smile which always melts your heart. Whatever you worship about her, whatever makes her *your* lady, that's what you try to show her."

He paused, the whole shop was listening to him now.

"It doesn't get any more romantic than that, gentlemen," he finished up, "giving a woman faith in herself, and faith in your love."

"Wow," a fellow at the back of the line murmured.

"That's what I'm talkin' about," Todd agreed and slapped a hand on Wade's shoulder. "I knew I couldn't get it across like you. Thanks."

Wade shrugged. Advice like that had always seemed obvious to him.

"Your friend's a real Romeo, Todd," the guy by the Pinots was shaking his head.

"Guess so. Who knew?" Todd replied, and exchanged a wrapped bottle for a credit card with the next customer in line. "Speaking of which," he added, waiting for a signature. "You can head right into the tasting room, Wade. Everything's ready."

Ready? What's ready? Wade almost asked. Then remembered. The talk hadn't quite made him forget, but it had distracted him. Tasting room. Everything ready. Of course it was. The nervous upset returned to his stomach and he had to suck in a few breaths before striding toward the back.

There was a separate room at the far end of the store with paintings of vineyards on its brick walls and a small fireplace with a glass screened hearth. Todd used it to teach classes in wine appreciation. On one side was a wet bar, on the other side several cases of champagne. Dead center between them was a large dining table with a floor-length, purple tablecloth.

Shutting the door behind him, Wade glanced about, but there was no one there. He didn't know whether to be disappointed or not. He did notice that there were six dessert wines on the table, along with six cordial glasses filled with a taste of each.

Then he saw what else was on the table: a blindfold and a note on a sheet of paper cut about the edges to resemble lace. *Sit down*, it instructed. *Put on the blindfold and sample the wines. Do not remove it until you're done.*

Until he was done? How long could it take? Wait. Maybe the card-giver was hiding and would come out when he was blindfolded? Maybe she (he?) was willing to speak to him or help him with the drinks but didn't want him to see them just yet? He chewed his lips, apprehensive, then removed his jacket and gloves. In for a penny, in for a pound. He settled into a chair and put on the blindfold. It was one of those black ones for sleeping. Comfortable with an elastic band.

"I'm blindfolded," he said aloud, although it felt silly. "And I'm trying the first wine."

Carefully, he reached out his fingers, found the stem of the first glass and lifted it to his lips. It was light and sweet tasting. "Nice," he judged as fruit flavors played over his tongue.

He went for the second, found it and tasted it. Very crisp and a little tart. "Like that one a bit better," he decided. "But I'm not sure." Nothing. Or... wait. Had he heard something moving? Clothing rustling? He carefully reached fingers for the third goblet. He smelled its floral aroma, then took a sip and savored it. Interesting. He was just about to set the goblet down when something touched his thighs.

He jumped, felt a splash of droplets on his hand from the glass he was holding. Jesus! Breath left him. Someone was under the table—

He felt the top of his jeans grabbed and pulled forward. He swallowed and quickly set down the glass. This strange game had just taken a very unexpected turn. The button of his jeans was popped open. The zipper was tugged until it split. Shit! Wade reached for the blindfold—and stopped as a hand squeezed his package through his cotton shorts. He wasn't sure if it was a warning or a promise, but it certainly stilled him. "Okay, sorry, yes," he murmured. "I'll keep my hands where you can see them. Okay?"

He took hold of the seat to show his good faith. No removing the blindfold. Fingers were now stroking across his underwear, teasing, promising what he'd get if he was good. Oh, god. Oh, god. *This isn't real*, he thought, trembling. *This sort of thing doesn't happen to me*. His dick, however, was stirring, wakening. It said that this was all very, very real, especially when those fingers slipped right into the opening in his shorts.

Wade's breath hitched as small, smooth fingers gently took hold of his naked, stiffening cock and drew it out. Female. They felt female. Weren't they? The thumb was rubbing over the tip, as if enjoying how slick it was getting with pre-cum. He was fully hard now, and feeling the pulse of that erection.

And then he felt the warmth of someone's breath on that tip. Shit! Lips touched down, soft and moist, jolting him. *Fuck!* He barely kept his hips from bucking up to meet that kiss. As the one hand held firmly to his cock, the other hand started fondling his balls through his underwear. Wade felt his face go hot with a mix of embarrassment and arousal. Profound arousal.

Another kiss to his sensitive mushroom head only this time, the lips parted and sucked.

"Ohmygod, ohmygod—" He moaned as everything below the waist seemed to catch fire. It had been so long. So damn long! Two years since he'd felt anything like this. God. That mouth was so soft and velvety.

"C-c-can I ask you...?" he gasped. He didn't want to destroy the magic, but he had to know. "Oh, fuck." He clutched at the seat as his sensitive tip was pulled and licked. "Are you a woman? Just tell me that. Please?"

A pause. The mouth didn't leave, but there was surprise in that suspended moment. It left him with a sudden terror that the mouth would vanish and he would be left begging for it to return. But then he thought he felt the lips smiling. There followed a nod, pulling his stiff cock up and down like the handle of a slot machine.

Yes. I'm a woman.

He released a sigh. "Does Todd know what you're doing?"

His cock, the upper half still trapped in her mouth, went side to side. No. This was ridiculous. He was having a conversation with his dick. Her warm, damp tongue was now swirling exquisitely over his helmet. It trailed underneath. Molten heat went with it, sizzling down his shaft. He groaned aloud and fought against an urge to release the seat he was holding and grab her head.

Oh, please, gods of love, he prayed now, *if I ever in my life did right by you, don't let this stop...*

His cock was rock solid, the veins pulsing. He could hear the woman's breath panting through her nostrils, the sounds of her slurping and sucking. Pre-cum was drooling out, mingling with her saliva. His thighs had spread apart, as far as his open jeans would allow, and his hips were moving, begging for release. Sweat trickled down the small of his back.

His lover's tongue showed him no mercy. It licked its way up the sides of his aching stem, rimmed his head. Flowed like warm water back down. He dug his nails into the wood of his chair. "You're killing me," he hissed and gyrated.

She was back to sucking him now, doing her own wine tasting and seeming to enjoy his vintage. Her hands milked and squeezed his straining shaft, and he began to lose control, his hips jerking, trying to fuck her mouth. The sparks in his groin bubbled and fizzed, rising and rising. That's when his ass finally tensed and his groin spasmed.

Wade clamped his teeth against a shout. It escaped as a deep growl from his chest as he shot like a cork from a bottle. His mind whirled drunkenly away as his cum slammed into the back of her throat, one spurt, and another.

"Oh my God," he panted, shooting out all he had, down to the dregs. The merciless mouth, with a final pull, finally released his spent cock, which twitched and bobbed as cool air hit it. Wade was shaking and gasping.

Sweat trickled down from his temples. God! Even his best moments with Joyce hadn't been like that. Then again, it'd been a long while since he'd been given such a gift.

His lover, very courteously, was now gently stuffing his damp and softening cock back into his underwear. A moment later, his jeans were zipped back up and buttoned shut.

"T-thank you," he managed. "God you don't know...." He tried to spill out his gratitude, but went dry. There were no words to say what he felt. He wasn't even sure she was still there. He finally dared to let go of the seat. No one touched him or tried to stop him from lifting his hands to the blindfold.

Do not remove till you're done, the instructions had warned him. Now he understood. He was certainly done in one sense, but not in the other. With a trembling hand he reached out and found the fourth wine. It spilled over his beard as he gulped it. He sampled the fifth and sixth wines before, finally removing the blindfold.

There was no one else in the room. Or if there was, hiding behind the bar or crates, he wasn't going to try and find them. He picked up the bottle of wine he'd liked best, a peach-colored Gewurztraminer that tasted of roses and honey.

"*I love your lips when they're wet with wine*," he murmured to himself, a love poem by Ella Wilcox. "*And red with a wild desire...* Bacchus, I hope our prayer pleased you." *It certainly*, he added to himself, *pleased me*.

Chapter 5
Love Charms

"This is turning into one of the strangest days of my life," he confided in Ralph. The cat lay on his desk, flexing out his claws with each caress he was given by Wade. The public radio station was playing French torch songs. Linda was out to lunch and there were currently no customers in the store. It was just Wade, Ralph and... that statue of Cupid.

"I mean," Wade continued, "what am I to say to this girl when I finally meet her? 'Thanks for the blowjob? Hope I picked out flowers and wine and candy you like?'"

Ralph blinked contented golden eyes and purred. The candle still burned at the foot of the Cupid. Wade gazed at the god uneasily. He could feel something profound happening to him, not just from the sexual release either. It was as if a tourniquet had been untied allowing blood to flow back into a limb, causing it to tingle.

Only it wasn't a limb. It was his romantic heart. Picking out the flowers and the candy, what had happened at the wine tasting. It was forcing that part of him to stir, very much like his cock had stirred and risen to life. It scared him. Getting it back meant he risked losing it all over again and he didn't know if he could bear that.

"It wasn't the break-up," he explained to the statue. "I wouldn't lose faith in you because I'd fallen in love and been hurt. Betrayed even. That happens. It was..." He hesitated. "It was seeing that romance had no power. Seeing the legs sliced out from under it. I watched it just topple over."

He sighed, and lowered his head into his hand. "And I toppled with it."

A banging at the door interrupted him. What the hell? The door was open, wasn't it? Had Linda accidentally locked it on her way out? Wade got up and hurried over. The door *was* unlocked. Why, he wondered as he turned the knob, was someone knocking? He threw it open.

There was no one there. Frowning, he glanced about then, by chance down. On the trampled snow-crusted mat was another envelope. Shit. Wade looked again in every direction. He saw folk moving up and down the mall, in and out of shops. There was no telling who had knocked and left the card.

He brought it in. It was red with a gold heart as the seal. Opening it, he removed the card and was greeted by the quaint image of an Edwardian gentleman putting a glittering necklace about the swan-like throat of a young lady. She gazed back at him adoringly. *Silks and diamonds, amber and gold,* the poem on the card read, *To thee I give my heart to hold.*

"Good grief." Wade shook his head. "With poetry like this, it's a wonder anyone agreed to be another's valentine."

Inside he found the pasted note: *Erzulie demands her luxuries. Go to Five & Diamonds. P.S. Glad you enjoyed yourself. Don't worry. No surprises this time.*

Wade was happy there was no one to see him blush. Erzulie, huh? Erzulie was the Voodoo goddess of love, a lavish gift-giver. He put on his jacket and gloves, hung the "back in ten minutes" sign and made sure, absolutely sure, to lock the door behind him.

Five & Diamonds was an eclectic store on the third and farthest block from the bookstore. It sold dresses primarily, but also jewelry, scarves, accessories and fragrances. It gave Wade yet another glimpse into the personality of the card-giver. She was mysterious and bold, that was already clear. Knowledgeable when it came to mythology... and making love. Now he added that she was also nontraditional.

The inside of the store smelled of sandalwood incense and like everywhere else it was filled with harried lovers in search of gifts. These, however, were younger, dressed in narrow jeans, their hair dyed in wild colors. There were women as well as men searching among the racks and shelves.

"Wade, how are you?" Slender Freda came forward, the tiers of her skirt swishing with her easy strides. Her blond hair fell about her narrow face in ringlets making it look like she'd stepped out of a fairytale.

"Fine." Wade, hands in his jacket pockets, wondered if she might be the one. Freda was certainly uninhibited enough to have been under that table. Wade could imagine her on her knees, giving his cock lingering tastes as those golden ringlets brushed over her shoulders.

Stop it, he told himself as his mouth went dry at the thought and his dick considered coming back up for a look-see.

"I— um— I guess—" He cleared his suddenly thick throat, "you know why I'm here?"

She smiled at him. "You're to pick out one luxury item for your valentine. Whatever you like."

Daunting, Wade thought, blinking around at the store. Freda had crowded it to the rafters with pillar candles and bejeweled clocks, painted boxes, snow globes and silver picture frames. There were bottles of bubble bath and hand lotion.

"You know," he sighed, "My old girlfriend would have called all this frivolous. She never went in for the luxuries."

"Love is a luxury," Freda pointed out. "But that doesn't mean you can do without it. If you don't have food, you wither and die. But if you don't have love, your soul withers and dies. I think I'd rather do without food."

Wade winced. It described him all too aptly.

"Take your time," Freda added.

He glanced about helplessly. How was he to pick out a single token of love for this secret lover? Well. Wait. He knew her from her old fashioned valentines and obscure mythological references. And from what she'd given him this afternoon: her generous, passionate attention. He knew her from the fact that she'd decided on this shop of all shops for a luxury gift. Maybe he *could* find the right gift for her. He wandered over to the jewelry display and scanned the section dedicated to Valentine's Day.

Not the silver love birds, no. Too soft and silly for his clever lover. Nor the necklace with the word "love" fashioned out of gold. That seemed a lazy gift. A rose pin made of tiny garnets? Nice, but he'd already given her roses in the bouquet.

"That bracelet," he pointed.

Freda left the register to unlock the case. She handed the bracelet to Wade. The links were cluttered with gold heart charms of all sizes and shapes, lockets, cameos, filigreed, bejeweled. There was even a small, winged Cupid. Yes, this was it. A dozen different hearts to reflect the different valentines he'd been sent. Fanciful, fun, but also beautiful.

"I'll wrap that up for you," Freda said.

Wade stiffened. "Wrap it up? But every other store has just... sent it on."

"This," Freda said, slipping the bracelet into a small, red box. "You take with you."

She tied a gold bow around it and passed it over to him. He slipped it into his jacket pocket and headed out. On the way back to his store he sensed it there, a small but significant bulge. Evidently, this was one gift that he, himself, was supposed to give his secret valentine. Something felt wrong about that, but he wasn't sure what.

Arriving back at The Bookkeeper, he found the door still locked. Linda had yet to return from lunch. As he stepped in however, he saw it. Another envelope on his desk. A black one.

"How the fuck—?" Only he and Linda had a key to the store!

Circling his desk, he eyed the envelope suspiciously. Strangely enough, this one wasn't sealed. Drawing in a breath, he drew out the card. It was the most straightforward of them all: A large pink heart.

Across that heart was the following couplet: *These tributes I have sent, and hope you will receive/ My heart is yours as well, from one who will never deceive.*

Opening it up, he found the sender's longest message yet. Also her final one: *It was thought to be bad luck to sign a valentine. So, I have not signed any of mine. I will be at the poetry reading tonight, my signature will be my poem. I do not know exactly why Valentine's Day is an anathema to you, but I hope I've made it less so. I will understand, however, if you've given all you can give. Hand me that final gift you carry, or return it. I have your flowers, chocolates and wine. I ask no more from my valentine.*

Wade read through it several times. Then he brought out the gift box from his pocket and put it down on the desk. He stared at it. He understood now why it struck him as wrong. *Your* flowers, chocolate and wine, she had written to him. None of it, however, really was from *him*.

He'd once read that fifteen percent of the women in the U.S. bought flowers for themselves on Valentine's Day. It had made him want to go out and find just one such woman so *he* could buy her the flowers. No woman, he sincerely believed, should ever have to do that for herself. Yet that's exactly what this woman had done. Not just flowers but everything, down to the charm bracelet.

She had, it appeared (and for reasons he couldn't fathom), allowed herself only the dream of having him as her valentine. The bouquet he'd buy her, the candy, even the thrill of an afternoon tryst. But she'd released him from the burden of actually *being* her valentine. He could, when all was said and done, decide that what little she had gotten of him was all she was ever going to get.

He could imagine her spending the night alone, just her and the gifts she'd bought, the ones he'd picked out for her. The thought was almost unendurable. How could any woman hand him that much power? The power to crush her heart? Yet the more he thought about it, the more he knew that he'd given Joyce, undeserving as she was, that very same power. And he'd never taken it back.

My God. He felt something easing in his chest, as if barbed wire had just been removed from his soul. Two years he'd been in mourning, blaming himself. He shouldn't have. There'd been nothing wrong with him. Nothing at all.

"My ambition," he ought to have said to Joyce on that fateful day, "*my dream and my goal for the future is to make you happy. To make us happy. That's what romance is all about.*"

The tingling was gone. The blood was back. He set his last valentine down beside the candle, still burning, at Cupid's foot and stared with wonder at the god.

"I did have objectives and aspirations," he said aloud. "And they were real, and they were important. I wanted to keep another's soul alive. What greater purpose in life is there than that?"

The playful spirit didn't respond, but then, he didn't need to. Wade knew what Cupid wanted him to do. What he must do if he was finally going to earn back Love's divine favor.

Chapter 6
Be Mine

The poetry reading had already started when Wade arrived. Linda had left an hour before closing for her date, and Wade had been caught short when last minute customers had shown up, men, of course, and one woman, all wanting advice on romantic books for their sweethearts. So he'd been late getting back to his apartment. It'd been hard, but he'd taken his time showering, trimming his beard and getting dressed.

He was still panting from rushing and running when he arrived at the coffee house, breath misting in the night air. Bodies filled the place, and he couldn't see who was at the mike.

"My heart is like an apple tree/Whose boughs are bent with thick-set fruit —" He heard a man's voice reciting over the speakers. Someone reading Christina Rossetti.

Wade patted his pockets, assuring himself that his gifts were there, then, gathering up his courage, he pushed his way in. He felt his chilled ears and nose begin to thaw as he escaped the cold for coffee-scented warmth. The first person he caught sight of was Jess. The chocolatier was sitting at a table with one of the delivery men from the flower shop. The two were sipping espressos and staring dreamily into each other's eyes. Wade grinned. Good for them!

The poet reading Rossetti finished. The room applauded and Wade started to edge his way through the press of bodies.

"Hey Wade!" Carla greeted him. She was wearing a velvet dress red as roses. It beautifully complimented her hazelnut skin. She was also holding hands with Rebecca Cho.

"Carla—" Wade blinked. "Rebecca." For a moment he didn't know what to say, especially when Rebecca, dressed in black leather pants and a lacy-white top, put her arms around Carla's neck and smiled her wicked, dimpled smile.

He gulped. "Um. Having a good evening?"

"Oh yeah." Carla stroked Rebecca's arm. "It's been very romantic. And thanks for that sexy suggestion you came up with this morning. I've all kinds of leftover flowers at home and I know exactly what I'm gonna do with them."

Suggestion? Oh, right. Wade felt his face grow hot. The flower scene from *Lady Chatterly's Lover.* He bit his tongue to keep from asking if he could watch. So, neither of these ladies was his secret admirer. Obviously.

"I've, ah, gotta get up to the front," he excused himself.

"Later," said Rebecca.

Shit. He'd never even suspected. Wade inched his way through the crowd as another poet came to the mike. *"Let me not to the marriage of true minds —"* the man quoted as Wade reached the front windows.

"Wade," a soft hand nabbed his wrist and Linda grinned at him. "You made it!" She looked stunning, all those glorious curves accented by a burgundy outfit.

"Um, yes I did."

"I'm so glad. I was afraid you wouldn't show."

Wade licked his lips, gazing for a moment at Linda's rosy cheeks and lips.

"It is the star," The poet at the mike was going on, *"to every wandering bark..."*

"Linda, I—" he began.

"Here you go," someone cut him off. And there was Todd, handing Linda the coffee house's Valentine's Day special: a raspberries-and-cream cappuccino. Wade saw a purple candy heart sinking into the foam. It read "Be Mine."

The wine storeowner leaned in and gave Linda a quick kiss. "Miss me?"

"Terribly," she cooed.

"Dude," Todd greeted Wade as he slipped his arm about Linda's ample waist. "Thanks for letting Linda off early."

Wade blinked. "No problem," he said, and from the grin and wink Todd gave him, got the impression that the young man was also thanking him for his advice. Evidently, he'd been more than able to express to Linda how beautiful she was.

The poet finished up the sonnet and received his applause. Wade didn't quite know what to do now. He'd been wondering all day if Linda's mention of a date had been a creative lie, if all those envelopes had been set there by his sly assistant. Evidently not. But if not Linda, then who?

"You offered Venus a rose garden—" The words suddenly came over the speakers. Wade spun around. The voice was female.

"You set a golden treasure before Cupid—" It was *her.* His heart raced and his throat tightened. It was her... and evidently Carla and Jess had let her in on how he'd decided on her flowers and chocolates.

27

"You gave your own wine to the Bacchae," she went on, as Wade edged round toward her, *"Though you risked your flesh in doing so. You put your faith in paper hearts and bad poetry, sending up these Valentine Prayers—"*

He recognized the voice now, and his throat seemed to lock up as he came out almost behind her. There was no dais, just a microphone and a small open circle. She wasn't looking around, and so didn't see him.

"—to a mortal woman unseen. In hopes of love, I hope." She had on pink boots and a ruffled lavender skirt. It went well with her strawberry sweater and its decoupage of fabric hearts.

"Hear now my prayers, sweetheart mine," Nora finished, *"Take whatever gifts you'll allow the gods to give you..."* She paused, and opened up her arms. *"Roses, candy, love and wine on this one day, known as Valentine."*

A beat, and then the crowd was cheering and whistling with approval. She curtsied and turned. That's when she saw Wade and hesitated before drawing in a breath and striding up to him.

"Hey," she said.

"Hello," he returned nervously. He couldn't quite believe it. He'd spent the entire day wondering which woman had sent him those valentines, and how he might show her his appreciation. Nora, however, hadn't even been on his list. Wade's long-standing crush on her notwithstanding, what she'd said this morning had made her sound too much like Joyce: a bright, hard diamond likely to cut him to ribbons. Not open to romance.

Now, having just heard her amorous poetry, Wade didn't know what to think. "Um, is there somewhere private we can go?"

"Come on," she motioned him to follow. "My brother can take care of the rest. It's his show after all."

Behind them, another poet came to the microphone. Wade heard the man's voice echoing as they headed through the storeroom. It cut off as Nora went through another door—labeled "Private"—which she shut behind them before leading the way up a narrow flight of stairs. At the top was a cozy living area with an open den and kitchenette done up in browns and blues. It was warm and infused with the fragrance of roasted coffee beans. Wade noticed the roses he'd picked out, a spray of pastel color, snug in a Chinese vase near the window. He also caught sight of his golden box of candy and the open bottle of wine by the sink.

"Eddie's got a place to crash tonight," Nora told him. "So, no disturbances. Wanna take off that jacket?" Her cheeks were flushed and her eyes sparkled with lust so frank it was scary. Wade fumbled off his gloves and scarf, then took out the gifts from his jacket pockets before slipping that off as well.

"Have a seat," Nora urged him as she got everything up on the coat rack.

28

He settled uncertainly onto the couch. He couldn't keep his eyes off Nora, her playful smile, the way she moved, like a nymph dancing to pan pipes. His heart pounded in his chest as he watched her tug off her boots, exposing compact legs and little feet.

"Nora, I don't understand—"

"Understand what?" she asked, gliding onto his lap all unexpected. Her weight and warmth nestled onto his thighs. And then her silky lips were brushing his. They melted into a kiss that heated his blood. Her tongue followed, warm and tasting of hot cocoa. It flirted with him. When she finally drew back, he was breathless and his cock was thick and throbbing. It remembered those teasing lips, that clever tongue, and would do just about anything for them.

"*My sweetheart.*" Nora said undoing the top button of his shirt and leaning in for another kiss.

"Nora, Nora—" He was left gasping for air. He didn't want to stop her, but this was absurd. "Please. I've been wondering all day what you wanted from me—"

"After what we did in the wine shop, I'd think you'd know." The way she was wiggling on his lap had him gulping. Her skirts were bunched up and from what he could see, she wasn't wearing much underneath. Her firm ass cheeks rubbed up and down his trousers, creating friction, her crotch nudged at the bulge in his pants.

"B-but why me?" She was running the tip of her tongue lightly around his ear, causing him to shiver. "And h-how long have you—?"

"Been interested?" She nipped at his neck, lightly, playfully, then nuzzled into his beard. "About six months."

"*Six months?*" He could hardly breathe now.

"Yeah. I was dating this cynical artist last year. He gave all his passion to his paintings and none to me." She opened another of Wade's shirt buttons. "We broke up. It was just after Valentine's Day, and I saw these re-created Edwardian cards on sale. I bought them. Now and then, I'd flip through them, and think about those soppy, romantic times. You know, it wasn't that Edwardian gents couldn't get any." The lower buttons of Wade shirt were falling away now, exposing his furry chest and stomach. The bulge in his pants had gotten hard and painful. "It was that they couldn't get any with one *particular* girl. All that restrained passion for one lady is what made the men surrender to romance."

"That's an... interesting theory," he choked as Nora jerked his shirttails free and pulled his shirt completely off him. "But what made you decide on *me*?"

"It was summer, and you and I were having one of our morning discussions," she said, lightly scratching his chest with her nails in a way that had him groaning, "and I started to realize that you weren't just well read and warm hearted. You were also pretty sexy. God," she purred, "I've been waiting to get at this chest ever since I saw you biking around shirtless last August—"

Leaning in she kissed her way over his pecs. Each touch of her lips left a little burn of arousal on his flesh. Then she started to lick at the hair circling his nipples. The sensitive nubs tightened up. He gasped aloud, squirming under her as she set her teeth to them.

"Oh, fuck," he groaned. His hands had found their way under her skirts to grip her ass. Damn. Her behind was so fucking cute! The skin cool and smooth. And the way she wriggled, there in his hands. God!

He forced himself to swallow, to focus. He wasn't done yet. "W-why didn't you say anything before now? Why like this?"

"I talked to Linda. She wouldn't give me any details, but she let me know that you'd been badly hurt, and probably weren't open to a new relationship." Nora was now working at his trousers. The button there gave way all too easily. "But the more I saw of you, the more I wanted you to be mine."

His zipper went down, giving him a deja vu moment back to the wine shop.

"That's when I came up with my Valentine's Day plan." She parted his pants and snapped open the long johns he'd put on for warmth. His eager cock sprung out to greet her. He trembled as she took hold of it. It pulsed in her hand, its swollen head already dripping with pre-cum. He couldn't hold back any longer. He released her ass to grab at her sweater. She let go of him long enough to help him tear it off.

She wore no bra; her breasts swung free, as cute as the rest of her. He took hold of them, suckling on one, dusky-rose nipple. He loved the way it turned into a pert little nub there in his mouth. He laved it and her pebbling areola, until he felt Nora squirming on his lap. Then he switched to the other nipple, adoring the sensation of that firm button pressing back at his circling tongue. Nora moaned and arched into him with abandon. Wade felt her crotch rubbing up against his naked cock. The fabric of her cotton panties was thin and wet. The swell of her pussy mocked him from the other side.

Jesus, how he'd missed this! Whether Nora was serious or just playing with him for the night, he didn't care. The chance to make love to a woman again was worth it all.

Releasing her breasts, he groped back under her skirts. Slipping into the front of her low-rise panties he found her soft folds. They parted for him and her lustful groan met his as her warm lotion slicked his fingers.

"Oh fuck!" she gasped grinding her hips and digging her nails into his shoulders. She was so wet his fingers kept slipping away from where he wanted to be. Nora didn't seem to mind, in fact, she was going crazy, biting his shoulders and throat in her excitement. Each nip took him higher and farther. He tugged at her panties, that scrap of cotton, wanting to rip them off. She rose to stand on the couch, her skirts falling to swirl about her thighs and got the panties down, off one leg, then the other and tossed them.

Her rich fragrance wafted down and he eagerly nosed his way under those skirts. Before him was a beautiful nest of soft curls. Sliding his tongue between those silken folds, he tasted that delicious mingling of salty-sweet nectar. Nora shouted, and jerked. He gripped her ass tightly, and felt her small hands squeezing his shoulders.

Her legs parted wider for him and he rubbed his bearded cheeks against her soft, soft thighs before seeking out what he most wanted. Her clit seemed to be floating there, like a candy heart.

"Yes!" She quivered in his hands as he danced his tongue over that swollen jewel. "Oh, fuck, yes!"

She writhed and gasped in his hands, her sing-song cries causing his balls to rise, his cock to throb and strain. For a heartbeat he felt himself drowning in her taste, her fragrance, then, quite suddenly, she orgasmed.

Waves of pleasure shuddered down her body, causing her pussy to clench and vibrate. Drunk and dizzy in that warm, fragrant humidity, Wade lapped frantically at her juices. He kept hold of her, lost and in love with the experience, as the shudders grew harder, then gentled to faint jerks,

Then he felt her pulling away. Startled, he came free of her skirts even as she stepped down from the couch. He almost moaned at the loss of her warmth; her delicious flavor was still on his tongue, her floral scent perfuming his beard. Even his hands could still feel her, vibrating there.

"N-Nora?"

She was breathing hard and visibly trembling as she made for the kitchen counter. For a moment she leaned there, face flushed, eyes shut, arms crossed over her bare breasts as if savoring the erotic bliss.

"In ancient times," she finally said, huskily, "a day like this belonged to gods of desire and passion. But then it got handed over to this saint known for marrying people. The passion got locked away and replaced with romance. Which created this belief that the two can be separated. That you can have one without the other."

She poured a little wine into one of the glasses and sipped at it. Wade had risen to his feet, though he had to make a grab at his open pants and long-johns before they dropped. His cock was poking out and up, reaching for Nora like an arrow after a target. He made his way over and sunk to his knees. Nora brought the glass down and offered it to his lips. The rose and honey flavored drink cooled his tongue.

"You could have made it easy on yourself, Wade." She went on setting the glass back on the counter. "Ignored the valentines or gone for a few standard red roses and a heart-shaped box of pre-wrapped chocolates. You didn't. You asked why I picked you. Because you didn't even know who your valentine was, and you still put all your heart into giving her the most romantic of gifts. I knew you would. You understand, as so few men do, that romance is a way of proving your passion. So, that's why you."

Nora's hands were in his hair now, brushing on down to his beard. He grabbed one of those hands, kissed at her palm and pulled, mutely asking for her. She snatched a white chocolate from the golden box before sinking downward. Taking a bite, she offered him the rest as she drifted, skirts fluttering, towards his lap. He let her slip the chocolate between his teeth. Her lips pressed against his as it melted in his mouth. Tastes mingled, the chocolate and wine, the residue of Nora's own flavor.

And then her moist pussy touched on his aching cockhead. Pleasure shocked though him. His hips thrust to meet her. She sheathed him in hot silk, and her arms locked about his neck. Her muscled legs came around his waist, imprisoning him. He held to her in turn, bucking and thrusting into her.

"Fuck! Fuck," she cried rocking her hips, "I love your cock!"

"And I love you!" Wade groaned back. He could feel the heat building; friction stoked the fire. His thighs strained as he pumped up and down. Her nipples brushed against his sweaty chest, her hair whispered past his cheek. Her teeth sunk into his neck and sucked, adding to the jolts of sensation. And with each thrust, the hot pulse from within her took him deeper and deeper into the fire until he found himself racing for the very heart of it.

Muscles tensed, and flashes of red and gold blinded him as his cock gave one last, eruptive throb. He came into her with a shout. Ecstasy, fierce as pain, took him. Her spasms of delight gripped him back, pulling and pulling at him, demanding more even when he had nothing left to give. And still Wade kept himself within her unable to bear leaving.

Finally, their breaths started to quiet, and Nora's legs relaxed. With the last of his shaky strength, Wade tenderly lowered her to the floor and eased out of her. Then he collapsed, gasping, onto his back, his exhausted cock falling wetly over his thigh. He suspected that he'd more than proved just how passionate he could be.

Chapter 7
The Gods' Divine Favor

"I love it!" Nora exclaimed, jangling the charm bracelet Wade had clipped about her wrist. She'd brought out a quilt and they rested under it, naked on the couch. Outside, snow was silently falling, drifting past the room's single window.

"It's so right!" She touched on each charm, flipping and delighting in them. "Like the flowers and the candy. Thank you."

"I just picked it out," Wade demurred, but his heart soared at the happy glow in her eyes. "Now the other gift."

"There was only supposed to be one," she protested as he handed it to her.

"This one's from me. Really from me."

She gently pulled away the wrapping paper revealing a slim volume with a brocade cover. "*Sonnets from the Portuguese!*" She brushed a hand over the gilt lettering.

"A special Valentine's edition." Wade flushed. "It's my favorite sonnet sequence."

"You said you didn't like poetry."

"I lied about that. But so did you. You said that you didn't want your guy reading verses to you—"

"I didn't say that. I said that I wouldn't make him read poetry to me in order to get laid." She winked at him. "Anything post-coital is fine."

He laughed. "You're so damn cute, you know that?"

"I know," she sighed and snuggled in closer. "I've tried to be other things: seductive, alluring, dominating. It always comes off as cute. Do you like cute?"

"I adore it." He did. And he loved holding her in his arms. It gave him such serenity and peace-of-mind that he finally ventured to explain why he'd been so averse to Valentine's Day. He told her about himself, about Joyce and his misfired love affair.

"Shit," she said when he was done, and hugged him tight. "I said that most men don't get that romance is a way of proving their passion. But it's as bad the other way around. A woman who won't let her man be romantic is keeping him from laying his passion at her feet. That's a horrible thing to do. I swear to you, Wade, you make me your sweetheart, and I'll never rebuff any of your romantic gestures. Never. I'll welcome them with open arms."

"Thank you," he whispered, both moved and shaken. "And you already are my sweetheart. You became that with your first valentine. Which reminds me... how did you get that last one into the office?"

"Linda gave me a copy of her key. She was in on it. I'm glad you decided to play along. I'm glad you enjoyed it. And I'm so glad you're finally mine."

His throat tightened. "I'm glad, too, but I don't get why you were so sure I'd come, through. Weren't you worried I'd disappoint you?"

"Nope," she said pertly. "I know you. I mean, I've been talking to you every morning for over a year, right?"

"When I come in to buy my coffee yes, but—"

"They might have been short talks, but they added up and told me all I needed to know. Like, you've got an imagination as colorful as those roses, and a mind as rich as those chocolates. Your passion is as heady as wine, and your heart as playful as my own." She grinned brightly. "I never doubted that you'd answer my prayers."

"I think it's the other way around," he murmured into her hair. "You answered mine."

She kissed him then, with lips sweet as sugar. "Can I wish you Happy Valentine's Day?"

"Oh, yes. And a happy, happy Valentine's Day to you too," he wished her back. And meant it.

If you enjoyed this story, you can sign up for a free membership at ForbiddenFiction and discuss it with other readers and the author at the *Valentine Prayers* story page at http://forbiddenfiction.com/library/story/JK1-1.000249.

We do our best to proof all our work, but if you spot a text error we missed, please let us know via our website Contact Form at http://forbiddenfiction.com/contact.

An Act of Charity

Chapter 1
Deck the Halls

Unlike most Christmas babies, Noel loved her natal day. Others complained about sharing their birthday with the season, or having it neglected altogether. "It's so unfair!" they bitched, especially on the subject of gifts, but Noel wouldn't have had it any other way. She loved having a birthday where giving was more important than receiving, which was filled with glittering decorations, sappy movies about Santa and angels, the fragrance of pine and gingerbread. She even liked her eponymous name.

Above all, she loved the music. Ah, the music. From the day of her birth, the melody of bells and carolers had played in her head. The beat and tempo of the holidays were a part of her and she considered herself blessed.

This year she felt more than usually blessed, which was why she was making extra generous efforts to spread the Yuletide spirit that started right in her own living room where she taught music classes in piano, guitar and harp. At the moment she was trying to help ten-year old Jill plunk out "Deck the Halls" on piano.

"It's the 'Fa-la-las' I can't get right," the girl bemoaned, kicking skinny legs back and forth under the bench.

"That's the hard part," Noel agreed. "But you can do this Jill. You know you can. Just imagine that your fingers are dancing to the song. Watch." Noel played the melody one-handedly. *Deck the halls with boughs of holly; Fa-la-la-la-la... la-la-la-la....*

Jill pushed back her glasses on her freckled nose and tried the part again. This time she got the first "Fa-la-la" right, but stumbled over the second.

"There's too many of that part," she complained.

"Yes, but once you master it, you've pretty much mastered the whole song. Why don't you try this: close your eyes," Noel urged. "Hear the music in your head. I mean really hear it. Soaring horns, jingling bells and your piano, the star of the show, in charge of it all. Let your fingers play along with that."

Jill nodded and tried again. Her fingers tangled up. Jaw tightening, she made another effort and another. On the fourth try, she got through the "Fa-la-las" with only a couple of hiccups.

Noel grinned. "There you go!"

The girl didn't smile back. She twisted a lock of stringy blond hair about a finger. "The party is tomorrow. What if I mess up in front of all those people?"

"You probably will. And you know what? It doesn't matter. Other kids will be messing up too. I mean heck, even professional musicians make mistakes, but the audience doesn't usually notice. The trick is not to stop. Keep going even if you slip up."

They practiced a little longer, then Noel walked Jill to the entrance hall and helped her bundle up in jacket, muffler, hat and gloves.

"You'll be there?" Jill asked anxiously. The girl had understandable issues with adults who didn't keep their promises.

"Of course," Noel said. "And I expect to see you enjoying the music you play. That's the important thing, especially with Christmas music. To enjoy it."

Closing the door on Jill, Noel nervously glanced at the clock. Her next appointment was due any minute now and she felt as jittery about it as Jill did about tomorrow's performance. She gave herself a quick check in the entrance hall mirror, smoothing her cedar brown hair and tugging her holly green turtleneck into place over her plaid skirt. *Hmm. Too tame?* She wondered. Then rolled her eyes at herself.

Of course it was. She was a "nice" young woman after all. It was something she'd heard throughout her life, and only lately admitted she wasn't happy about. Outside of comments on her music, every remark about her included that damn word.

"She has a nice face... she has a nice personality... she has a nice figure... she wears nice clothes...."

When she was younger, she'd been fine with it, but now it sounded like a backhanded compliment. Of course, she had only herself to blame, she knew that. She was... nice. In fact, given what she planned on doing this afternoon, that troublesome adjective was only going to get glued onto her tighter.

"I guess that means a change of clothes isn't going to make much of a difference," she murmured to her reflection, and headed back to the living room.

The Christmas tree, as always, dominated this most central area at this time of year, bedecked and glowing within the nook of the large bay window. At the top, guarding and blessing both the tree and the instruments in the room, was the Music Angel. The angel had been in Noel's family for decades, and even before Noel's birth had been known as the Christmas

37

Music Angel. Dressed in Grecian robes all gold and royal purple, the Angel held a lyre in her arms. Her wings where cupped around her as if to hold in and amplify the holy music being summoned from those strings.

Noel, gazing up at her, felt a wave of peace and smiled.

"I bet you'll be glad when you no longer have to teach music to ungrateful kids," a cool, masculine voice startled her.

She'd forgotten all about Benjamin. He was seated at the roll top desk in the alcove, half hidden by a fortress of cardboard boxes, files and accordion-like folders. Only his narrow shoulders and the back of his dark-haired head could be seen.

"Jill isn't ungrateful," Noel said stepping into the alcove.

"She can't play," he said bluntly, and finally turned his chair around. His youth always surprised Noel; she had a hard time remembering that he was only a year or two her senior because he acted like such an old man. As if he'd been born in another, less charitable century, she reflected. It didn't help that he was almost always dressed in black: black sweater, black trousers—a stark contrast to her own preference for scarlet and green. The clothes gave him a pallbearer's appearance, which was only enhanced by his aquiline nose and angular face.

"So?" she said defiantly. This time of year Christmas music was always playing through her head. For some reason "Have yourself a Merry Little Christmas" came to mind when gazing at Benjamin. Nostalgic, evocative. "And why do you think I'm going to give up teaching?"

He waved to the papers around him with a long-fingered hand that Noel had always secretly wanted to see playing piano. "In a few weeks, you'll be a rich woman. You won't need to."

"Jill is one of my foster kids. I teach them for free."

He snorted. "You're too charitable."

"There's no such thing." She glanced up at the Music Angel. "Especially at this time of year when every angel is an angel of charity."

"A lovely sentiment, but you need to remember that you're on planet Earth with heartless human beings. How many of those pro-bono students of yours bother to practice? How many of them whine and moan and give you a hard time?"

"It doesn't bother me."

"Even if you do teach them to play a few tunes, what good is that going to do them? By the time they're adults with jobs and kids they'll have forgotten all you ever taught them. Your act of charity will have made no difference."

They won't forget the music, Noel thought, but didn't say. *That will make a difference.*

"Some of us," she patiently responded, "are willing to give of ourselves, even if we don't have to, even if we don't see any immediate or even long-lasting benefits."

Benjamin's mouth twisted derisively at that, and not for the first time she wondered why she put up with him. Actually, she knew the answer to that. He was a damn good accountant, and he'd been the only one on her lawyer's list of recommendations willing to come over to her house and dig through decades of paper rather than having her haul boxes to his office. For almost two years, he'd been making monthly visits, sometimes for a day, sometimes for a week, diligently working through all the assets and hidden bank accounts left to Noel by her mother. And for two years he'd chided her for her "acts of charity."

Especially at this time of year, she felt as if the two of them were reincarnations of Bob Cratchit and Ebenezer Scrooge with Scrooge as Cratchit's clerk this time around. If that were so, she shouldn't give up on him. As a Christmas baby, it was her job to prove that goodwill towards men was not humbug.

The doorbell rang. "Oh, jeez; that's them."

Benjamin's expression went even more sour, his lip curling with distain.

"I was going to put out some coffee and cookies," Noel sighed as the doorbell rang again. She shouldn't have let Benjamin distract her.

"Why bother?" he groused and she hurried to the entrance.

"Hello—" she said, throwing open the door. There they were, bundled up warm, an older woman and a young man. Noel's eyes fastened on the man, and she forgot the rest of what she was about to say.

She hadn't seen Hank Bole since high school and to say he'd matured was an understatement. His smile, however, was the same as she remembered, bright as holiday lights.

"Noel," he said, leaning in to kiss her cheek. His warm breath smelled of peppermint. "You look fantastic."

To her embarrassment, Noel giggled, much as she had back in high school. Rubbing sweaty hands down her skirt, she managed to invite them in. Mittens were stuffed into pockets, coats and mufflers hung up on hooks and she finally got to see Hank in all his adult glory. His golden hair was darker than she remembered, but then he'd often bleached and spiked it back in his wayward youth. His features were more chiseled, his bearing more serene. Those bright blue eyes, however, were as mischievous as ever, and, with a wink, could still melt her into a puddle.

You've got a boyfriend, she sternly reminded herself, even as the song "Let it Snow" began to jingle in her head... *The weather outside is frightful,* it suggested, *But the fire is so delightful...*

"This is Mona Criden," Hank introduced the woman, "the real founder of our charities. I'm just the poster boy."

"It's such a pleasure to finally meet you." Mona vigorously gripped Noel's hand with bone thin fingers. She was wearing a bit too much make-up, but her tone was sincere.

"Thank you for taking the time to come here," Noel said. "I really should have visited you—"

"See? " Hank said, "What'd I tell you? I said she'd thank *us* for coming to take her money."

Noel blushed and herded them into the living room. They settled in the plush armchairs about the tea table.

"In high school, whenever anyone was in need, they went to Noel," Hank continued. "For a shoulder to cry on, help with their homework. I even remember her giving away her lunch to those who forgot theirs."

"I didn't think you'd noticed," Noel admitted, her face very hot. "You were too busy with the drama club."

He chuckled. "You mean I was too full of myself to notice anyone else. I wish I had taken more notice of you then," he added, a sparkle in his eyes.

I wish you had, too, Noel thought, finding it very warm in the room.

"Was he a good actor?" Mona asked, apparently enjoying the reunion she was witnessing.

"He was a ham. And the rumor was he used his acting talents to lure gullible girls into bed."

"I've reformed!" Hank protested, looking so comically aggrieved that they both laughed. Their merriment was cut short by the sound of rattling china and the appearance of Benjamin, a silver tray between his hands. Noel caught her breath and felt her face pale as he intruded.

"Your coffee, Miss," Benjamin said drolly, and set the tray down. At least he'd used her good holly-leaf china, Noel thought, rather than the whimsical snowman mugs. It would have been just like him to mock her with those. Benjamin viewed her Christmas paraphernalia with all the scorn of an art critic eyeing paintings of clowns.

Her guests glanced at him, then at her, eyes wide. Great. What a time for her accountant to show off his weird sense of humor.

"This is Benjamin," Noel said through her teeth. "He's my accountant, not my butler." *And right now I'd like to slap his superior face.*

"Oh." Mona looked disappointed. "Pleased to meet you."

"Could you bring over the checks, Benjamin?" Noel asked sweetly. That killed his cheeky expression. Reluctantly, he crossed to the alcove.

Noel poured coffee.

"I remember these!" Hank said, holding up a gingerbread reindeer. "Every December you'd bring batches to school."

"Yeah, and that was the only time you bothered to pay attention to me," Noel said. "You'd come over and flirt until I gave you a handful, and then you'd ignore me again till I brought something else to school, like cupcakes or pie."

"I was incorrigible," he admitted, biting off some antler.

Benjamin came back, checks in hand. If the money had been his own, he couldn't have looked more distrustful. "Disadvantaged Children's Christmas Choir," he read off one check. "Is that doing well this year?"

Noel flushed and angrily opened her mouth, but Mona responded gamely, "Very well, actually," then to Noel, "The kids have been invited to sing everywhere, especially at Church services. They even got a small role in a holiday hip-hop video. Music makes such a difference in their lives. I only wish that we could maintain the choir year round."

"Well, I hope this donation helps you do that." Noel pointedly threw a look at Benjamin.

"The Mission of Music," he read off the other check. "Clever pun." he said without a smile.

"I thought so," Hank retorted. "You probably won't believe this, Noel, given what a narcissist I was in high school, but I did some volunteer work in a shelter last year. It's how I hooked up with Mona. Anyway, all these impoverished musicians would come in asking if we had any instruments they could play. They didn't want food or a bed. Just to make music. They made me think of you and how you were always playing tunes on the backstage piano, which is why I contacted you when I came up with this idea. Of course, all I was hoping for was a used guitar or two, not money."

"I recently came into some funds," Noel said shyly.

Benjamin rolled his eyes and handed the checks to Mona.

"Oh, Noel," Mona's lipsticked mouth dropped open. "This is too generous. Especially the one for the musicians."

"Hank said you weren't getting many donated instruments. This way you can buy new ones as well as food and beds." She glanced away uncomfortably. It seemed so wrong to be flaunting her donation; she would have rather given the money anonymously, or at least made it direct deposit. Benjamin, however, wouldn't hear of it, insisting that she make out checks and hand them to the founders herself. He'd been ready to go on strike if she tried to do it any other way. Noel wondered now why he'd insisted. Perhaps he'd hoped making out the checks would be too much trouble for her, or that she'd change her mind once she saw all those zeros. Well, if so, he failed. She was never happier than when she was sharing what she had with others, money included.

His humbug thwarted, Benjamin drifted back to the alcove and Noel enjoyed a quiet hour with Mona and Hank.

At the front door, Mona warmly gripped Noel's hands then made for the car. Hank, however, hung back. "I hear you're going to be at the foster kids' brunch tomorrow," he said. "We'll be there to support some of our choir kids. I hope we can do more catching up."

Let it snow, let it snow, let it snow... the music played in her head. "I'd like that."

He winked, and left. Noel closed the door and leaned against it with a sigh. *You have a boyfriend!* She wagged a mental finger at herself.

She returned to the living room to practice for tomorrow's party. Christmas tunes were drawn from her small, Celtic harp, soulful hymns and playful melodies, carols both sad and jolly. Benjamin stayed at his desk throughout, saying not a word. Noel was so deep into the music—floating on it—that she almost missed the sound of the door opening and a deep voice calling her name.

"In here," she shouted, setting the harp aside. She fussed with her sweater and hair.

"There she is!" Roland appeared. Before Noel knew it he'd swept her up and off her feet. Noses rubbed, hers warm, his still cold. A second later and their lips were locked in a deep kiss.

"What are you doing here?" she breathed. Did that sound guilty? "I thought you were going to be working late again and sleeping at your place."

"Got a lucky break and I'm so friggin' glad." He nibbled on her earlobe. Strangely, the song "Here Comes Santa Claus," started running through her head; maybe because, of late, Roland had been as hard to catch a glimpse of as St. Nick.

"I've been thinking about you," he whispered suggestively, "... in between selling drum sets and electric guitars of course." Another kiss. Their tongues tangled and caressed, sending heat down Noel's thighs.

"Ah-hem," Benjamin loudly cleared his throat and Noel unintentionally broke from Roland, which infuriated her. How dare Benjamin make her feel like a wanton maid caught 'fornicating!'

"Sorry," the accountant said unconvincingly. He actually looked pleased, as if dousing their ardor in ice water was a rare treat. "I just wanted to let you know that I'm going."

"Will you be coming back tomorrow?" Noel asked. She wouldn't have asked it of anyone else, tomorrow being the day-before-Christmas, but Benjamin Snowden had made it clear to her over the year-and-ten months that she'd employed him that he was on the outs with his family and so never had any holiday obligations marking his calendar. He not only worked on December twenty-fourth but, if necessary, on the twenty-fifth—which was a kind of sacrilege to Noel.

"No." He lifted up his briefcase. "I've everything I need. I'll finish up this last bit at my office."

"Oh." Noel felt an odd mix of relief and disappointment. No final chance to redeem her personal Scrooge before Christmas then. "I'd better give you your present then."

For a split second, Benjamin's habitual, cold expression vanished and it seemed as if a veil had been dropped. A look of naked pain crossed his face. It was gone in the next instant, and but for a flush to his cheeks, Noel wouldn't have thought she'd seen it at all. But she had... hadn't she?

"You shouldn't have," Benjamin said in a clipped voice. "You already gave me a very generous Christmas bonus."

"I did the same thing last year," she reminded him, which caused him to touch on his watch. It'd been her gift to him the previous Christmas—a forties, deco-style watch with a leather band. She'd mailed it to his office and gotten a very polite thank you card in return. Every time she saw him, however, he had it on his wrist.

"Here you go," she grabbed a small box from under the tree. Inside was a fountain pen she thought he'd like. He accepted it and stuffed it away in his pocket.

"Thank you," he said apparently in a hurry. "And Happy Holidays. I'll see myself to the door." He didn't look back on his way out.

Roland slipped up behind her, wrapping his protective arms about her. "Let's go back to what we were doing before Benjamin interrupted," he suggested, "only in the bedroom."

Noel was in favor of that.

Chapter 2
Holly Jolly

Music was always playing in Noel's head, even during sex. That evening she found herself lost in the Christmas lullaby "All Through the Night." Inappropriate as it was, she couldn't stop trying to make slow, sultry love to it. Roland, however, was moving to a different beat. He pushed deep inside her, then bucked his hips as if drumming, growling all the while, "Oh, yeah, fuck, yes!"

Noel rocked with languid eroticism in response, keeping to the cadence of the song. *O'er thy spirit, gent-ly steal-ing,* Her clit pulsed. *Visions of delight re-veal-ing...* She gasped as Roland pinched her nipples. Shock and stimulation followed, but she wished he'd stroke her areolas instead, that he'd take the time to really tease her. She ground her hips, hoping to cue him. He missed the hint entirely and raced ahead. Noel finally surrendered to his rhythm and allowed herself to respond.

"Fuck yeah!" Roland shouted, leaving Noel drowning in white noise.

A while later, feasting on honey-glazed ham sandwiches, Noel forgave Roland for not being in tune with her. He was the manager of a store specializing in electric guitars, drums and amps; his beat, marked with unpredictable accelerandos, often ran counter to her own. As she had the wider musical range, from jazz and opera to rock and country, she felt it up to her to keep pace with him; but she wished he'd at least try to match her tempo now and then. She couldn't help wondering what Hank's musical tastes were like.

"It's good to see you again," she said to Roland. "I was beginning to doubt your existence."

"Hey, I miss you, too, babe. I especially miss catching sight of you walking into the store, a basket of sandwiches like these," he waved a half-eaten wedge, "over your arm. The food from the convenience store is shit."

"That's it? You miss me bringing you lunch?"

He grinned. "That and our strolls through the park, and hearing you talk about your day. How was your day?"

An awkward segue. They really weren't harmonizing tonight. She told him of her students, her concern for Jill and her meeting with Hank and Mona. When she mentioned Benjamin's antics, he stopped eating and frowned.

"He's almost done, right? With all this inheritance stuff?"

"He'll be finished once and for all by New Year's. After that, I'll only have to see him at tax time."

"I wish you wouldn't see him at all after that," Roland asked. "I really don't like him. I mean, I keep feeling like... I dunno, like he's got dead girls in his basement and you're going to be next."

"What a thing to say," she laughed. "He might be a bit of a pill, but he's hardly that bad."

Roland touched on her hand, his expression gone serious. "You're too charitable; I mean, I love that about you, how you always want to believe the best about people. But sometimes you shouldn't. For my sake, once things are settled, drop him. Better yet, let me introduce you to my accountant. He's friendly and he never wears black."

Noel laughed, though the idea unsettled her, as if she were being asked to give up the long, dark nights that made Christmas lights so bright. And that, if anything, made the point to her. Roland was right. Time to shoo away the bleak raven and find a cheery blue bird. "After New Year's," she agreed.

The day before Christmas dawned gray and overcast with a new blanket of snow on the ground. Noel, up at seven, sat at the kitchen table drinking down coffee and yawning.

"Did you stay up late watching another holiday movie?" Roland asked pouring java into one of her snowman mugs.

She yawned again and nodded.

He dropped toast into the toaster. "What was it this time? Another version of *It's a Wonderful Life*? A modern remake of *A Christmas Carol*?"

She shook her head. "Good-hearted elves nearly mess up Christmas."

"Ah. That one," he said tolerantly, and Noel couldn't help but compare his friendly acceptance to Benjamin's scorn.

"Do you mind?" she found herself asking, "The way I indulge in Christmas, I mean."

"You mean: candy cane hand towels, sugar-cookie scented shampoo, a poinsettia patterned welcome mat and that comforter on the bed with nutcrackers and ballerinas? Not at all."

She laughed. "It's a duvet, not a comforter. And I did warn you when we got together what you could expect."

"Babe, there was no warning you could have given me back in August that could've prepared me for this—this transformation of your home into Santa's Village."

"It's not that bad!"

"Close enough." The toast popped and Roland brought it over. "But hey, it's all very you: sweet and charming. I get it. All except watching every single holiday movie no matter how awful."

She smiled and reached for the apple-cranberry jam. "All year long we're bombarded with the message that we need to be ruthless. To always want our side to win, even if it means destroying the opposition. If someone hurts us, we're supposed to bring out big guns and start shooting." She shook her head. "It's like, if you're kind or giving, you're an idiot. In December, however, the world changes its mind. For only twenty-five days, but still. Everything you see or hear reminds you to care about others, to think about them and not yourself."

She took a nibble of toast and jam, enjoying the tart-sweet flavor. "That's why I try to catch all the Capraesque movies... and listen to all the Christmas carols and display every holiday card. Because I don't want to miss a minute of those precious, twenty-five days. When else is the world in sync with me?"

"That's very nice, but you've got a brunch to perform at and those movies have left you half-asleep."

"I can play any Christmas song you'd care to name with my eyes closed."

"The way you're yawning, you may have to. Speaking of which, I'm really sorry, but I don't think I'm going to be able to watch you play today."

She sighed. "You said you could get a few hours."

"I know, I know, but one of the part-time salesgirls came down with the flu yesterday, and, well, I've some last minute shopping to do myself." He wagged his brows. "See you tonight? My place? I'll be picking up that dinner you ordered; all you have to do is remember the wine."

Noel forced away her disappointment and smiled. He was right. They were going to have all night together and all tomorrow: her birthday and favorite day of the year. What else mattered? "Tonight's movie features a wayward angel who saves a family's Christmas. I'll keep a spot open on the couch."

Noel sat on the red velvet divan, eating her brunch and listening to the shrieks and laughter of children. So far, the party had proved an unqualified success. It had started at nine in the morning on a steep, snowy hillside.

Armed with a dozen donated sleds, the kids had taken to that hill, racing each other on down, sometimes tumbling off, sometimes crashing.

Noel had watched with the other adults, cheering them on, until, of course, gloved hands had grabbed hold of hers. "Come on, Miss Larken! You have to give it a try—"

So up the hill she'd trudged. Flat on her stomach, clinging to the sides of the sled, she'd had second thoughts until someone had given her a push. Snow had spit up, pelting her in the face, and she'd screamed as she hit the bumps. At last, she'd reached the bottom, gliding to a stop. She'd dragged the sled back up and done it again, and again. She would have kept doing it, but the whiny kids had demanded their sled back. Spoil sports!

Hungry and frozen, the party had retired to the farmhouse for brunch. Owned by a retired author of children's books, it was a wonderful place, filled with a mix of rustic furniture and eccentric pieces like the divan. Divested of jackets and galoshes, the kids had grabbed hold of TV trays with Christmas-tree-shaped waffles in the largest area. The adults had been treated to crepes stuffed with caramelized pears and pecans. There were maple sausages, orange slices and hot chocolate or coffee to round it out.

This, Noel thought, as she forked up bites of crepe, was heaven. Exactly what a holiday home ought to be like, the fire blazing, toy trains zipping about the tree, a gingerbread house detailed with marzipan wreaths and gumdrop cobblestones. And guests. A great many guests all warming themselves in each other's company.

Christmas had been like this when Noel was little, a big gathering of family and friends, noisy and lively. She remembered tearing about the house with other children, new toys in her hands, parents picking up torn wrapping paper and discarded ribbons. Her birthday had been the best day of the year back then. As the years passed, however, so did the friends and relatives. Some left due to age or illness, others moved away or married and started spending Christmas with their new families.

By the time Noel's father died, only she and her mother had been left to sit around the tree opening presents. These last two Christmases there'd been only Noel.

Well, she reflected, *this year I'll have Roland*. Oddly, however, that thought didn't warm her in quite the way it should. Why was that?

"I saw you racing down the hill," a charming voice said, and she felt her heart jump like a spark from a fireplace log. Hank was smiling down at her. "I had no idea you were into extreme sports."

Her pulse sped up. "There are a lot of things you don't know about me," she said, which was deliberate flirting and so what? She glanced about. "Where's Mona?"

His face darkened and his eyes slid away. "She had to stay behind and take care of some business. In fact, I need to talk to you about that. Not now, but maybe later?"

Noel was taken aback. This sounded serious. "Of course," she said, and was about to say more when Mrs. Rothmore, the organizer of the party, rang a bell.

"Welcome, foster parents, to our annual party," she said once everyone had quieted down. "I don't know if the children have managed to keep it a secret from you, but they've got some special presentations."

The adults reacted with an "Ohhhh," as if surprised and applauded as the first child was introduced. A series of vignettes followed: a girl in pink tights dancing to the *Waltz of the Snowflakes*; a boy performing a couple of magic tricks; another reciting a portion of "Visit from St. Nick." In between were the musical performances. Hank's quartet of choir kids sung a lovely rendition of "Oh, Holy Night." Then there were Noel's students: Tom strumming out "Jingle Bell Rock" on guitar; Debra picking out "Sleigh Ride" on banjo.

Jill's turn and Noel held her breath as the girl settled onto the bench, pushed up her glasses and bravely set her fingers on the keys. *Deck the hall with boughs of holly...* the notes diligently marched along, then, *Fa-la-la-la-la...* hesitation so brief only Noel noticed it, *La-la-la-la.* Perfect! Noel silently cheered. Go Jill!

The girl got through the second set of "fa-la-las," her tempo picking up. There were stumbles, but Noel couldn't have been more proud. The final "La!" note played, Jill stood and basked in her achievement. And Benjamin said these kids wouldn't remember this, Noel reflected, as she joined in on the applause.

"Fantastic!" she mouthed to the girl.

The last child performed and now it was Noel's turn. She brought forward her harp and everyone in the room stilled as her fingers dropped that first glorious note. People so rarely heard harp music that they forgot how beautiful it was, the instrument of angels. Sensing that she had them, she started in on "Bring a Torch," using those strings and the carol's novel, 3/8 time to take everyone back to early yuletides. From there Noel melted seamlessly into "Merrily on High," with all its tingling notes. Smiles appeared and the kids bounced along, like raindrops on a sidewalk.

"A Holly Jolly Christmas" was her finale. A jazzy, laughing tempo that allowed her to surrender to that melodic current. She felt the stings under her fingers, the vibrations through the frame of the harp, the rapt attention of the audience. There was no more intimate connection for Noel than this, as she gifted herself to people with the music she loved. Finished, she accepted the applause. Then, calling the children forward, she led the room in a rousing if off-tune rendition of "We Wish You a Merry Christmas."

"*And a Happy New Year!*" rang to the rafters. Everyone cheered and hugged and then the kids were urged to look under the tree. They excitedly pounced on the gifts, searching for and finding books, candy, and secret-Santa presents. Paper was torn, boxes opened, and the prizes within shown off.

"We should talk now," Hank reappeared at Noel's side.

"Yes, certainly," Noel said, and they retired down the hall to an empty sewing room.

"Nice playing, by the way," Hank said, shutting the door behind them. It wasn't the response she'd hoped from him, especially in regards to her music, but he obviously had other things on his mind.

"Thank you." She nervously tugged at her sweater. "Um... has there been a problem?"

He looked very grave, as if the light within him had been doused. "I... have to give you back the checks," he admitted, pulling them from his pocket.

Noel's stomach dropped and she felt her cheeks go hot. The first thing that popped to her mind was that Benjamin had made a mistake, fouled things up. "Didn't they go through?"

"It isn't that," Hank said, running a hand through his blond hair. "We're being investigated."

"*What?*"

Hank shrugged and tried to smile. "Mona and I have been accused of siphoning off funds, child exploitation and well, fraud." He offered a half-hearted laugh.

"That's terrible!"

"I just wish the accuser, whoever they are, had waited till after the holidays," he said sadly. "We learned this morning that our assets have been frozen. There are a lot of things we bought on credit that we'll have to return."

"You don't... know who filed these charges?" Noel murmured. The crepes she'd eaten were threatening to come back up. *No, no. He wouldn't.*

"Not a clue."

He wouldn't, Noel insisted. But in her gut, she knew he had.

"On the day before Christmas," Hank sighed. "Can you believe it?"

No. she couldn't. "I'll take back the checks," she said, "And see about getting you some cash to tide you over."

"That's beyond the call of duty, Noel," Hank said, gazing at her with warmth and relief. "Even for a saint like you. But thank you. I knew you'd understand."

She understood all right. And her charitable thoughts toward Benjamin finally reached their limit.

Chapter 3
Let It Snow

Benjamin's office was locked, but Noel knew what that meant and where to find him. A block down from his building was the red door of the *Crow's Nest Coffee Bar.* Painted blackbirds in Santa Hats decorated its window, and green candles flickered in the decorative, snow filled fountain by the outdoor tables. A couple sat at one of those tables, well bundled up and smoking cigarettes.

Stepping in, Noel was greeted with the music of low voices and the hiss of cappuccino machines. There were garlands of holly on the dark walls and silver ornaments dangling from the ceiling beams like stars. Offbeat and charming, she could see why this was Benjamin's favorite haunt. Of course, knowing frugal Benjamin, he probably just came here because it was close to his office.

She found him seated at a table near the wall, documents that might have to do with her inheritance scattered about. He looked as cold and phlegmatic as ever, no hint or sign of his covert activities. Stuffing hat and gloves into her pockets, Noel marched over, scraped back a chair and seated herself across from him. He glanced up, startled.

"You must have arranged for those investigations days ago. Weeks maybe," she said. She was surprised at how low and steady her voice was. She had to lace her hands tight, however, to keep them from shaking. "And what's why you had me write up checks and give them to Hank personally. Because you knew what was coming and if you stalled me the money wouldn't go through. That's what you were after, wasn't it?"

The heavy lids of his eyes fell and rose in a slow blink. His saturnine face expressed neither surprise nor guilt. "Those *charities* didn't deserve your money."

"Didn't deserve my money?" she echoed. "When did second guessing my choices become part of your job?"

51

He offered her that hawk-nosed profile of his, not looking ashamed so much as worried, as if he hadn't expected her to come at him this way. "A good accountant should have your financial interests at heart."

"Is that the best excuse you can think up?" Her tone was clipped. "All that trouble, those charities turned upside down, reputations destroyed, Christmas ruined, all because you had my financial interests at heart?"

His thin lips pressed together, a stubborn expression that suggested she was being ungrateful. That angered Noel even more.

"You know what I think?" she said, "That you've been working on my finances for so long you think they're yours."

That got a reaction, a real one. Benjamin looked like she'd slapped him.

"That's not true!" he protested, but his voice wavered.

She rose from the table. "I think it is. And I think it's a good thing we're almost done, you and I, otherwise I'd fire your ass. Roland was right, you can't be trusted."

"Can't be trusted?" His cold eyes were back on her, blazing. "Roland said that? *That?* About me?" He laughed. It was the first time she'd heard him laugh and it sounded ugly. "Oh, that's rich!"

He soared to his feet, towering over her like some dark tornado. Noel shrunk back a step. She remembered what Roland had said about dead bodies in the basement.

"Ask Mr. Trustworthy why he's been working late," Benjamin said. "Ask him why he can never meet you for lunch."

Her mind blanked out. What? She replayed the words. They didn't make sense. "I don't... " she fumbled. "What are you saying?"

Like that, Benjamin's stormy expression vanished. Face paling, he gazed at her in anguish, like a child realizing he'd just broken something very delicate and precious.

"Oh, God, I shouldn't have— I mean— I— N-Noel—" He held out a pleading hand.

She was already making for the exit. She bumped into a chair, a table, the couple who'd been smoking outside as they stepped through the door. Next thing she knew, she was hurrying down the street, cold air hitting her face. She struggled to tug on her hat and gloves.

Church bells were chiming the hour. She half ran, half stumbled toward the park where Roland liked to take his breaks. It was one-thirty, late for lunchtime, but Roland, she reflected, always took a late lunch.

The bare branches of the trees were dotted with white ornaments, as if they were catching fireflies, and the park, itself, was quietly active. There were skaters circling the frozen pond, and boys kicking up snow as they threw a football. Noel passed a woman selling caramel corn and a man with a hot chestnut cart. A cloud of nutty smoke drifted from the wide, shallow pan where he roasted them.

She glanced about furtively as she walked, hoping and not hoping to see Roland. "Winter Wonderland" played in her head, her feet tapping in tempo as they inexorably headed for Roland's favorite lunch spot. More than anything she didn't want to see him there. She could almost bear the thought of him lunching with someone else, so long as it wasn't at *their* spot.

She heard the melody of a babbling brook, and her heart started to pound as she came in sight of a red, covered footbridge, its snow weighted roof gaily festooned with holiday lights. There were benches within, set to either side of the footpath. Pedestrians could stop and sit and gaze out through the latticework trusses at the park. Noel had lunched with Roland on those benches almost every day since they'd become a couple, back in August. During the months of autumn they'd enjoyed tomato soup out of a thermos while rain pattered on the bridge's roof and tore colored leaves from the trees. When the first snow had fallen in early November, they'd been here to see it, drifting down quiet and gentle as the kisses they'd exchanged.

It was right after that, however, that Roland had gotten busy, too busy to meet her except for dinner now and then. She'd accepted that this was due to the demands of the holiday season. Overly generous as always, she'd even urged him not to worry about it, to think of himself, not her.

Only now did it occur to her how curious it was that he hadn't asked her to meet him at the bridge since then. Not for lunch, nor for one of his breaks, nor even after work. Not once in all those weeks.

Voices joined the rush of the brook below and Noel saw people within sitting on the bridge's benches: parents with children, elderly couples, dog walkers—all chatting amiably and gazing out at the winter wonderland of the park. And then, as she'd dreaded, she heard Roland's deep voice carrying like a baritone in an opera.

"...about tonight," he was saying regretfully. "But I just can't ruin Christmas for her."

"Well," a woman's amused voice harmonized with his, "you're going to have to ruin something. New Year's or Valentine's. Unless you want to hold off till the Fourth of July?"

"No. No. It's just... she was born on Christmas day—"

"Ah. Yeah it *would* be harsh to break up on her birthday...." the woman reflected.

"—and she's completely gaga about the holidays," Roland finished. "I mean, it's all real for her."

That made Noel wince, as if he'd driven a spike into her heart. God. He made her sound like a child who still believed in Santa Claus.

"She's a *nice* person," he added.

And that was the nail in the coffin. *Nice.* She couldn't think of a more damning description. Dead accurate, but damning. Funny, she didn't feel nice at all right now.

Roland and the woman were still talking, but Noel wasn't listening. She strode in. There they were, seated near the mouth of the bridge, sharing a bag of hot chestnuts. All the music in her head vanished. For the first time in memory, her mind went quiet. Stone, cold quiet.

Roland saw her first. His eyes going wide with shock and guilt. The woman, seeing him freeze, paused and blinked at Noel. "Oh," was all she said.

She was a willowy brunette dressed in neon pink and black; her hair was sassily cut and accented with snowy white streaks. Noel recognized her from the pictures of local bands that covered one wall of Roland's music store. She'd been dressed in hot pink leather, flailing away on an electric guitar.

So, Noel thought, Roland had left her for a metal girl. Left, yes, probably since November, maybe before that. Strange to realize she hadn't had a boyfriend all this time.

"Noel—" Roland managed at last.

"I want my key back," she said quietly. "Now, please. You can give it to me out here," she added. She was not going to put on a show for electric guitar girl or anyone else.

She hurried away from the bridge on down the path, stopping at a lamppost. She leaned there, gazing at the brook. Roland came jogging up behind her, key in gloved fingers.

"I'd appreciate it," she said, taking it from him, "if you'd erase my e-mail from your address book and my phone number from your cell. Don't bother contacting me. We won't be getting back together. I don't even want to be friends."

He was stunned, so much so that she almost laughed. *Yeah, Roland,* she thought, *I've never seen this side of me either. Who knew I could be such a stone-cold bitch?*

"Noel, I was planning to—"

"Don't. You can't make it better, and there's no point trying. Just tell me: Why sneak around? Why not just say it wasn't working and you'd found someone else? Why, for God's sake—" She flashed on last night's sex, "— pretend that you cared for me?"

He flushed to the roots of his hair and stammered. "I wasn't pretending. I mean, I do care about you, and things weren't exactly wrong between us. They were just... out of step. She and I are more in tune."

For some reason Benjamin flashed to mind, in particular what Roland had said about getting her another accountant. She hadn't thought her heart could sink any lower, but it did, as if through the brook's icy waters to the soft muck at the bottom.

"So you weren't waiting for me to come into the money?" she heard her voice accusing him, loud and clear as a bell in the still air. He hesitated.

"Jesus, Roland—"

"It's not like you think," he protested, "I thought if you had the money it'd be easier. You have all these plans, things you're going to do with the money. I thought that would take your mind off, well, me. Give you something else to focus on... if we... after we broke up."

"Honestly?"

"Yeah, honestly," he snapped. "But if you really want me to be up front, I gotta tell you, I was pissed that you never asked for my opinion about the money. It would've been nice to know that you cared about what I wanted, about making *our* dreams come true. I mean all you ever talk about day and night is granting other people's wishes; why not ours?"

"Charity begins at home?"

He looked angry now, his guilt turning to self-righteousness. He did have a point, though. She'd never once thought of how she might use the money for them, for their future. She'd only thought of giving it away to foundations.

"How about her?" Noel lifted her chin toward the bridge. "Does she want to make your dreams come true?"

Roland blushed. "We're going to pool our cash and start an internet radio station," he admitted, "at the music store so we can feature live bands."

"Wonderful." She was cold. Time to get home. "I'll pack up your stuff. You can come pick it up next week."

"I'm sorry if I hurt you," he said as she turned from him. "You're a really —"

"Nice girl," she said in unison, and gave him the finger as she walked away.

55

Chapter 4
All Through the Night

Noel stood in the dark, staring at the Christmas tree. Once she'd gotten home she'd stripped off everything and gotten into her red-and-white striped, footed pajamas, a one piece with a zipper up the front. The pj's were totally absurd, but very soft and cozy. Her plushest robe had gone on over that.

Feeling well armored, she'd taken Roland's stocking down from the mantle and scoured the house for anything belonging to him; clothes, electric razor, coffee cup, the presents under the tree that were from him to her, still in their wrapping paper and ribbons. Everything had gone into a box in the hall closet, even his toothpaste. As for the Christmas presents she'd gotten him, those she tossed into a different box, one she'd drop off at Goodwill day after tomorrow.

She did keep one thing: the wine. The plan had been for Roland to pick up a pre-ordered crown-roast supper for two. No doubt he and electric-guitar girl were feasting on it now. Roland wasn't the sort to let that kind of thing go to waste. Which left Noel with a bottle of merlot. She poured a second glass and wandered over to the tree.

The ornaments glinted and glowed on their branches, asking to be admired. Almost all of them were musical in theme, ones she'd picked up herself or been given by family, friends and students: Miniature pianos, violins, saxophones, lutes, French horns, even an accordion. There was a little drummer boy and a fiddling Santa, varnished scrolls of sheet music, silver and gold notes, and a dozen different harps and bells.

Usually, she had only to glance at an ornament and a snippet of music would come to mind: the xylophone of The Nutcracker's sugarplum fairies or the trumpet of Handel's Messiah. Not tonight.

"Noel?"

She sipped her wine. There was no music tonight, only deafening silence. That's all there'd been in her head since the bridge. She didn't even notice the sounds around her: the crackle of the fire, the wind blowing down the chimney. Footsteps.

"Noel?"

No music, and no desire to give. She'd always believed that giving was its own reward. Yet now she wondered about that. It seemed like she'd spent her time on earth meandering in and out of people's lives, offering them music, money, time, everything she had. They'd drunk their fill of her and then? Students stopped with their lessons and never contacted her again. Friends moved away, relatives passed on. Lovers sought greener pastures.

Maybe that was why she'd been so eager to throw money at charities? Because she'd known that they would keep coming back. But likely they'd just drink her dry and head off to another well. How the hell had she ended up so lonely?

"You left the keys in the front door," Benjamin said. Not Roland, nor Hank for that matter, come to rescue her from solitude. Benjamin. She could feel him there, waiting for her to face him.

"I put your key ring on the hook. There were some documents I didn't think I'd need," he added, "and it turns out I do. I— I wouldn't have come here otherwise."

Tomorrow morning, Noel reflected, still staring at the tree, she'd sit here opening gifts that meant nothing to her. Things she didn't want and couldn't use, poor substitutes for love and companionship. She would open the presents alone, just like last year and the year before. And just like last year and the year before, she'd spend the rest of Christmas day, her birthday, alone.

"Noel?"

"I found Roland with his new girlfriend."

"Oh, Jesus, Noel, I'm sorry—"

"We broke up," she cut him off. Then, "When did you find out about them?"

She didn't hear him shift, but she felt the movement, his discomfort.

"A few weeks ago. I wasn't spying on him. I was on my way to a meeting with a client, and I passed by the music store and saw him and—and her. Kissing. Fooling around. Noel, you have to believe, I didn't mean to tell you that way, to hurt you—"

"No, no," she sighed and sipped her wine. "It was a good thing you did. I went looking for him rather than going to the bank and withdrawing a large amount of cash to hand over to Hank Bole."

She heard Benjamin suck in his breath.

"That would have been bad, right?" she added. "Because he's a crook."

Silence.

"Come on, Benjamin. Right now I'm feeling my whole life's a lie. You're the only honest thing in it. So give it to me straight."

"Hank Bole is... " A pause. "...still doing what I overheard you say he used to do in high school. Only he's not using his acting talents to get girls into bed. He's using them to bilk women out of their money. He and Mona are con artists."

No different from when they were teenagers, Noel mused, not Hank or her. He'd flirted with her to get what he wanted, and she, dazzled by the attention, had been ready to give it to him. What was especially galling was how easily he'd lured her in: all those depreciating regrets about his selfish youth, as if he were sorry for his wrongs and now wanted to do right. Oh, yes. The girl who loved holiday movies about redemption and discovering the Christmas spirit had swallowed that hook, line and sinker.

"You wouldn't have believed me," Benjamin's gruff voice cut through, apologizing. "If I'd told you flat out about Roland or Hank. You... like to give people the benefit of the doubt."

"I'm a nice person. Yes," she finished, setting down her empty wine glass. Maybe she ought to refill it again? "You're right. I probably wouldn't have believed you. Like you said, I'm too charitable, a gullible Pollyanna. No wonder you're always looking down your nose at me. You must think I'm a real idiot."

"No," he said roughly, and she finally turned around. He looked terrible, pale and lost, as if he'd been walking the streets for hours. "I think you're the most generous, most wonderful person I've ever met. And I can't stand that people use and hurt you."

Noel didn't know how to respond to that.

Benjamin started pacing, restlessly crossing and crisscrossing the room. "The people I meet always want to cheat the system. They don't care if someone ends up starving on the streets; having what they want is all that matters. It's like life is one big game, and the aim is to screw everyone else while hoarding all the prize money for yourself. I was convinced everyone was like this. Then I met you." He flapped his arms about like an outraged bird. "An impossibility. A character out of a Christmas story. You really and truly think only of what you can do for others. You'll lie down and let people step on you if it'll help them get to the other side. I've seen it.

"You're cheerful, charitable, forgiving," he went on. "You even think the best of me!" He tapped his chest. "I can tell. No matter how awful I am, you think I'm worth..." he caught a breath. "Worth something. And yet your students never thank you, and their parents always want you to perform for this event or that without pay. Assholes like Hank Bole want to fleece you. And Roland," he growled the name. "You'd think a guy who sells instruments would understand your music, but he doesn't get it. Doesn't get you. When I'm at the desk, and I hear you play, it's like— like—"

"Like?"

He stopped in front of her. "Like you're gifting yourself to me."

She was amazed to see that he was trembling. She'd never imagined her accountant could be like this, so ardent and stormy. Nor had she ever imagined she'd find him so strangely attractive: that wavy, black hair, the dark eyes, even the aquiline nose. Why hadn't she ever noticed how sexy he was? Like some negative angel come down to Earth in search of redemption. He smelled good, too, all Christmas spice.

She found herself leaning towards him, and before she could reconsider, her hands were behind his head. Her fingers combed through that wavy, black hair and drew his head down. His spicy fragrance filled her nostrils, and she heard his shallow and rapid breathing. Was his heart thumping loudly in his ears?

Their lips touched. She expected him to seize the opportunity and kiss her roughly, but he was surprisingly tentative about it, brushing his lips over hers, as if exploring their softness. His mouth opened and so did hers. He tasted of nutmeg and brown sugar. The kiss deepened, making her tingle, making her hunger for more. She forced herself to break off and step back. She didn't want to make another mistake.

He didn't come after her. He just waited, Adam's apple bobbing. She'd always thought him cold, but she could see now that he'd been wearing a visor all this time, one that disguised his feelings. It'd been lifted at last and his emotions were plain to see: He wanted her. Badly. But he was sure she was going to change her mind, renege on that kiss and throw him out. He was right to be worried; she wasn't feeling charitable or nice; what she was feeling was that it was time to reclaim her Christmas Eve.

She grabbed hold of his sweater and pulled it up. He was startled, but hurried to help her snatch it off him. Underneath was a thermal shirt. He quickly crossed his arms and pulled that off too, tossing it aside. His body wasn't as skinny as she'd feared it'd be; the ribs were showing, but his shoulders had breath, his chest definition. She raked her eyes over him, saliva pooling under her tongue as she followed a line of hair down from breastbone, to navel and below. *All mine*, she thought, nabbing him by the belt and dragging him into the bedroom.

A push landed him flat on his back, and she busied herself with getting his boots unlaced. They hit the carpet. Socks next. He had long, boney feet. She climbed up next to him and reached for the buckle.

"You've got ballerinas and nutcrackers on your bed," he said. He was blinking at the quilt in disbelief.

"Yes I do." She leaned in, nose to nose. "This is my Nutcracker Suite duvet and you will *not* disrespect it."

"That's a tall order," he responded, cupping her face in his long hands and giving her a lingering kiss. The desire in her rose quickly, strongly. His tongue was caressing hers now, teasing the roof of her mouth, making her feel flush and dizzy.

"But anything you want, I'll do," he said in a thick, husky voice. "Anything."

She swallowed hard and stroked a hand down his belly, liking the way it fluttered under her touch. Back up and across his chest which rose and fell with excited breaths. "Take off your pants," she told him.

He unbuckled and unzipped, lifting his butt to push off the trousers. A few kicks and he was free of them. He wore a charmingly simple and cheap pair of white briefs, under which his erection was evident. Noel tossed off her robe. Benjamin's eyes widened as he got a good look at the striped, footed pj's. He bit his lip.

"You can laugh at my elf suit later," she grumbled, lying down beside him. Roland had always wanted to rip off the clothes and get down to business, rarely giving Noel time to explore. She was determined to indulge herself now. In no rush, she fondled Benjamin through the cotton briefs, toying with his thick tool, even scratching it with her short nails till he squirmed and moaned.

"Let's take them off," she whispered in his ear. He couldn't wiggle out of them fast enough. His shaft popped up from a nest of black hair, pearl drops welling at the tip. Scooting down, Noel took it in hand, and gave it a taste. Benjamin gasped and bucked and Noel licked her lips. He tasted like honey and nutmeg.

She ran her tongue down the side of his rod, between his hairy thighs to his balls. His spice fragrance was potent down here, and she lapped at that furry, crinkly sac very leisurely, enjoying his intoxicating scent. By the time she glided back up he was rocking, his dick swaying like a metronome. She took him into her mouth.

This was one of those things she savored, when the velvety soft skin of a man's member grew slippery with her saliva and she could just swallow him down. She let the crown hit the roof of her mouth, sucking on that satiny candy cane. Then she let it glide back out so she could tongue his slit, sip at that spiced punch flavor, then back again to bobbing and sucking.

Benjamin groaned and clutched at the duvet. It was clear that he was fighting against his urge to buck up into her throat, which impressed her. Roland had always lost control and ended up gagging her.

"Oh, Jesus, Noel," Benjamin suddenly cried, and before she knew what was happening, his cock had left her mouth. He grabbed her and rolled them over so that he was kneeling above her. He caught her mouth, biting her lips, fingers searching for the zipper. His skin had a sheen sweat and he was trembling with desire, but he held off. His gaze meeting hers, asking permission to open his Christmas present.

She nodded and he slowly drew down the zipper. The pajamas parted from neck to crotch. It was his turn to rake his eyes over her, and she watched him carefully for signs of disappointment. His Adam's apple bobbed with a hard swallow as he drank her in, eyes traveling from the exposed breasts with their dusky rose nipples, to that soft bit of belly she couldn't seem to exercise away, down to the cinnamon-red triangle of her pubic hair. Then his gaze came back up and he used that beak of a nose to slowly caress her neck.

Down he went from there, his lips pressing at the base of her throat, shoulder, and finally her breasts. He rubbed his hair over her nipples, an exquisite sensation, and they stiffened. Then his cheek went up against them, the faint, sandpapery hint of stubble sending a burn down to her groin.

"I know you're doing this as an act of charity," he whispered, "and I don't care, I don't care—"

"Fuck that." Noel impatiently pulled him toward her nipple. "I'm not being charitable. I want something and I'm using you to get it. Without reservations, without hesitation. This is all for me."

"Good for you!" he breathed on her breast, and then he was tonguing her areolas and pulling gently at her nipples with his teeth. Each light tug sent a jolt to her pussy, wetting her thighs. She groaned and struggled out of the pajamas.

With impatient tugs, Benjamin helped to get her naked, and then he was down between her legs, his hands, those long, hot piano hands, at her waist, following her curves. His kisses feathered over her belly making her hips grind.

Her breath was coming short now as he left that soft spot right below the navel to nip and suck at her tender, inner thighs. She writhed and moaned, and spread her legs wider. When his tongue hit her swollen inner-lips it came as such a shock that she cried out. It was as if he'd rung a bell. She'd barely had time to catch her breath when he licked her again and again. Long, slow strokes, his tongue flat and trying to lap up every taste of her.

She had her hands tangled in his hair, and her ass was rocking up to meet him. Sweat broke out across her body. That's when the music came back. No set tune, just a full orchestration of licks and rocks and jolts and waves. The steady caress of his tongue over her sensitive clit, the beat of her ass against the bed, the ripples of sensation, spreading up and out to her limbs—

The tempo sped up, until, like the climax of a cadenza, she was swept up. Her body jerked and spasmed and she cried out, eyes shutting tight. When she opened them again, Benjamin was over her, his cock ready to enter.

She grabbed hold of his lanky body, drawing him inside. His cock rubbed those tight, still-squeezing walls within her. Another orgasm, the intense beat of it a counter point to his strokes. Faster and faster—

Benjamin shouted, coming hard, and Noel thought she screamed. The music crescendoed and a sensation sweeter than any music carried her up. She kept hold of Benjamin throughout, as she might hold onto an angel flying her into the dark Christmas sky. Finally, she became aware of their ragged breaths, their sweaty bodies, and the matching hammer of hearts.

Releasing him, she collapsed onto the bed, wrung out, exhausted, and marveling at the fact that for once, and without a single, recognizable melody in her head, she'd enjoyed a perfect improvisation with a man.

Chapter 5
A Merry Little Christmas

Christmas morning, Noel's birthday, she came awake in her bed, naked and alone. During the night she'd woken now and then to hear Benjamin's breaths beside her, his warm, solid body curved possessively about hers. The oddest thing was that she hadn't mistaken him for Roland. His presence in her bed had felt right in a way Roland's never had. Which was ridiculous. She wasn't even sure she liked Benjamin. Yet she couldn't deny that there'd been chemistry between them unlike any she'd ever experienced before.

She gazed over at the empty side now, the dent in the pillow. Well, she thought, what did she expect? He'd gotten what he wanted from her, just like everyone else. Noel slipped out from under the blankets and, finding it shivery cold, got her footed pajamas back on before heading into the bathroom.

It was as she was stepping out again that she heard the piano music. It started awkward, full of mistakes. Stopped. Started over again as if the fingers were trying to remember how to play. *Have yourself a merry little Christmas...* . The notes carefully and timidly stated.

Stepping into the living room, she found a fire blazing in the fireplace and Benjamin seated at the piano. He was dressed in his trousers and sweater, his usually impeccably combed hair tousled. His long hands were making their way over the keys and they were as beautiful as she'd imagined they'd be. Surprisingly, he seemed to have both natural talent and a passion for playing. He looked quite wrapped up in the tune, until she took a step closer. Then he fumbled to a stop, blushing with embarrassment.

"Merry Christmas," Noel ventured.

"Happy Birthday," he returned, which made her feel pleased and shy.

"Why didn't you tell me you played?" she asked.

"I only play for myself. Also... I was one of those awful, bratty kids who gave my piano teacher a hard time."

Ah-ha. "Why am I not surprised?"

He rose from the bench and waved to the tea table. "There's cinnamon toast. Also Christmas coffee. It's got cocoa, sugar and some nutmeg in it."

Her brows went up and she wandered over to the table. There were her holiday mugs with snowmen, the matching plates with toast on them, the coffee pot, and a bowl of whipped cream. The chocolaty beverage smelled delicious.

"I thought we could have some coffee, then open your presents." Benjamin said and paused, his eyes going unexpectedly cold and hooded. "Unless, of course, you want me to leave."

"Why should I want that?" she said, settling down into an armchair and pouring out two cups of mocha. She was reaching for the whipped cream when she saw, by the bowl, a small, gift-wrapped box.

"What's this?"

"Your birthday present," Benjamin murmured. He was still on his feet, standing behind an armchair as if ready to bolt out of the room.

He hadn't called it a Christmas present, she noted. She pulled off the ribbon and opened the box. The ring inside took her breath away. It was a gold channel setting with tiny diamonds. Small rubies and emeralds alternated between the white, sparkling gems. For several minutes she was utterly speechless.

"This is an engagement ring," she managed.

"It's a birthday present," he insisted.

"When in the world did you buy this?"

"Six months ago," he admitted, almost defiantly. A jerk of his head toward the office. "I've been keeping it in one of the drawers there in the roll top."

"You hid it here? In *my* desk?"

He nodded. "I had it all planned. I'd ask you out, and we'd date, and if we were still together come Christmas morning, I'd get it out of the desk and... propose."

"You're kidding." She felt bowled over, and, thinking about it, a little angry "So... what the hell happened? How is it you dropped the ball and I ended up with Roland the cheat instead of you?"

His lips tightened with offense. "You make it sound like you'd have said yes, and been happier with me. What would someone as ni—"

"Don't you dare say 'nice'!"

"What would someone as wonderful as you want with a dull, cynical, killjoy accountant? I've yet to come up with a single answer to that question, which is why I never asked you out."

"How about you're the only person who's completely honest with me? That's a reason. Everyone thinks I'm so nice they don't want to hurt my feelings. You say what you think. I like that. And I like that you're not ostentatious, and that you stand on your own two feet. I even like that you plan things out to a ridiculous degree. But why don't you tell me what would someone as sharp and intelligent as you want with a rosy idealist too blind to see that her boyfriend is fucking another woman, and her high school crush is a hustler?"

He broke eye contact. "Well, you did give me a very large Christmas bonus."

Noel snorted.

"...And so what if you err on the side of optimism?" he went on, "You're unapologetically you. For two years I've been amazed by that. You put it all out there from your passion for music to your weakness for sappy movies, even your ridiculous affection for Christmas paraphernalia—"

"Hey!"

He lifted a brow. "You're the one dressed like a runaway elf."

She pursed her lips. "So you're saying it's all sweet and adorable? My gingerbread cookies and yuletide spirit? The poinsettia welcome mat?"

He winced. "You had to mention the welcome mat. No, I don't think it's sweet and adorable, I think it's delusional."

She grinned. There was her Benjamin. She'd take his honest scorn over Roland's patronizing bullshit any day.

"My point," he continued, "is that this isn't an act of charity. It's... love. Love of you and all you are. And just so you know," he added quickly, "I've worked out a rudimentary pre-nup."

"You what?"

He quickly held up his hands. "For me! Stipulating that I can't touch your inheritance. I didn't... I don't want you thinking I'm after your money."

The man was besotted. Crazy. "An accountant who tries to take everything into account," she murmured liking that as well. She held up the box so the ring flashed in the firelight. "So what am I supposed to do with this?"

He shrugged. "I don't know if last night meant anything to you, but I couldn't live with myself if I lost another chance. So be charitable and accept it... as a birthday present or Christmas present or whatever."

He finally stepped around the armchair and sat down, almost upsetting the cups and coffee pot. "I know I'm not someone you'd normally consider, being that I stupidly err on the side of pessimism. I'm not sure I'm someone you'd even want for a friend. But I swear, Noel, if you give me a chance, you won't be disappointed."

Her heart turned over. "Emeralds and rubies. You know me pretty well."

Truth was, she thought, she didn't want Benjamin gone from her life. Yes, he was bleak and suspicious as a raven, but he was her raven. And yeah, he'd stuck his beak into her business, but that was his way of protecting her.

She could see that now; all he wanted was to be her knight in black armor, shielding her from predatory dragons, giving of himself to her.

Downbeat he might be, but he was selfless and generous, and he harmonized perfectly with her upbeat melody. She slipped the ring on her finger and leaned across the table to kiss him.

"Six months from now," she said, "if you don't want this ring back, we'll talk about changing its status from a birthday present to something else."

His intense, dark eyes were back on her again and she saw what she was beginning to think of as the real Benjamin. A man who was anything but cold. He blinked at her, and blinked again, his Adam's apple bobbing.

"I'm not going to want it back," he said hoarsely. "And I'll keep December 25th marked on my calendar."

She grinned. One thing was sure, if this all worked out she'd have a husband who'd never forget either her birthday or their anniversary.

They took the coffee and toast with them over to the tree and Benjamin helped Noel open her gifts. She felt bad that there were none under there for him, but he seemed happy enough to watch her exclaim over her presents.

They talked afterwards, and with a little coaxing, Noel got Benjamin to sit at the piano while she took up the harp. They didn't get into sync on the first song or the second, but on the third, Benjamin started to relax and enjoy himself. By the fourth, they were in tune and Noel knew that she wasn't the only one with music always playing in her head.

That morning their holiday themes soared about the Christmas tree, making the ornaments glint and swing. And the angel on top, her wings cupped to catch it all, sighed with wonder.

If you enjoyed this story, you can sign up for a free membership at ForbiddenFiction and discuss it with other readers and the author at the *An Act of Charity* story page at http://forbiddenfiction.com/library/story/JK1-1.000235.

We do our best to proof all our work, but if you spot a text error we missed, please let us know via our website Contact Form at http://forbiddenfiction.com/contact.

A Many-Colored Lantern

Chapter 1
Yule

The festive lights illuminating the word "Charity" made Ethan feel worse, sick to his stomach with shame. There'd been more than a few such moments over the past seven years, things he'd done that he'd rather forget. But he'd never sunk this low.

He couldn't believe he was robbing a children's charity three days before Christmas.

It was late afternoon on December 22nd, and dark even though the sun hadn't officially set. The thrift shop was closed, but someone had left on the holiday lights. Flickering red and green, like stop-and-go warnings, illuminated the worn bills in the envelope. It was only float money, meant for the register, so it wasn't much. Ethan, however, didn't need a lot, just enough for a little food and to pay off his shitty hotel room. Enough to get him through the holiday season.

The store was in his neighborhood and he'd often caught sight of volunteers clearing out the register, taking the money into the back room. A few nights ago the old man responsible for closing out had forgotten to shut the door to that room behind him. Through a side window Ethan had seen him slip the stuffed envelope between two books on a high shelf. Not a very good hiding place.

It was almost as if the universe was inviting Ethan to take advantage of the place. Having worked odd jobs as a handyman, he'd had no trouble jimmying open the window and unlocking the back room.

His gloved hands shook while he fumbled the money out of the envelope. He told himself it was from hunger.

"HELP!" The shout made him drop the money.

"Help! Murder! Rape!" The screams came through the open window, riding on the frosty air.

Before he even knew what he was about, Ethan was tumbling back out through the window, his boots crunching on slush. He saw shadows against the brick wall of a tenement.

"You fucking son-of-a-bitch!" the girl shrieked as he reached them. She was fighting with a man over a canvass bag, kicking at him. Her face was white with fury.

"Hey!" Ethan didn't think; he ran with shoulders down right into the man. The robber, heavy and reeking of garbage, fell over. And so, unfortunately, did Ethan, slipping on ice and hitting the pavement. The girl snatched back her canvass bag and then tumbled onto her ass. Packages fell out and scattered, but the startled robber was no longer interested. Kicking splatters of slush into Ethan's face, he ran off.

For a moment there was just the sound of the robber's footsteps echoing down the alley and the pant of their breaths, Ethan's and the girl's.

"Son of a bitch!" she swore.

"Are you all right?" Ethan managed to push up on hands and knees. The adrenaline rush was gone and he felt he was about to faint. It'd been two days since he'd wolfed down those half-eaten burgers fished out of a fast food trashcan. Shit.

"I'm mad as hell." The girl was alternately brushing slush off her jeans and reaching for packages. There were several parcels, gift wrapped and tied up with pretty ribbons lying like fallen stars on the dirty snow.

"Let me help." He picked up one and tried to clean off a bit of mud with his gloved fingers.

"I hate that," the girl said getting up, "I really hate it. Some asshole tries to take your purse or your groceries. Makes me so mad. I want to kick the living shit right out of him."

Ethan swallowed, his throat suddenly tight, and slipped the package back into the canvass bag. As he did so he finally got a good look at the girl. He felt faint again, only this time it was not from hunger. He'd seen prettier girls, sexier. But he'd never seen one with such a glow about her, as if she'd been formed out of moonbeams. Thick, midnight hair came down from under a woolen cap to frame a cute, round face. The lips were full and kissably soft, the twilight blue eyes that met his so dark as to be almost black.

"I'm Sophie Cauldwell." Her voice, down to a normal register, sent a shiver right to his nuts. "Thanks for coming to my rescue."

She was staring back at him and Ethan felt a flush of embarrassment. He hadn't shaved in a couple of days, and he knew he looked thin and hungry as well as unkempt. His clothes were second-hand and tattered, from jeans to moth-eaten sweater. Even his beloved leather jacket was frayed and getting gaps at the seams. She must be wondering if he was going to try and rob her, too, and who could blame her?

"Ethan Rowe," he said roughly. "My pleasure. Um...Rape and Murder?"

She laughed. "Sorry. '*Help, someone's taking my stuff!*' doesn't get the same response."

69

"I suppose not."

"Police!" barked a hard voice from behind them.

Shit! Ethan got to his feet as a pair of cops came into sight—a pair of very brawny, very tense cops. Both eyed him with accusation; one had his gun out, the other had hands hovering near jacket pockets that undoubtedly held handcuffs. Ethan's heart was racing. No running. Surrender and comply. The last thing he wanted was to make them mad.

"You all right, Miss?" The one with the gun hung back, while the other, larger one, stepped up close, making Ethan, average in height and build feel positively scrawny.

"Fine," Sophie said. "Fine, just shaken. I guess you heard my screaming."

"Actually, it was the alarm at the Thrift Shop that brought us," the cop said. "Someone set it off."

Alarm? Ethan winced. He'd hit the place because he'd heard they couldn't afford an alarm. Evidently some good Samaritan had taken care of that.

"Probably the same junkie who jumped me." Sophie was still indignant. "He was really out of it. Tired to take my bag. If this man here hadn't come running I don't know what would have happened."

The cops frowned at Ethan; they didn't buy him as a rescuer. "Can you describe this junkie?"

Sophie gave the police a quick précis of her assailant. The cops asked for names and addresses. Ethan gave them an old address and a phone number that no longer worked.

"Oh, geeze," Sophie glanced at her watch, "I'm going to be late. Is it okay if I go?"

"Yeah." The cops had finally taken on "at-ease" positions and were even offering smiles. "There's not much else you can do."

"I'll walk with you," Ethan said quickly.

"I'll be fine," Sophie began.

"You shouldn't be on your own," he pressed, hoping his desperation wasn't too evident. Was that one cop scowling at him?

She shrugged. "Okay. Thank you for all your help, officers. I hope you get a chance to enjoy the season."

"You, too, Ma'am," they wished her warmly, "very happy holidays."

Ethan took her elbow. They got to the sidewalk and started uptown. He held his breath until they were well out of sight of the cops, and even then he waited in fear for the police to come running after them. A few blocks down he finally relaxed.

He'd escaped.

Sophie couldn't believe she was feeling this way. Infatuation-at-first-sight was a myth, a story. Or so she'd firmly believed until Ethan had come barreling to her rescue. One look at that face, so sad and wry, that untidy dark hair, eyes brown as earth and she'd been pulled right in.

Infatuated. Totally infatuated and she'd only just met him.

Not that she expected this heroic stranger to reciprocate. Though he looked to be in his mid-twenties like her, it was clear that he was far more grounded. Too worldly wise for loony Sophie, the girl—her big sister had always said—who fell from the moon.

"What am I keeping you from?" she asked Ethan now. "A concert? Poetry reading?" He was probably one of those creative types, the kind that always intimidated her. "I excel at derailing people. Someone has an important meeting and somehow or other they end up driving me to the towing yard or bringing me flu remedies instead. Happens all the time."

"You're in luck then. You didn't derail me at all, at least, not in a bad way." He grinned ruefully.

Damn. So that was what everyone meant by a "soulful" smile. Sophie felt her heart speed up. She glanced away acutely aware of his presence, the matched beat of their footsteps, the fog of their mutual breath.

"They're predicting heavy snow," she said inanely. "Humidity's in the eightieth percentile."

He glanced at the gray clouds overhead. "Looks like it's going to snow," he agreed.

Now she just felt stupid. "Really, you don't have to walk me all the way." She shifted the awkward sack of gifts on her shoulder. "You've been more than a gentleman."

"Not gentleman enough." He reached for the bag. "Let me take that. My mother, God rest her soul, would have had my head for not offering sooner."

Sophie blushed and gave it to him. "Thank you." She knew she ought to be more suspicious, not so trusting, but to hell with it. She'd rather believe in him.

They'd left the disreputable part of town and reached the renovated center with its upscale stores and apartments. Lights twinkled in bare tree branches, and holiday decorations reached across the street, lamppost to lamppost: sparkling banners and Santa in a sleigh with eight tiny reindeer. Muted holiday music could be heard through glowing display windows. Sophie took in dioramas of the North Pole's workshop and miniature tableaus from *A Christmas Carol.*

71

"So," she said, "what do you do when you're not rescuing damsels in distress?"

The rueful grin returned. "You weren't in distress. In fact, I think I saved the junkie's life."

She laughed, which helped as what had happened was only now beginning to hit her. She remembered the robber's stink and his grubby hands. She remembered screaming and kicking. God, she shivered. If that asshole had hit back, if he'd had a knife—!

Ethan, seeming to sense her distress, moved a little closer. He wasn't tall or broad, but there was something about him that was solid and real. She could almost feel his heat. It made her heart flip over and her mind spin.

This couldn't be real. And if it was, it couldn't last. Could it?

Chapter 2
Longest Night

"What do you do when you're not rescuing damsels in distress?" Sophie had asked, and Ethan's stomach had gone sick again. *Search through garbage cans*, he'd thought. *Steal packs of cigarettes and liquor and cold medicine to sell for pocket money.* Jesus, what was he doing still escorting her? It wasn't like there could be anything between them.

And yet he couldn't pull away. She was too... comfortable. From her thick hair to the oversized coat she wore, everything about her was as soft and welcoming as a warm bed. Even her name exuded a kind of coziness: *Sophie.* He wondered what it would be like to snuggle with her under the covers, to have her naked body next to his, skin to skin.

She was waiting for a response. He said the first thing that popped into his head, something about saving the junkie's life, and she laughed—which only made him want to lean in closer.

"I've got a crazy temper," she admitted, "but I mean, can you believe it? That asshole broke into a thrift shop run by a *children's charity*! That's like stealing from kids. Who would do something like that?"

The warmth stirring in his crotch went cold, and he looked away.

"I dunno. Someone desperate, I guess."

Sophie turned them at a corner, past a café that smelled of mochas and sugar cookies. Behind the glass doors, Ethan saw couples intimately sharing tables. There were carolers performing, singing songs of wassailing and decking halls.

God, wouldn't that be paradise? Sitting in there with Sophie, listening to the carols, indulging in an eggnog latte. He let out a snort. How pathetic was it that he hadn't the resources to do even that? To buy a girl a cup of coffee.

He glanced away and almost stopped. A block down from the café was a street of beautifully renovated Victorian homes. God. Porticos and mansard roofs, turrets, oriel windows.... For a moment the carpenter in Ethan took over, heart swelling at the sight of all those expertly refurbished gables and cornices. And then regular Ethan was back absorbing the expensive decorations, and the way the windows glowed behind their frost, rather than being dark and ominous. The plowed snow, piled up on either side of the tree-lined lane, was white, not muddy black and gray as in Ethan's part of town and the air smelled of firewood and dinners cooking.

Ethan's mouth watered helplessly and he found it hard to swallow. He couldn't walk down this street. He didn't belong here, not for years now. They'd take him for a vagrant and a thief and they'd be right.

"I work with kids," Sophie was still moving, walking backward and nearly falling over a fire hydrant. Much as his instincts told him to hold back, Ethan couldn't help but follow her.

"At the Natural Science Museum," she elaborated. "Programming, tours, teaching, it's the greatest thrill to see that 'wow' expression on kids' faces when you show them how the human body works or explain the connection between electricity and magnets. I *love* my work. I'm annoying you aren't I?"

Shit. His misgivings were showing. "Um no, it's not that."

"I bet you like girls who are quiet and supportive." Her expression fell, as if she'd just ruined a job interview. "The kind who wouldn't dream of disturbing you while you paint."

It was his turn to laugh. Was she kidding? Not just about the painting, but about the kind of girl he wanted. He'd been seven years on his own, and during the first few he'd kept the television on for the illusion of company. Forced to sell the set, he'd replaced it with an old clock radio he'd found in a dumpster. He never switched the damn thing off. Silence was deafening, terrifying. Sophie could babble all night long and he wouldn't tire of it.

"I like your voice," he said, which was an understatement. She had charming intonations; they flowed and hummed like a harp.

"I have a mother and sister and we're pretty close," she was still apologizing. "We chatter incessantly. You'll see when I introduce you. Here we are."

"Introduce me?" he said with alarm, even as he trailed her down a path and up the steps of a restored gingerbread. It had been lovingly repainted in mistletoe-green, and gold. Violet-blue holiday lights outlined the bay windows and hung like droplets from the eves.

On the door was a pine wreath accented with small apples, pomegranates and shiny stars.

"Mother!" The door wasn't locked and Sophie was already in before Ethan could stop her. For a single heartbeat, he thought about running off with her packages. Then he guiltily stepped in, shutting the door behind him.

The first thing that hit him was the smell: holiday spices and something savory on the stove. The delicious aroma left him weak in the knees. The second thing he noticed was the bench, its cubby holes and hooks occupied by a motley collection of scarves and coats, boots and gloves. He'd lived alone for so long, the evidence of a family seemed strange. Wondrous.

"Mother!" Sophie stood by the bench shedding her hat and gloves and finally her coat to reveal a black turtleneck. It sparkled with silver thread and displayed a sweet figure. Then, "Here let me take that."

Before Ethan knew it, she had relieved him of the canvass bag and his jacket. The house was nice and toasty and he could feel his chilled nose and cheeks thawing. Sophie was busy tugging off his gloves when a copper-haired woman in a purple cardigan and woolen skirt appeared.

"Amazing. You're only a little bit late," She said with mock surprise. Crow's feet accented the corners of her blue eyes, yet she still had girlish freckles across her nose. Her generous mouth matched that of her daughter. She checked her step on seeing Ethan.

"This is my mom, Kay Park," Sophie said, falling onto the bench and removing her boots. "Mom, this is Ethan Rowe. He saved my life."

"What?" Ethan said. "No, no, I didn't save her life."

"I was attacked by a crazed junkie," Sophie went on. "Ethan, slip off your shoes. We all go about in our socks around here."

She launched into an explanation, making the robbery and Ethan's rescue sound far more harrowing than he remembered and leaving out the part where they'd both ended up on their asses and crawling after scattered packages. Sophie's mother, arms crossed, listened with a mix of wonder and bemusement, like she knew Sophie had to be exaggerating but was still impressed.

"So can Ethan stay for Solstice Supper?" Sophie finished.

Ethan stiffened. Desperate as he was for a free meal he couldn't possibly stay. He didn't belong and it wouldn't take but a minute for someone to realize that. He looked to Kay, expecting to see her uneasy and disturbed. "But, of course he can," she said with surprising enthusiasm. "It's the least we can do. Welcome to our home, Ethan. Now get your shoes off and come on, we're about to start."

"About to start what?" Ethan asked as Kay vanished and he set about unlacing his boots.

"Yule," Sophie said.

He blinked at her.

"Winter Solstice celebration," she elaborated. "Mom's a pagan so we have a little ritual. Um, oh heck, I should have asked. Is that a problem?" For the first time, Sophie's expression was suspicious, as if she feared Ethan would disrespect her family. It bothered him more than he thought it would. He wanted her to trust him, even though he knew he wasn't trustworthy.

"It doesn't bother me. So, you're pagans?"

"Just mom." She led him into a generous living room. Ethan was amazed. In his childhood, when things had been good, his parents had favored spare but elegant furniture. Almost the first lesson he'd learned was not to put his dirty hands or muddy feet on anything. The homes of friends had been the same: filled with hard-to-clean carpets and rich fabrics, delicate crystal and other rarities that kids were only allowed to look at, not touch.

What he saw here was the complete opposite: the velveteen and leather upholstery was softened and discolored from hard use, the armchairs wide and welcoming. The couch was as deep as a bed and piled with inviting cushions. There was a small, upright piano, its keys yellowed from years of playing, and shelves overflowing with well-thumbed books. No precious vases or antique statues, nothing off limits. Heaven help him, even the Christmas tree was homey, a shaggy sort of fir dotted with old ornaments and topped with a papier-mâché sun. Underneath, on a quilted skirt, was a collection of gifts. He could scarcely breathe for fear it would all vanish, as in a dream.

"Everyone, this is Ethan," Kay introduced him from where she stood before the fireplace. "Ethan, this is everyone. Benji, could you turn off the lights?"

A brown-skinned boy of perhaps nine started snapping off lamps. There were three other people circling the fireplace: a graying, bearded Asian gentleman, a lean black fellow, and a very pretty young woman with hair coppery red like Kay's. *Sophie's sister* was a good guess. Her sunny blue eyes flickered at Ethan, and then she exchanged a wry look with Sophie.

Ethan flushed a little as everyone regarded him curiously and rather too much like a prospective suitor, but he bravely stepped up. A single, large log occupied the cold hearth. It was decorated with holly and nested on a pile of dried oranges, pinecones and cinnamon sticks. The last light went out and Benji rejoined them. It was too dark to see anything clearly, but Ethan felt slender fingers slip into his as the circle clasped hands. The sister was to his left and he could smell Sophie's fragrance to his right, an alluring mix of mint and roses.

"There are many stories about the Winter Solstice," Kay began. "It is one of the oldest celebrations on earth, a celebration of belief because to the ancients it came at a time when birds and animals were gone and the trees were bare. In much of the world the ground was icy and hard. Worst of all, the sun, the life-giving sun, was fading away. How frightening it must have been for them to huddle through that long, cold night wondering if the light would ever return?"

A pause. Kay's words hung over Ethan, and he almost felt she was speaking directly to him, not about the solstice, but about his life.

"There *was* belief in the sun's return, however, and out of this belief came stories. What's your favorite Benji?"

"The one where the Holly King does battle with the Oak King," the boy's voice pierced the dark. "They fight all night long, and come morning, the Oak King has won and can now make the days longer."

"Until they do battle again at Summer Solstice," Kay agreed. "What about you Sophie?"

"The one where the sun wanders away," that vibrant voice said nostalgically. "And we light fires to call it back."

"That's my favorite, too," said the sister.

"And then there's James' favorite." Kay's tone was fond, "Where the old sun dies and we keep the fire burning in hope of his resurrection. When we wake up in the morning, the sun has been restored to us as a child of light."

Ethan could hear the smile in her voice. Everyone in the room had moved closer together, and he felt Sophie's arm reach about his waist. His own hand slid over her back and found a comfortable curve.

"Which ever belief we hold to," Kay went on, "we are all together in being far, far from the sun on this, the longest night of the year. And in order to maintain hope, we must share, and gather together, and warm each other's hearts. That—and to hold the darkness at bay—is why we celebrate this time of year with light."

A spark flared into flame as a match was struck, bringing almost blinding light into the room. It touched upon portions of the log which must have been prepped with some kind of lighter fluid because it caught immediately. Flames engulfed the dry wood, illuminating the circle of faces and filling the room with the inviting fragrance of oranges and cinnamon.

"Here comes the Sun," Sophie began to sing a bit off key, *"Here comes the Sun."*

The other family members chuckled and joined in until they were all singing of how the long, cold, lonely winter would end, how the ice would melt and everything would be "all right." They finished up, laughing and exchanging hugs.

"Happy Solstice!" Sophie gave Ethan an embrace so sweet and comfortable that it fairly melted him. Then she joined the rest of her family in taking down candles from the mantle and lighting them. Soon the living room was aglow with candlelight.

"Let's eat!" said Kay. Cushions were snatched, quilts were unfolded, and in moments they were all sitting cross-legged before the blazing fire, teacup shaped bowls of turkey and dumpling stew balanced on their knees. Ethan, blind to everything else, bolted down that first serving and was scraping his spoon through the savory gravy when Kay stepped up to him.

"Hungry?" she asked.

"Very."

She got him a second helping. He slowed down enough to taste it this time. While he ate, he listened to the family discuss mutual friends and relatives. He picked up that the black man, Isaac Wilkins, was a mediator in labor disputes and married to Sophie's sister, Nikki. Nikki taught ESL to adults, and son Benjamin was an aspiring piano player. Mother Kay and her husband, James Park, jointly owned a computer store and were planning on visiting his ex-wife and sons in Hawaii.

The stew eaten and the bowls taken away, the family kicked back. Benji was given a long-handled pan and the task of roasting chestnuts. James brought in mugs of spiced apple cider and a bottle of brandy for those wanting to lace their brew. And that was when everyone's attention finally turned to Ethan. Sophie told the story of the robber again and the family radiated approval. It was downright embarrassing. Ethan was used to being eyed with distrust, not favor.

"So, what do you do?" James asked. The tone was familiar. The man might be Sophie's stepdad, but he was clearly as protective as any biological father.

Knowing he couldn't put them off as he had Sophie, Ethan cast his mind over various truths: he'd been a janitor and worked at a car wash, held innumerable positions at fast food restaurants. He'd even been a singing waiter once. He didn't think any of those would go over well, but lying would only catch him up later. He'd have to go with the one vocation he felt was honestly his.

"I'm a handyman," he said, and waited to hear the disappointed, "oh" that usually followed that pronouncement.

"Really?" Mother and daughters perked up and the men exchanged glances. Ethan was confounded. Why did everyone suddenly look so pleased?

"My dad started out as a handyman," Sophie explained. "That's what he was when he met mom. Then he got into construction and restoring old houses. He rebuilt half the places around here."

"That's...wow." Ethan murmured. He didn't quite know how to feel, relieved that they actually liked his humble profession, or embarrassed because he'd told them a half-truth and didn't deserve their support.

"I don't suppose you have time to do some repairs?" Kay wanted to know.

"Mom, it's the holidays!" Sophie objected.

"That doesn't stop things from breaking. Why should I hire a plumber to fix the leak in the bathroom or an electrician to get the light working over the stairs when I can pay Ethan?"

Why indeed? "Sure, I can do those things," he said quickly. His pulse was racing. God, yes, he could do them if it would earn him enough for another month at the hotel. So long as no one checked to see if he was legit, he would be fine.

"Don't let her bully you, Ethan," James warned. "If you've better things to do over Christmas—"

"No, no, really, it's fine. But I ought to get going." He rose to his feet.

"I suppose you have to," Sophie looked crestfallen.

"No, he doesn't," Benji said, shaking his pan over the burning Yule log. "It's like a blizzard out there."

"What?" Ethan made his way to the darkened entry hall and peered out through the front window. Huge, white snowflakes were storming down, covering the houses, burying the cars. It looked bad. News stations would probably be advising people to stay off the roads and remain indoors. Shit.

"The temperature took a real plunge while we were eating dinner." Sophie was there with him, gazing out at the flurry. "Which, combined with the humidity, probably makes those snowflakes stellar dendrites. Gorgeous crystallization. You know, you can capture snowflakes with glass slides and superglue. The slides have to sit in the refrigerator for two weeks but the superglue...." She faded to a stop and flushed as Ethan just blinked at her. "Benji says you can share the attic with him if you want. He can use a sleeping bag and you can have the bed."

"The couch will be fine." This was ridiculous. How had he ended up trapped in a place like this?

"Want some hot chestnuts?"

God. "Sure. Why not?

Chapter 3
The Workshop

Ethan woke from a wonderful dream of roasted chestnuts, hot apple cider, and a late night game of cards—hearts?--where everyone had laughingly cheated. It was only as he rolled over and felt the plushness of the couch instead of his lumpy mattress, the snug and downy comforters that Kay had piled atop him, that he remembered it was no dream.

He smelled fresh coffee and sighed with wonder. Heaven. He'd found heaven. Not that he could stay. It was a very dangerous thing for him to start hoping. In his experience, life would pull the rug right out from under him if he did that. So, he would have a cup of coffee and leave.

Reluctantly, he stretched, stood up, and rubbed the grit from his eyes. Following the fragrance, he found his way to a pale blue kitchen dominated by an old stove. The coffee was to the side, filtering through a modern drip machine.

"Morning." James, dressed and reading the news on an iPad, lifted his mug in salutation. "Sleep well?"

"Very well, thank you. I was just going to get a cup of coffee and be off."

"I don't think so." The black, almond eyes twinkled. "You promised to fix a few things last night. Or was that the brandied cider talking? Trust me, even if you were drunk, you don't want to go back on your word to Kay. Cauldwell women are very strong-minded."

"I haven't any tools or materials," Ethan objected, which, he reflected, he ought to have remembered when he'd made the offer. Rug right out from under him. So much for a paying job.

"No trouble there. Pour yourself a cup and follow me."

Under the main stairs was a door. James led Ethan down to a finished basement with the usual washer, dryer and water heater. Purely practical. Beyond that laundry room, however, was a workshop. A vast, beautifully stocked and organized workshop that would have put Santa's to shame. Ethan's breath went shallow as he took in planks of wood, sheets of colored glass, old tiles, spools of electrical wiring and copper piping. Lining the walls were labeled storage containers filled with hammers, nails, bolts, screws, measuring tapes, drills and wrenches. And right in the middle of it all was a huge work table with a circular saw, a small lathe and even a glasscutter.

It would astonish Ethan later that he didn't even consider stealing anything. His only thought at that moment was that he'd found his heart's desire. Sheer elation filled him. Then he recalled that this wasn't his. Like everything else in the house, it was only on loan. He began to wonder if it might not have been better to go to jail last night instead of suffering in this sweet purgatory.

"When I married Kay," James said, "she offered to have all this cleared out. But I thought one of the girls might become a craftsman like their dad." He shook his head. "They both turned out like their mother, all thumbs. Especially Sophie, God bless her."

Ethan was still staring. He didn't know what to say.

"Think you can do the repairs?" James asked, clearly amused.

"Yeah," Ethan said as he swallowed past the pain. "Yeah, I think so."

Sophie rolled and rubbed herself across the comfort of her old, childhood mattress. She had on a thin, flannel nightgown that caressed her bare skin. She was imagining the fabric was Ethan's hands. A light stroke over her breasts, teasing her nipples, gliding down her belly.

His hands were warm, she knew that from last night, and broad and just a little calloused. She could almost feel that tantalizing roughness between her thighs, parting them, discovering how wet she was. She released a sigh of desire. *Moon dreams.* That was the name for daydreaming in this house. She'd talked with her sister about it last night.

"He's sooo cute!" Nikki had approved as they'd lolled on Sophie's bed, half-tipsy with spiked cider. "And what a way to meet! I'm so jealous. All the guys I ever dated I met the normal way."

"By getting drunk at a bar?"

Nikki had punched her in the arm for that.

"He probably has a girlfriend," Sophie had said then. "Or he thinks we've got nothing in common or he's just not interested. What was I thinking? I drag him in, all unasked, to a pagan ritual, and then, when he learns he's stuck here with us, I natter on about crystallization. And superglue!"

"So he thinks you're loony. What else is new?"

"I could have started singing 'Let it Snow,' or suggested we catch snowflakes on our tongues, but noooo. I had to talk about trapping snow between glass slides! Could I have been more geeky?"

"Nope. And stop it." Nikki had smacked her again. "You are not going to undermine this. What if I'd done that with Isaac? *I'm not the sort of girl he wants to marry, it's going to be too complicated, he'll chicken out*...blah, blah, blah. I didn't. I decided what I wanted and I went for it. You can't just moon dream about romance, little sister, you have to make it happen."

"I'm just glad you're married," Sophie had sighed. Nikki was four years older, but she still shone brighter than Sophie, she always had. Sophie recalled her preteen years, watching her sister put on her make-up, going out on innumerable dates with the best looking boys. The kind of boys who hadn't given Sophie a second look when it had come time for her to date. Even their father had preferred Nikki's company to Sophie's, though he'd tried not to show it.

Enough musing in bed she decided rolling off the mattress. She headed down the hall to the bath and yelped in surprise. Ethan was under the sink. He jumped in response, whacking his head on a pipe.

"Shit!" he hissed.

"Oh, gosh," Sophie was mortified. "I'm sorry! I'm so sorry. I was startled."

"Yeah, I gathered." He rubbed at his forehead and stared at her.

"Fixing the sink?" she said then winced. Duh. Of course he was.

"Yeah. Do you need me to get out?"

"No, no, I can use the other bathroom." She wrapped her arms about her then moved her hands to her hips. *Say something, Sophie. Say something.* "You know, I remember when my father retrofitted all these pipes. I must have been nine? Ten? I got this screwy idea to study up on waterflow because dad was always looking at me strangely when I talked about supernovas and stuff. I thought it would give us something in common. Anyway, I tried to discuss laminar flow and vortices—that's where you get turbulence." She spun a finger to demonstrate.

Ethan was still staring. Just staring.

"I suggested less bends, different diameter pipes...." She trailed off, shifting again. Crap. Well, at least he was looking at her directly and intently. Her father had just fiddled with the pipes and murmured, "Uh-huh."

"There's an annual skating party put on by the neighborhood," she said desperately, not the best segue. "This afternoon, at the local park. I don't suppose you'd want to go? We've collected all these extra pairs of skates over the years. I'm sure one set or another would fit. Unless you're busy? You probably have family obligations or friends or a date or something."

Here's your chance to tell me about your girlfriend. Or just run away from me, Sophie thought swallowing past a knot in her throat.

"Nothing." The rueful smile was back. "Not unless your mother wants more things fixed."

"Really?" Sophie didn't think he was lying but the inference was almost too painful. No family? No friends? No plans for the holidays? She felt relief, but also a wave of great sadness for him. "Would you like to come then?"

He looked uncertain. God. He would have said yes if she'd been Nikki. Maybe he was even thinking that. That if she was more like Nikki he'd want to go.

"Okay," he said at last. "But I really will have to go home after that. I need a change of clothes, a shower."

Ethan in the shower. Now there was a moon dream. She licked her lips. "I'd better get dressed." She hurried out. It wasn't until she was brushing her teeth in the other bath that she noticed how threadbare her nightgown was, how evident her breasts and nipples were.

Maybe...maybe that's what he'd been staring at?

As he watched Sophie skate across the frozen pond, Ethan flashed back on how she'd looked this morning. He hadn't meant to stare, but she'd appeared out of nowhere, like some winter sprite. Her bedroom hair had been wonderfully disheveled, her pale blue nightgown so delectably soft and transparent. She must have thought him a moron, lying there on the floor gawking at her. But he hadn't been able to look away as that nightgown revealed, with every shift, a delicious part of her body: a hip, an erect nipple. Shift again and there was the outline of a mesmerizing pubic triangle. He'd barely kept from moaning. A drop of her arms and the breasts had swung. It was like a striptease. And always there was the winter sun coming through the bathroom window, backlighting and illuminating her.

He hoped Sophie hadn't noticed his hard on. His cock was still aching, lustful and restless in his jeans as he watched her now. She twirled with her arms out as if to hug the world. He really liked that about her: that she tried to find a way to embrace everything, to make it important to her.

This was not good, he thought. Not good at all. The longer he stayed, the more he wanted all of it: the house, the workshop, the family and, most especially, Sophie.

"Aren't you going out there?" Isaac sat down on the bench beside him. He was one of those tall and angular men, with sharp features and very dark skin. He waved at the frozen pond. It was located in a bucolic glade surrounded by birch and maple trees. The air had that tang of fresh snow, and under the overcast sky the ice shone like a mirror. The circling skaters, moving to the holiday tunes piped over a loud speaker, resembled dancers in a music box.

"I'm trying to get up the courage. It's been a while since I've skated," Ethan hedged. Truth was, he wasn't just out of practice, but he felt, once again, like he didn't belong. Those out on the ice were all part of the neighborhood, laughing and waving to each other. They owned homes and were part of families. They could afford a cup of coffee at the local café.

Going out there would be like breaking into someone's home.

"Benji said you showed him how to use the lathe," Isaac remarked.

Ethan tensed. Oh, shit. He hadn't thought twice when the nine-year-old had sundered down into the basement, bored and asking questions.

"I'm sorry," he began, "I didn't think."

"No, no, it's fine. Except now Benji likes you and wants to know if you're going to be at tonight's festivities."

"Festivities? Isn't Yule over?"

"Technically, no. It lasts twelve days. But that's not what I'm talking about." He smirked. "In this family the greeting is '*Happy Holidays.*' And we mean it. We're not just interracial and multicultural, we're interfaith. James is Christian. Methodist before he married Kay and they both went Unitarian. So tomorrow night we'll be having a little Christmas celebration."

"And you'll be presenting Kwanzaa?" Ethan guessed.

Isaac lifted a wry brow and pulled at a chain bringing forth a Star of David.

"Um, oh."

"You got a problem with that?"

"Um, no, of course not."

The other man laughed. "I'm just fucking with you. I get that sort of reaction all the time. Not all of us are Baptist or Muslim, ya know?"

"You converted?" Ethan ventured.

"Nope. Jewish law is if your mom is Jewish, so are you. Which my mom technically was thanks to her Jewish mother who scandalized her family by marrying my Afro-American granddad rather than a nice Jewish boy. Mom was non-practicing, but grandma introduced me to the faith and it took." He shrugged. "It's what I am. Nikki is the convert. We got married and not long after she started coming to synagogue with me and decided that my faith was hers, too. I joke that she found both her soul mate and her spiritual path in one."

"Oh. That... that must have been a powerful thing," Ethan ventured, "finding a faith that called to her so strongly that she left all she'd been behind."

Isaac gave Ethan a reassessing look. "You find something like that and you go running towards it. You don't even look back. You know, in Judaism, you're not supposed to remind coverts that they're converts or inquire about their past. Not that it stops people from asking—like you just did me--but the idea is that the convert has always belonged to the tribe. They just didn't know it. Now they do, and it's like... like they've come home."

Can't be that easy, Ethan almost said, then reflected that it probably hadn't been easy at all for Nikki or Issac for that matter. But he understood. If he were ever able to finally find people and a place he could call home— he'd be willing to go through a lot for that.

"Anyway," Isaac grinned, "what I was trying to tell you with this long-assed saga, is that even though Hanukah's over, we'll be reprising the eighth night for the family. And Benji'll be disappointed if you're not there. And you should go join Sophie before some other guy snatches her up."

Some other guy? Ethan stood up and took a few awkward steps. Sophie was skating with another guy— Benji. Ethan sighed out a breath of relief that surprised him. How could he feel such possessive jealousy for a girl he'd only just met? And yet he did.

His skates touched the ice and he wobbled a bit before remembering how to balance. Childhood memories flooded back, and he found himself pushing and gliding. Stopping, however, was another matter.

"Incoming!" he warned. Benji backed out of the way but Sophie did not and suddenly he had her in his arms. They both swayed and fought to stay upright and just barely managed it.

"Sorry," he breathed. She felt very soft and right in his embrace. Her face was close and he could smell peppermint on her breath. "Forgot how to stop."

"It's okay." Her hand was brushing up and down his back, down near enough to his ass that he felt a tingle. She seemed to realize what she was doing and broke away. "I was just teaching Benji some physics. It's one of the ways we instruct the kids. You can learn all of Newton's laws in a skating rink."

"Really? Okay, I'll bite. Instruct me."

She eyed him skeptically, as if she thought he was humoring her, then, "Um, well, you just demonstrated Newton's first and third laws. Let's try something a little less precarious for the second."

They started gliding about the pond. Sophie let him push her as she skated backwards. "Newton's second law" she informed him, then she crossed her arms, grabbed his hands and got them into a spin. "And this is how we demonstrate how planets and satellites orbit around each other."

Can I stay in your orbit? Ethan almost asked her, and even after they'd come out of the dizzying spin, he felt as if he was magnetically locked on her.

They skated for a while longer, joining others for a crack-the-whip, and a conga line. And there must have been something in what Sophie said about the effects of gravity because Ethan began to feel more and more like he belonged not only with Sophie but on the ice with this group of warm, welcoming neighbors.

Breathless and chilled, he and Sophie finally returned to the benches, took off their skates and retired to the refreshment tent.

"I really enjoyed that," Ethan said as they nibbled on gingerbread cookies.

"That's nice of you to say."

"No, I mean it. I mean, I look at pipes or snow and I just see plumbing or bad weather. You see a whole new universe. That's really wonderful."

She blushed and ducked her head. "Thanks. So, um, how about you? Did you always want to be a handyman?"

"No, though, as a teen, I was addicted to home improvement shows. The ones where the handyman would show up and restore some rundown place to its former glory were my favorite."

"Where he'd come to the rescue you mean?" Sophie nudged him with her elbow.

"Yeah," he laughed, "I guess so. But I never thought about going into that profession, never even imagined I'd fall into it, which I kinda did."

He paused, recalling how he'd started as a day laborer, hired to tear down or dig up, to lay tile or hammer wood. Naturally, he'd picked up a little knowledge of wiring and plumbing along the way. Figuring that the more he knew the more he'd be hired, he'd hung with the plumbers and carpenters, electricians and contractors, learning what he could. He'd been as surprised as anyone to find he was good at it—and that he loved it.

"I like knowing how things work," he admitted, "and I really enjoy figuring out what's wrong and making it right."

"That you do," she breathed, gazing at him with a glow in her eyes, like she'd just found her knight in shining armor.

He coughed uncomfortably at that, and glanced away.

"Yes, well," she said and shifted, "Um, so, I guess I'm giving you a lift home?"

His stomach flipped. They'd driven to the park in two cars and it was no short walk back. It made sense for Sophie to take him directly home but the last thing he wanted was for her to see his shithole hotel.

"Actually, Isaac convinced me to stay for tonight's festivities. I can walk home after that."

"Really?" Sophie's face lit up. "I mean, that's great. My family really likes you."

"I like them. But I need to shower and shave, and wash my clothes."

"No problem." Sophie gave notice that they were leaving and got them back to the house. Ethan refused to let her do his laundry, not wanting her to see his tatty underwear. After getting everything into the washer, he showered, and finally scrapped off three days of beard with a disposable razor. Wearing a borrowed bathrobe, he switched his laundry to the dryer, and headed in search of Sophie.

He found her on her bed, facing away from him as she flipped through a magazine. She'd also taken a shower and was dressed in nothing but a silky blue robe. It was short and riding high on her thighs. As she shifted, Ethan caught sight of her ass cheeks. She bent a leg, and he glimpsed moist, pink pussy lips.

His pulse pounded in his head and his breath came short. He sunk back from the door, flattening himself against the wall. His cock was stiff and poking out of the robe. Shit. He couldn't let her see him like this. He had to think of something to wilt the erection, anything.

He winced as a memory flashed into his mind, one he really didn't want to remember, but it did the trick: His family had once been well off. He'd attended a private school with kids from good families, and he'd dated Brianna, an Amerasian butterfly with dark eyes and a bright, social personality. Then, just before his senior year, his family's fortunes had crashed—spectacularly and scandalously. Forced to drop out and mortified to his soul by what had happened, he'd cut himself off from all his former friends, Brianna included. He'd figured that was better than watching her turn away from him.

Two years later, coming up to a table in the restaurant where he worked as a singing waiter, he'd found himself face-to-face with her again. It was a humiliating moment. Some of her friends had joked to break the ice, but Ethan saw the way they looked at him. Curious but uneasy, like he was an ex-con who'd committed some infamous crime. He'd pretended it was all good. He'd even sung, as he was supposed to, as he wrote down their orders. But, in the end, he'd gotten another waiter to service the table and gone out into the alley.

Sitting through his break with his head in his hands, it'd hit him that there was no going back. He wasn't part of that world anymore and never would be again. If he was being honest, he shouldn't have been part of it in the first place, should never have been with Brianna. Girls like Brianna weren't for him. Girls like Sophie weren't for him.

"Ethan?" Sophie was at the door, eyeing him anxiously. She must have noticed his shadow in the hall.

"Oh, hi... I um... was just looking for you."

"Come on in," she nabbed him.

"My clothes should be dry," he tried to say, but she was drawing him over the threshold, and he couldn't seem to resist. And to his chagrin, his deflated cock was beginning to twitch again

Chapter 4
Festival of Lights

Make it happen, Sophie kept thinking. That had been Nikki's advice and after this afternoon, still feeling herself light up every time Ethan smiled or laughed, she wanted to do just that. Make something, anything, happen. She suspected she had a good chance as during their ice skating, Ethan's grip on her waist had seemed possessive, and he'd eyed her with interest. So maybe what she was about to try wasn't crazy.

Locking the door, she faced him, threw her arms about his neck and kissed him. He smelled of her mother's herbal soap and felt wonderfully warm and solid. A sick pang of anticipation hit her all the same. She fully expected him to push her away and tell her there'd been a misunderstanding.

Then, to her relieved delight, his arms snaked about her and his tongue was in her mouth. It tasted of gingerbread. She felt his erection stiff against her bare thigh as he got them on the bed. Her robe was half off already, it took only a tug on the bow to part it completely. She ran her fingers through his damp hair, and broke from the kiss to bite at his throat. She was only a little disappointed, as she brushed her face against his, that she hadn't gotten a chance to experience his very attractive and poetic stubble.

His calloused hands were gripping her bare ass now, squeezing her cheeks, tracing the curves and crack in lazy, maddening circles till she moaned and squirmed against him. She wanted to rub herself over every part of him, burrow into that delicious spot between his neck and shoulder and scratch her nails slowly down his ribs until he arched up with desire.

What she wanted most, however, was lower down. Ripping open his robe, she began to explore, her tongue licking over his sparse chest hair then following the line to his navel. She savored the spot marking the beginning of his tantalizing treasure trail.

"Sophie," he moaned, as she moved down lower. And there it was, stiff and shiny with desire. It wasn't a long cock but it was admirably thick and cinnamon-colored with excitement.

Ethan felt Sophie's breath on his cock, which was enough to make him want to come. And then her lips had him and she was sucking at the tip. He jumped and groaned, and tangled his fingers into her satiny hair.

Oh, sweet Jesus! Her hands took possession of his rod, fondling and stroking so teasingly he almost screamed. Her mouth never left the tip, and he fought the urge to thrust deeper. Her tongue swabbed his slit, lapping the juices that leaked out in copious amounts. And now he was thrusting as her hands jerked him and tumbled his nuts like a pair of dice.

"Oh, Christ, Sophie, keep that up and I'm gonna come!"

Her response was a kind of purr, which he heard and felt, and then that beautiful mouth was gone and she was crawling back up. Silky hair tickled his belly and sides, teeth grazing his hot skin. Unable to take it any longer he rolled them so that he was on top, cupping an impossibly soft breast. This time, he initiated the kiss.

Sophie writhed as Ethan first bruised and then sucked on her lower lip. His hand, rough and smooth, moved over her breast, each stroke sending a shock through her sensitive nipple. She pushed up, trying to get more friction, but he continued to torment her breast while his tongue tasted the roof of her mouth.

His hard, hot body ground against hers, his slick cock against her wet crotch. She could still taste him, a flavor musky-sweet like pecans. A shift, and now he was torturing her other breast, squeezing it, licking and sucking till she whimpered and her pussy dripped.

Reaching back to the nightstand, she nabbed the little foil packet, one of several she'd found in her bag, left over from a stay with her last boyfriend. She handed it to him, and he quickly got the rubber out and on.

"My hero," she whispered as he leaned back over her, and nipped at his earlobe, "my hero!"

She ran her hands over his shoulders and down his back as he entered her, loving his solid strength, loving his ass which tensed as it bucked and pounded into her, loving his breath in her ear, so regular and warm.

Ethan was in love and like gravity there was no escaping it. In love with Sophie's dreamy, twilight eyes gazing at him as if he were a hero, with her voice, murmuring and crying out in delight. He was in love with her plush curves and the soft, soft interior, which he could feel gripping him even through the protection. He was locked in her orbit and god, it felt so right. Like he belonged.

He felt her come, those clenching inner muscles seeming to wrap him up tight and safe. And when his own moment arrived, it was more release than explosion, a thrust that set free all his insecurities, all his doubts. He shot and shot again even as she cried out, and hugged him tight.

It came to an end, and yet even that felt wonderful, like he was stretching his muscles after years of being locked in a box. He sunk down into her arms, limp and more relaxed than he'd been in years and stayed that way for a long time, drifting on moon beams.

It was fairly clear that the family sensed the change between them, which made Ethan flush and feel like he'd been caught with his hand in the preverbal cookie jar. But Sophie seemed pleased. She unabashedly touched him and leaned against his shoulder. It was endearing how proud she was of him, humbling as well. The worst of it was, everyone seemed to agree with her. James slapped him on the back, Nikki gave him the thumbs up and Kay smiled as if he was already her favorite son-in-law. Even Benji gave him a man-to-man nod. It was a little overwhelming.

After a supper of braised brisket and crispy potato pancakes, they retired to the living room where an eight-armed Menorah waited on the mantle. Isaac stepped up and stood before it, relaxed as a teacher before his favorite students.

"In 165 B.C.," he began, "the Jews fought the Syrians, conquered them and regained control of Jerusalem. While in power, the Syrians had desecrated the temple. They believed, as so many sadly do, that a religion, a faith, even a god can be destroyed if the place of worship is destroyed. But God isn't a temple, and belief doesn't rely on having a place to pray.

"Having won the war, the Maccabees sought to re-dedicate the temple. They had only enough oil to light the holy flame for one night; they didn't reckon, however, on the power of their faith. The oil lasted eight nights, exactly enough time for them to get more and keep the fire burning."

Ethan blinked and drew in a breath. Once again, he had the strange feeling that the story being told was his own. As if Isaac knew all about him and was trying to show him something he'd missed.

"When I decided that my grandmother's faith was my faith, some in the Christian branches of my family didn't understand." Isaac went on, "I don't know if I understood myself, except that I felt kinship to those who kept belief alight even though their temples were destroyed, their homes lost. What I've come to realize, however, is that whatever lights us up inside, a faith or a person or a place, whatever keeps that inner light burning, that's ours. And we, in turn, need to tend to it and keep it burning. Light brings light."

He stepped aside for his son who struck a match and lit the center candle. With that candle he ignited the other eight while reciting a Hebrew prayer. Once again, hugs were exchanged along with wishes for a "Happy Hanukah." And then, Benji sat down at the piano.

Ethan was prepared for a student recital, but the kid turned out to be honestly talented. He played with jazzy ease, first a Hanukah song, then a haunting rendition of "O Come Little Children," and "Silver Bells." Ethan was impressed and said as much to Nikki as he sat down beside her to sip coffee and nibble on little jelly donuts.

"He loves music," Nikki said brightly.

"I was wondering," Ethan said, "I know you're a convert to Judiasm. What if your son converts? I mean, you let him participate in pagan rituals, and celebrate Christmas, don't you worry that he'll follow a different path?"

"We've a family motto," Nikki smiled. "*Belief is a candle inside a multicolored lantern.* It's modified from a quote by Mohammed Naguib. Putting it another way: It doesn't matter what color Benji wants his lantern. All that matters is that he has a something to light his way."

That made Ethan thoughtful. He rested back on the couch and considered his own situation, coming up with a very grim picture. In his case, the hue of his faith didn't much matter... because the candle was out. Dead and cold. It had been for years now. Yet he found the image of the multicolored lantern compelling. It gave him an idea.

The phone rang and Kay went to answer it. A moment later, she shouted for Sophie. Benji snatched up some donuts and sat with his step-granddad by the fire; Kay came back to joke with her daughter and son-in-law. On the mantle, the eight lights flickered and glowed. Ethan felt a wonderful sense of peace and acceptance, one he honestly couldn't remember ever feeling. It was an odd realization. He'd thought falling into poverty had set him apart, but he was beginning to realize that he'd always felt that way. He'd never felt at home anywhere... till now.

"That was the police," Sophie announced returning. "They caught the bastard who tried to rob me!"

Ethan went cold.

"All right!" Isaac approved.

"Nothing much is going to happen over the next couple of days, what with Christmas and all, but I can go down on the twenty-sixth to fill out a complaint if I want. I wonder if they'll charge him with breaking and entering that children's charity shop? Trying to rob me was nothing compared to that."

Ethan's heart sank, as if an ember within him, working its way to flame, had just been doused. Of course it had all been too good to be true. A holiday, and now it was over. He couldn't possibly maintain this charade, not after getting to know these people, not after what they'd made him feel, what Sophie had made him feel... trusted and welcome.

91

He was subdued after that but no one seemed to notice. Bedtime came and Sophie looked at him expectantly. He wanted to refuse, but her expression grew hurt when she saw him hesitate. He relented. He just hoped making love to her tonight wouldn't make things any worse.

There was no desperate, urgent desire this time, just her and Ethan, naked on the bed and illuminated by the candle she'd lit. Sophie couldn't stop looking at him, touching him. The men in her life tended to fuck and leave her, and she expected Ethan to do the same. Sex was one thing, a relationship quite another and most guys found her too strange for a relationship. She had vowed, however, to enjoy and cherish Ethan while he lasted, like the holiday lights and music and treats, and not be sad when it came time for him to go.

Ethan, evidently, had similar thoughts. He ran hands down her arms, raising goose bumps, then gently cupped her breasts and teased her nipples hard with his thumbs. His kiss this time was gentle, tender enough to make her shiver.

"Lay down on your tummy," he whispered.

She did as he asked, resting on a pillow. He brushed her hair back from her face, fingers combing through it reverently, as if it were the finest silk. For a good long while he stroked and massaged her shoulders and back, getting her into a dreamy, relaxed state.

Then he began to kiss down her spine, down her sides, making her giggle as he tickled her ribs. His hand slipped between her thighs. She blushed and trembled. A curious finger between her legs sent a spark up her groin. The smell of her desire mingled with the fragrance of the candle as he finally rolled her over to face him.

Sophie had the most beautiful pussy lips, thought Ethan as she spread her legs for him. Like rose-petals, red and velveteen. She even smelled of roses. His dick hardened and dripped as he bent and gave her a lick, causing her to gasp and jerk. For a moment he shut his eyes, letting her flavor play over his tongue. It was elusive, like the taste of a snowflake, but he knew he wanted more of it. He licked again, and again. Sophie began to moan and thrust at him. She reached back to squeeze the pillow under her head. He wrapped his arms about her thighs to hold her steady, and kept on licking those soft petals. Her groans grew louder, her writhing more urgent. When he finally licked her clit she cried out and bucked. A new surge of juices flowed out and trickled down like snowmelt.

He was growing quite heady now on the fragrance of roses, on that pure, tangy flavor and at the sight of her swollen, blushing pussy. His cock ached and he had to work hard to concentrate. He flicked his tongue at her clit again, moving it like the clapper in a bell. He loved the way she was squirming in his arms, growing slippery with perspiration, loved the muffled cries she screamed into the pillow.

She came quite violently, shuddering and jerking. The condom was waiting on the nightstand again. He nabbed it, and got it rolled down over his rod, then grabbed her about the waist and plunged in. He caught her mid-orgasm, a pulse that took hold of him and beat like a heart. Sparks shot up his throbbing cock, curling his toes and leaving him dizzy. His nuts drew up and he came, firing into her, giving her all he had.

He kept thrusting till he was long done and both of them were gasping for breath. Withdrawing from her at last, he sunk down onto the quilts. By the candlelight he could see that she was trembling, her thighs quivering.

"Fuck!" she breathed. "You are by far the best moon dream I've ever had."

Ethan had no idea what that meant, but he supposed it was a good thing. She had a damp towel ready for him, and after he got himself cleaned up they snuggled under the quilts. Sophie was even more comforting to lie with than Ethan had imagined she'd be. Her head rested on his chest, her hair spread over his arm like a silken blanket, and her naked body fitted to his.

Swallowing past a lump in his throat, Ethan kissed her, and closed his eyes. It was a good way to end a holiday.

Chapter 5
A Christmas Gift

Sophie was disappointed to find Ethan gone when she woke. She slipped into her nightgown, socks and robe and padded downstairs. Everyone else was up and they gave her sly looks as she stepped into the kitchen. Even Benji grinned knowingly, which was just wrong.

"Good night?" Nikki innocently asked.

"None of your beeswax." Sophie poured herself some coffee. "Anyone seen Ethan?"

"He's down in the workshop," her mother said. "He ransacked the kitchen drawers, made off with some cookie cutters, and no one's seen him since."

"He's working on a secret project," Benji announced.

"I guess that gets him out of kitchen duty for the day," James remarked. "If you all would finish up and get dressed."

There was a general groan at that, typical and only half serious. The tradition was that James made the Christmas Eve meal, and the rule was that he could draft anyone and everyone to help him. It wasn't that anyone really minded, but the family liked giving him a hard time about it.

Sophie's groan was a more honest one this year as she'd hoped to spend a little time with Ethan. Okay, a lot of time.

James put her on vegetable duty, peeling and cutting up carrots and parsnips and trimming brussel sprouts. She sat at the table with Benji, who was busy scraping seeds out of a butternut squash. Mom, the family baker, made chocolate ganache for her Christmas Eve bûche de noël while Nikki and Isaac polished up the silver and prepared the centerpiece.

"Good morning!" Ethan suddenly appeared toolbox in hand. He paused to give her an unabashed peck on the lips before kneeling down to check out a loose floorboard.

"Um, good morning." Sophie exchanged a glance with her mother. "What are you doing?"

"Fixin' stuff."

Sophie wasn't sure what to make of that, but apparently Ethan meant it literally. Over the next few hours she heard him moving up and down the stairs, going in and out of rooms. There was hammering, sometimes cursing. Now and then he appeared, brushing dust out of his hair or asking for a Band-Aid.

James finally got everything into the oven or the refrigerator, and his crew took a much needed break. They went out for a game of football, which quickly turned into a snowball fight. Ethan joined in. To Sophie's chagrin, he sided with Benji and James against her, Nikki and Isaac.

"Hey, Sophie! Newton's first law!" he shouted, throwing a snowball and hitting her right in the head. There was fierce retaliation, and they all ended up back in the house wet and cold. A change of clothes, in Ethan's case another trip to the dryer, and it was time for Christmas Dinner.

There was a candlelit centerpiece of roses and pears and all the good silver and crystal sparkled. James set out the roasted vegetables and wild rice stuffing. Then with fanfare he brought in the glistening brown goose. Wine was poured, grace said, and everyone started in.

"What have you been up to?" Sophie asked Ethan as James carved the bird and dishes went round.

"What hasn't he been doing?" her mother interrupted. "He fixed a dozen things I didn't know were broken. Plastered over cracks, adjusted picture frames. You remember that one door lock that never worked? Well now it works."

Ethan smiled shyly. "Just wanted to repay your hospitality."

Sophie didn't know why, but somehow that comment made her uneasy. Ethan had clicked into place with her family yesterday, yet now he was back to sounding and acting like a guest. All she could figure was that he was trying to put some distance between them, to make what he planned on telling her easier.

The meal passed at a leisurely pace till nothing but bones and scraps remained. As everyone had helped make it, they now all helped to clean up. Trash was removed and the prize silverware and crystal washed and restored to the cupboards. Finally, they all went into the living room. Her mother plugged in the Christmas lights while James and Isaac served up the chocolate bûche de noël.

Ethan sat by Sophie, pressing his leg near hers, resting his arm over her shoulders as if they were a couple. But he seemed tense, unsettled. She couldn't understand it. He obviously liked her family a lot and she would have sworn that his passion for her was genuine. Why was he acting like he was there under false pretenses?

"I've got a little gift for everyone," he said, putting aside his dessert and getting up. They heard him head down the basement steps. A moment later he was back, cradling something in his arms. The gift wasn't wrapped. Ethan just set it down on the table. It was rectangular and made out of hammered copper with a wire handle at the top. On the sides were four pieces of cut, colored glass.

"What is it?" Benji asked.

In response, Ethan got down the box of matches. Unlatching the top of the object, he fished out a tea candle, set it aflame and returned it. The thing lit up and the glass on each side threw colored shapes onto the walls. There was a golden sun on one side, a violet dove on another, a green Christmas tree and a blue snowflake shaped like a six-pointed star.

"The multicolored lantern!" Sophie's mother was the first to say, and she looked at Ethan with awe. "You made it real."

"It was already real," he murmured.

"It's wonderful," Sophie said. It was—as wonderful as its creator.

"It's an apology," Ethan said. And that's when Sophie knew that her moon dream had come to an end.

"Sophie," Ethan said, his heart pounding, "I've something to say, and then I'll be going. I wasn't entirely honest with you. With any of you."

The family exchanged anxious looks, and both Isaac and James scowled. They were probably wondering if they were going to have to beat the living shit out of him. In truth, they might after they heard what he had to say. But it was Sophie's pained expression, the way her eyelids dropped in anticipation of something terrible that ripped his soul apart.

"I want you to know," he said quickly, lest she get the wrong idea, "if I had one wish, it would be to stay. To stay with you, Sophie, and be your hero. But I'm not what you think I am. You see, that robber I knocked over wasn't the one who broke into the thrift store. That was me."

"You?" she echoed. Her tone said she didn't believe it. Didn't want to believe it.

"I picked the charity because I knew where they hid the float money. I was about to take the cash when I heard you scream for help. Rescuing you saved me from being arrested."

"You're—" Sophie swallowed. "You're a *thief?*"

"Lately, yes. I was a handyman of sorts some months ago. It was an under-the-table thing, a bunch of us unlicensed, unemployed guys doing whatever needed doing. We had a boss who provided us with the tools and stuff. He got arrested for, well, running a fake contracting business." He shrugged. "So I misled you there, too. I'm not really a bona fide handyman."

He felt the rest of the family shifting, but all he could look at was Sophie and her cooling expression.

He took in a breath. "After that I took to stealing. Petty theft: cigarettes, a bottle of liquor, that sort of thing."

"Why?" Benji wanted to know. The boy had moved himself close to his mother for comfort. His disillusioned gaze hurt Ethan almost as much as Sophie's.

"I was broke and hungry, and too proud to go to a church or a shelter. I know that probably doesn't make sense. A person should feel worse about stealing than about accepting hand-outs." He glanced down at his stocking feet. "But I kinda lost myself—my better self--over the years. You, all of you, helped me find a bit of that lost self. I don't know if it'll make any difference to you, but I'll be going to the police station tonight. I won't let that other guy be blamed for what I did."

Deafening silence. Oh, for a clock radio. Ethan released a breath. It was done. He turned and made for the entry hall, then paused as one last thing occurred to him. "I'm sorry if I ruined the holidays for anyone. Really sorry. I never, ever meant to do that."

He got his boots and gloves on and took his jacket down from the hook. The sound of the front door shutting behind him seemed very final.

Chapter 6
Holiday Lights

The world outside was frosty cold, the sky overhead shadowed with clouds once again. But the neighborhood lights still blinked bright and welcoming. As inviting as the first time Ethan had seen them. God, had it only been three days ago?

His footsteps echoed around him as he headed down the sidewalk, his pulse sounded in his ears. He tried to enjoy the solitude, but after living with Sophie's active, chatty family, all he felt was lonely. Profoundly lonely. And back at square one. Providing he managed to stay out of jail, he'd have to find a way to pay his rent, buy food.

He heard the sound of a door opening and shutting. "Ethan!" The shout was followed by the sound of hurrying steps down the sidewalk. He winced. It was his own fault for thinking he could escape without a confrontation. Shit and shit again. Shoulders hunched he turned.

Sophie, her big coat flopping about her unbuttoned, came running. She stopped in front of him, shivering in the cold, breath puffing out in clouds before her.

And then she kicked him in the shin.

"OW!"

"You asshole!" she barked as he hopped about on one foot, hissing.

"Jesus Christ—no, no, don't kick me again!" He stumbled back as she took aim.

"How dare you drop that bombshell and just leave!"

"I kinda... kinda thought you'd want me out of there. You know, *'Never darken our door again!'''*

"You thought wrong! God damn it! And by the way, Isaac says that if the police have no evidence of who did the breaking and entering and nothing was stolen then there's no point in giving yourself up. They can't charge the other guy, and they're not going to want to do the paperwork on you."

"Well, that's good to know. Thank him for the advice and I'll think about it."

"You'll *think* about it?"

"Look, Sophie, whether I do what he says or not, it doesn't change anything."

"What's that supposed to mean?"

He sighed. Why was she making this difficult? "You were all outraged about someone trying to rob a kid's charity, and now you're not?"

"No, I'm pissed at you and so is my family. Angry and disappointed. So what? That doesn't mean we want to lose you." She grabbed his wrist. She wasn't wearing gloves and her fingers were freezing. "Fucking up doesn't make you worthless."

God. Why did she have to have so much damn faith in him? He was going to have to confess it all. "Sophie, I've got nothing. Absolutely nothing. I can't even buy you a cup of coffee. And I know that shouldn't mean anything, but it does."

She was staring at him with those penetrating blue eyes of hers. "Why is that Ethan? What happened? Where's your family, your friends?"

Right to the heart of it. He moved his arm, forcing her to release him and turned away. "My father believed that it was important to have expensive things. A Lexus, a house in the right neighborhood, a son going to private school. All this was proof that a man was a success. When I was seventeen, however, he was arrested and we learned the truth. He'd gotten his wealth from defrauding investors, some of them our friends and neighbors. He was a crook, a con man. He left us not only broke, but disgraced. Stigmatized."

He felt the old pain, that knot of betrayal. Sophie stood listening, hands in her pockets.

"All those righteous lessons he'd taught me about a man standing on his own feet, meeting his responsibilities was all bullshit." Ethan swallowed. "And then, just as this all came to a head, the son-of-a-bitch had a heart attack and died, which saved him from going to jail, but left us to deal with the aftermath."

"Oh, Ethan."

"We had to sell everything. Mom and I ended up living in a one-bedroom apartment. I quit school, got a job to support us, but then mom got sick, leukemia."

Sophie winced. "I'm sorry."

"Don't be. She never got over the loss of it all—of her elegant lifestyle, her rich friends, her beautiful home. She was depressed and angry till the end. Her passing was a mercy." Ethan chewed on his lip.

"So you were left all alone, in the dark," Sophie said softly.

"I was on my own," he agreed, avoiding her gaze. "And I was no good at it. Over the years I've sunk lower and lower, becoming as much of an unreliable, irresponsible, immoral fuck up as my father. Do you see? I'm not someone you would have invited into your home or your bed! I led you and your family on in order to steal what I could from you."

"Is that why you think you should go to jail? For taking advantage of us?"

He flinched. Damn, she was good.

"Come on," she added with a jerk of her head. "We're going to be late for the Christmas Eve ceremony."

"Sophie—"

Her eyes met his, not dreamy this time, but rather like they were drawing him in, locked on him and pulling. "You just admitted that you wronged me, and owe me. If you mean it, then come on."

He couldn't argue with that. He followed her back down the peaceful street to the house. She did not, however, go up the front stairs. Instead, she took them through a gate into the backyard. The family was standing on the snow-crusted porch. They were bundled up, candles in hand, out under the stars.

Only Benji glanced at Ethan and Sophie as they joined the circle. The adults acted as if nothing had happened, but Ethan could sense the effort of that nonchalance. He wasn't sure if he was grateful for it or not.

James stepped forward and the family formed a circle around him.

"The Christmas story," he began, "is a very simple story. And yet I think that the most important part of it is often overlooked. We see the divine child, the kneeling wise men, the winged angels and the star, but the most important element of this tale, to me, is the manger."

A pause. Distant church bells could be heard, ringing from town.

"It's important to remember that the light of the world was born in the most unassuming of locations offered off-handedly, if considerately, by a busy innkeeper."

Ethan glanced away. Was James implying that letting him sleep on the couch was like offering Mary and Joseph the manger?

"This should remind us," James continued, "that in looking for our inner fire, we should examine not our greatest achievements, but our most modest. In looking for those shining stars in our world, we should consider not the highest and most powerful people, but those who are simple and unpretentious. Because it is in the most humble of places that the greatest light is born. Finally, we should remember that it doesn't matter if we're in a castle or a manger or under the stars."

He opened his hands and gazed up at the night sky. "So long as we're with the people we love, we are blessed."

This time Ethan hung back as the family sang "Silent Night," then hugged and wished each other a Merry Christmas. But then James came up and quite deliberately stood in front of him. Quiet descended and Ethan finally met the older man's gaze.

"You want to hit me over the head with a hammer for good measure?" he asked James.

"I'll leave that to Sophie," the older man said, squeezing his shoulder. "But I will say this: The birth of His son on Earth was God's gift to the world, a gift of love and absolution. On this night of all nights, why can't you believe that we'd forgive you?"

Ethan shrugged. He knew the answer, but couldn't say it aloud. It involved being able to forgive himself.

James sighed. "Kay and I are off to church services, and Isaac is taking Nikki and Benji to look at Christmas lights. So you and Sophie will have the house to yourselves. I hope we'll see you in the morning, Ethan."

The family drifted away, candles floating like fairy lights before them. Ethan was left with Sophie, there in the dark, stars twinkling overhead.

"Well?" she asked.

Late the next morning, Christmas morning, Sophie stood outside on the porch gazing up at Ethan's lantern. Her mother had lit and hung it. The sky was gray and dark enough that the rainbow glow was easily seen, beams of colored light and symbols of the season, shining in every direction.

It had been quite a morning with the family seated around the tree opening presents. They'd sipped hot chocolate and nibbled on cranberry coffee cake while tearing at wrapping paper and prying the lids off boxes. Gifts were tried out or tried on, paper was balled up and thrown, and bows were placed in everyone's hair.

Intimidating for Ethan, who'd huddled in an armchair, uncertain of his welcome. It hadn't been easy convincing him to stay the night. Dragging him upstairs and fucking his brains out had helped. He'd still spent this morning looking ready to bolt.

"One last gift," mother had said and handed James a small box. James had passed it to Nikki, who'd passed it to Isaac who'd given it to Benji, who'd paused in playing his new game tablet to present it to Ethan.

"Um...thank you," Ethan had murmured, sounding both surprised and apprehensive. Slipping off the ribbon he'd popped open the box and lifted out two keys. "What's this?"

"Keys to the basement," Mother had said and when Ethan gawked at her. "You can take the stuff that's down there and sell it, or you can use it to help out these people." She handed over two sheets filled with names and addresses. "Old homes in desperate need of a good handyman."

Ethan's mouth had fallen open, nothing coming out.

"You can also sleep in the basement if you like," James added, "We'll work out payment for room and board later."

"I can't—I can't—" he'd tried.

"Yes, you can," Sophie had jumped in, feeling the same determination to make things right as she had last night. "That workshop is going to waste. It should belong to someone who can use it to fix and save things."

"Sophie, I'm not--"

"You are. You came to my rescue, didn't you? And I was a total stranger. You'll do good things with this gift, Ethan, we all believe that. That's why we feel you should have it."

Ethan had gone quiet after that and Sophie could only hope she'd convinced him. One thing she was sure of, however, was that whatever else happened between them, he would no longer be stealing from charities.

She heard the door open and shut behind her, and Ethan joined her at the porch rail. She leaned in close, unable to resist his pull. She remembered how he'd smelled last night—all spice and musk. How he'd touched her, his calloused hands hot as they stroked her curves, her breasts, like he was using a lathe to carve every inch of her into his heart.

Just thinking about it warmed her right through.

Standing beside Sophie, Ethan flashed on last night's passion. "I'm not giving up on us before we even try to make it work," she'd informed him. And then she'd rubbed her burning body over him, and tickled his skin with her hair till he couldn't stand it any longer.

For you, he'd wanted to tell her then, *I will convert and believe in it all: In forgiveness. In being able to leave behind what I was and become who I really am. I will believe that my inner self can be set aflame, and that I, in turn can set yours alight. I will believe in us.*

He hadn't been able to say it, however. Only show her with his hands and his mouth and his passion. When he'd finally plunged into her, holding her tight, he'd felt how she was making him come and how he was making her come and it had been like flames meeting and merging. He'd envisioned the two of them creating one brilliant light.

He looked at her now and still couldn't quite come to grips with what had happened. He'd been so sure that Sophie and her family were karmic payback—all he wanted and, because of past and present sins, couldn't have. He'd been wrong; they'd been a blessing of the season, a chance to restore and renew himself. All that had been required was that he accept them and have faith.

"What religion are *you*?" he ventured now. "I mean, I know the faith of everyone else in your family, but no one ever told me yours."

Sophie looked surprised. "I'm a scientist, you know that."

"What? Are you... are you saying you don't believe in anything?"

She laughed, "I'm saying I don't believe in everything. That doesn't mean I don't believe in anything. I believe in the laws of gravity and in quantum physics. Not all people do, you know. I believe in the power of life, which can flourish in the most amazing places. Most of all, I believe in our species. I believe we can grow and do better. I believe we can perform miracles."

She was glowing again, or seeming to, like a candle in the dark. "What do you believe?"

Ethan thought about it, about all that had run through his mind last night in bed with her. And finally he said, "I believe that the sun is coming back, and that everything is going to be all right."

"I believe that, too," Sophie smiled.

He put an arm about her then and drew her close. "Your mother paid me for my repairs. Can I buy you a cup of coffee?"

"I'd like that."

They headed down the block, hand in hand. Holding the café door open for Sophie, Ethan paused to glance back, his eyes seeking out the verdant Victorian house standing like an evergreen in the snow.

The multihued lantern could be seen even from so far, colorful, and bright as a star. Whenever they decided to return, it would guide them home.

By Travelers' Moon

Chapter 1
Demonic Dealings

I was just about to take a much needed break from fortune telling when the Devil walked into my tent.

Devil with a capital "D," that is. I'd gotten plenty of impish tykes throughout the afternoon, all wearing red Wal-Mart PJs with paper horns and silly pointed tails, also giggling adolescents, hair highlighted with fiery colors, mini-bat wings harnessed to their shoulders.

This particular fiend, however, was a very grown-up hellion. Stepping through the flap to the sound of carousel music and the sticky fragrance of cotton candy, he wore a blazing red suit with a shiny black shirt and tie. This was no cheap costume; it was fine wool and real silk, and its impeccable tailoring made it clear that he had a body taut and fit underneath. His matching red-and-black wingtip shoes gleamed. Even his horns were elegant and understated, black enamel points crowing his artfully disheveled black hair.

His glossy goatee, the finishing touch, was real, and recently trimmed to frame his ironic smirk. I could easily envision him resting back in the barber's chair, a glass of whiskey, neat, to hand as the stylist meticulously clipped away. Devilishly handsome, oh yes. For a moment, half out of my chair, I froze and just stared; he was so beyond anyone I'd have ever expected to see in that tent.

Having taken a gander at my palmistry charts, Rota Fortunae poster, bead curtains, and cheap paisley tablecloth, his dark eyes finally found me. As his gaze locked with mine, I felt my face and, more embarrassingly, everything below my waist, grow hot. I was sure he knew, and was about to grin with evil delight, but he glanced away, as if I wasn't nearly so interesting as he'd thought.

I felt like I'd been jabbed with a pitchfork. Which was stupid—there was only one hanging lamp in the tent, leaving a lot of me in shadow. I was swaddled in a cheap, lace-up, flouncy-skirted costume and several shawls. No man could possibly tell if I even had a figure, let alone if it was worth admiring. I also had lavender colored contacts in my eyes, age make-up on my face, and a crazy pink-gray wig covering my head.

So he hadn't dismissed me-me, he'd dismissed my fortune teller get-up. But even if he had seen my actual self and rejected her, so what? I didn't know him from Adam. All the same, I felt like crying out "Wait! This is just a mask," as he started to back out.

"Oh, no you don't!" a laughing female voice said, "You said you'd do it!"

The succubus who'd appeared was clearly the Devil's partner for the night. Her form-fitting, scarlet-and-ebon dress was as expensive as his suit and corresponding red enamel horns poked up from her golden blond hair. I had to admit I was envious of that soft and easy coif; it was like the stylist had captured the wind breezing through a field of flame grass.

Given the sheer fabric and plunging neckline of the outfit, I did wonder why she wasn't shivering. The chill of mid-October had arrived, and even swaddled in shawls, I was cold. Then again, she did have the Devil to keep her warm.

"Must I?" Mephistopheles sighed like a sulky teen.

Her lips, artfully painted red-and-black, parted to display a cute pair of plastic fangs. "You said you would if I won."

"What did you win?" I ventured, resting back in my chair.

"The pin-the-leaves-on-the-tree dart game," she said.

"I got three out of five!" he protested.

"You missed the two top branches," she countered and said, to me, "I did not. He has to get his fortune told. That was the bet."

I heaved a sigh of my own. No break yet. "Five minute read, ten or fifteen?" The prices were posted outside, all very affordable; way lower than I usually charged. This was a school carnival after all.

"Five—" Beelzebub began.

"Fifteen," his demoness corrected, her fingers running over his firm shoulders, as if playing piano. I noted that her long nails had tiny flames painted on them. That made me conscious of my own nails, which I'd coated with childish purple polish and star decals. I'd thought my costume pretty fine, certainly good enough when I'd looked at myself in the mirror this afternoon. Now it seemed bargain basement.

"You said you'd go for a whole fifteen minute read if you lost," Lady Lucifer chided.

"Fine." He reached into his jacket, pulled out an expensive looking wallet and withdrew three five dollar bills; as my sign pointed out, I was only accepting cash. I slipped them into my box as he drew back the chair across from me.

"Read on, Madame Marzanna," he said with a grand, sarcastic gesture. It was the name over my tent, and my tarot reader alter-ego.

"This is so exciting," the demoness declared, pulling up the other folding chair and setting a hand on his crossed knee.

"If you say so." He was trying to sound bored, but the feeling I got from him was more like a big cat prowling a cage. I, in the meantime, surreptitiously set the timer on my phone and picked up my deck. A multitude of cheap bangles clanked on my arms as I shuffled.

My client raised a black brow, evidently impressed at how adeptly I was handling the cards. "Worked tables at Vegas?"

I set down the deck. "Are you right handed?"

"Left, actually."

"Cut the cards with your right hand."

He did so. I put the cards back together and flicked five out onto the paisley tablecloth. The Princess of Darkness leaned in to examine them, but the Prince did not. He checked his watch, which, sure enough, had a red dial and a gleaming, black-linked band. His disregard cooled my already cooling interest in him. Even if he didn't want to be here, he could at least be polite, and look at the cards. This was going to be a very long fifteen minutes.

"Two of cups," I tapped the first one. "Love's on the horizon."

"Oh!" His companion wiggled in her chair. *"Love!"*

The Devil rolled his eyes. "Please. What kind of a vague prediction is that? And if you're after getting my attention," he said more directly to me, "and being far more accurate—you should say that *sex* is in my near future." His voice purred and he flashed a salacious grin, all the whiter thanks to his inky goatee.

"No one needs a card reader to predict that!" Mrs. D. laughed, and somewhere in my hindbrain there flashed this image of him, well... That mortifying heat returned to my loins.

I cleared my throat. "This is a cups card. Cups don't predict sex. They do predict friendship and love. So, however much guaranteed sex is in your future, it's not being foretold by this card."

He gave me a started look and tilted his head, as if only now realizing I wasn't one of those mechanical psychics that spits out a fortune on a strip of paper. For a moment, his perpetual air of mockery dropped away and his face went very serious. His eyes, a penetrating brown flecked with rust and gold, certainly saw me now. Then he actually glanced down at the card still under my finger.

"That looks like us, actually," he remarked. "A man and woman across a table. Sharing some wine, it seems. That's love?"

"The beginnings of it." Embarrassingly, I had to clear my throat again. "The possibility of it. The next card..."

I moved on to the Five of Wands, featuring a circle of five, colorfully dressed youths with staves, striking out at each other.

"All those sticks," The Devil's eyes glittered. "Don't tell me I'm going to have to compete to get that sex."

"You're going to have to compete to get something," I corrected.

His lady threw him a look, telling me I'd hit the target.

"Others want what you want," I added. "You're going to need to stand out and prove you're better than they are."

"Oh, I will," he said, utterly confident. Surprisingly, the young woman beside him lifted her chin and gave him a skeptical look. Whatever the challenge, she doubted he'd win so easily. I got the feeling she didn't think much of his casual bravado, either.

Maybe I'd underestimated her, and misread the power dynamic here? I sucked in a breath, and moved my finger to the third card, the one at the apex of the curve. "Hanged Man."

"Someone is going to want to string me up by my heels?" The Devil smirked. "That's no surprise."

"A lot of someones, I'm sure," I said, reflecting that doing so probably wouldn't make him any less arrogant. "Something is going to give you pause. Maybe during the competition, or because of it. You will step back from your life and see it from a different perspective. You might even do the opposite of what everyone else expects you to do... Much to their surprise."

"Is that so?" he murmured almost lazily. Then "Hey, it's my card!" He tapped the next card down from the Hanged Man. The Devil card as it happened. "Kinky," he added eyeing the chained and naked figures beside the throned and winged demon. "People are going to attach themselves to me? I *am* very desirable."

This time his companion rolled her pretty eyes. "Talk about not-a-prediction."

"Don't get too excited," I cut in. "This card is usually more about *your* desires than theirs."

"Unquenchable desires, I hope." He wagged a brow, and the demoness, laughing, gave him a playful shove.

I had to clear my throat again. "Desires, addictions, ambitions. You might find it hard to free yourself from them."

He snorted. "Who wants to?"

I sighed. "Exactly. This is the outcome." I tapped the last card.

"The Lovers!" His voice dropped in pitch and got husky. He was mocking me again, but that tone still burned through me like molten fire. Damn him. "That looks like the flip side of the Devil there," he pointed out.

The observation was astute. Not many first-time sitters noticed that the Lovers featured a naked man and woman, just like the Devil. The Lovers, however, had a garden setting rather than a rocky landscape, and an angel between them rather than a fiend.

"Are my evil desires going to lead to heavenly love?"

"Possibly," I shrugged.

"Possibly? What kind of fortune teller are you? You said this was the outcome. Doesn't that mean it's going to happen?"

"No," I said. "The outcome means you're on your way there, but now that you've come to me, and you know what's ahead, you can change things."

He and the young lady exchanged puzzled looks.

"This is the map." I waved over the cards, "It shows what's going to happen at each stop along the way. But you don't have to stay on this road. Right now, you're here or almost here." I set my finger back on the Two of Cups. "Change your plans for this week and none of this might happen."

"But it will," the demoness said, "if he sticks to his plans?"

"If he keeps traveling the road he's on, yes. He'll hit each one of these cards and as he does," I tapped the Lovers, "this will become more and more inescapable. But right now, he can easily escape it if he wants."

"Free will, huh? How convenient." The Devil was back to being cynical. "If it does happen, you foretold it, and if it doesn't, I did something to change it." He pushed up and out of the chair. "Well, thanks for the reading, and I'm glad to know I'm on the road to true love... If I want it."

"You've got seven more minutes."

"That's okay. Keep the change. I could do with a hot drink," he said to this companion. "An adult one. Shall we head to the bar booth?"

"Sure," she said and rose, but her eyes remained on the cards, and her expression was thoughtful.

"Thank you, Madame Marzanna." The Devil took her by the elbow and steered her toward the exit, while offering me a dismissive wave. "It's been... fun, in a naive, children's carnival sort of way."

"You're welcome, and you should be aware that the true love in your future isn't going to come free." I said this loudly, and half-regretted it. Why should I care what he thought? Just let him go and forget it. But damned if I was going to let him have the last word. Not on my turf.

"Huh?" He glanced over his shoulder. "What's that?"

I lifted the Devil card in my left hand, and the Lovers in my right. "It's in the cards. To have this kind of love, you'll need to leave the underworld and go celestial. Change from fallen angel to rising. Which I predict you will willingly do... If you get to this outcome."

"Ha!" He laughed, and the tent flap dropped down behind him. "Like hell."

I ran into Lucy and the twins while waiting in line for a cider.

"Beauty and the Beast?" I ventured, as the seven-year-olds, munching on funnel cakes, came running up. They'd refused to give me even a hint as to their costumes, wanting to surprise me. Eden was wearing a pretty blue pinafore dress and white apron, brownish-black hair in a ponytail with a big blue bow. Her brother, Ardie, had gone for the equally casual beast look with a white pirate shirt and dark trousers. He had gold faux fur wrapped about calves and forearms, and an abundance of it circling his head as a lion's mane.

He gave his best try at a roar, mouth full, and waved about the fake claw on his free hand.

"And I suppose you're the good fairy?" I added as my sister, Lucy, caught up with them. She resembled our mother, meaning she was taller than me, sharper featured, and her brown hair was wavy rather than curly. It also had polished brass highlights rather than my coppery ones.

"Enchantress," she corrected, taking down her own funnel cake. "And I'm in disguise." She was, in fact, wearing a hooded cloak over a simple peasant dress. "I'll go full on glitz for Halloween. And you need to stop me from having any more snack food."

That was Lucy's constant refrain this time of year. *"Stop me from eating too much candy. Stop me from eating too many hand pies."* I'd never been able to figure out why she asked this, as no matter what she ate, she stayed skinny. All I could figure was that she liked the *idea* of resisting temptation.

"I can't stop you from doing anything while I'm busy telling fortunes, which I've been doing non-stop since this place opened." I waved about the school's soccer and baseball field, filled with illuminated booths, rides, games and concession stands.

"Ooo. Lotsa money for the school."

"Yeah, too bad I don't get a cut. This is my first break." I glanced at the line, moving at a snail's pace. "And I think it's going to be a long one."

"Are you going to want a ride home afterwards?" she asked. Her tone and side-wise glance at the kids told me she was hoping for an early night.

"Naw. I rode my bike."

"That old thing? In that costume?"

"Don't worry. I tie up the skirts so they don't get caught in the wheels."

"If you're sure..."

"Arlo! Arlo!" Ardie tugged at my sleeve.

"Yes, Dee?"

"There's a haunted hayride tomorrow night. Will you go with us?"

"I will absolutely try to go with you," I told him, "Remind me sometime in the afternoon."

"Can we have more money for the games?" Eden interrupted, brushing her sugared hands on her apron. "I want to go on the pony carts." She pointed towards where bored little horses pulled kids in carts up one side of a dusty road and then back down the other way.

"Oh, high striker!" Ardie bounced on his toes. "Mommy, you said I could."

"Don't tell me you used up all your tickets! Already?" Lucy sighed.

"High Striker?" I repeated, glancing over to where young men and some athletic women were taking turns swinging a hefty looking mallet. Each time they hit the target, a series of lights went up the tower. If they got it to the top a bulb flared and bells rang out.

"They've got smaller mallets for kids, and adjust how much force has to be used," Lucy assured me even as the twins grabbed her hands and dragged her towards the ticket booth. "See you later!"

"Try to win a prize for me!" I called after. And then, finally, it was my turn at the window. I treated myself to the buttered-pecan cider and settled at one of the picnic tables. While I'd been stuck in the tent, it had gone from late afternoon into early evening, and for a moment I just absorbed the snap in the air. I don't know why, but the coming of night in October always feels different from any other time of year. Velvety and magical, as if arriving on stealthy paws.

The flashing lights of carnival rides and the glow from inside booths and tents grew brighter. The shrieks and laughs of kids grew louder. The carnival always took me a little by surprise, appearing, it seemed, all at once from the mists one day; gone the next. A kind of strange illusion; silly, delightful, and, given all the ghostly-creepy decorations, shivery scary...in a good way.

Fortune telling in costume might be a pain, I thought, scratching under my wig, but I did love the fleeting enchantment of this once-a-year festival. I loved the mingled scent of popcorn and burning leaves that perfumed every autumn breeze and I loved the butter-pecan cider. I smiled and lifted my cup for a deliciously hot sip.

"Can you explain the logic of having a costumed Halloween carnival the weekend before the weekend before Halloween?" a familiar voice jolted me and that first searing sip splashed across my knees. I bit back a curse as Mr. Mephistopheles settled across from me, a toddy reeking of Crown Whiskey in hand.

111

"Hope you don't mind drinking with the Devil." Completely ignoring the upset, he grinned and toasted me.

Chapter 2
Bespelled by Pentagrams

"October thirty-first falls on a weekday this year," I said, mopping at the spill with paper napkins. It wasn't all that bad, or visible, but I was pissed. Also I didn't want to meet his wicked brown eyes. "So, not so good for a school carnival. And they hold it on this weekend so they don't spoil the weekend parties that happen right before Halloween."

"Don't spoil them or don't compete with them?" He flashed his white, almost irresistible smile.

"Compete with them," I granted.

"I didn't mean to impose," he added, likely knowing it was too late for objections. "But after we left you, it occurred to me that I'd been a bit of a jerk, and that I ought to apologize."

"'S'kay. Dealing with jerks is part of the job description."

"Still. Apology tendered." He offered a half-bow.

"Accepted." I gave him a regal nod.

"So," he leaned in head on hands. "What do you look like without the wig and contacts?"

"Don't know what you're talking about. This is my real hair and eye color."

'You're not going to give me a clue, are you?"

"Nope. Where's Mrs. Lucifer?" I tried to sound casual.

"Kelly? She's not Mrs. anything, and she's off with her friends on the tilt-a-whirl." He lifted his chin toward the ride where cars spun like tops while dipping and rising. I caught a glimpse of the demoness in a seat with two other ladies. They were screaming with terrified delight.

"That's why we're here," the Devil went on. "She used to go to this school, and every year she comes back to nostalgically attend this carnival and reunite with her old BFFs. I got invited along. We're sorta business partners."

"Sorta?"

"S' complicated." He shrugged, then held out a hand. "Piers. Surname: Tatham."

"Arlo Symons." I shook his hand. His grip was firm, and warmer than warm. Hot. Dry. I had to force myself to release it.

"Arlo? Really."

"Really."

"Short for—?"

"Short for nothing," I said firmly. "A-R-L-O. My mother liked the name."

"Hm." He stroked his short beard, eyes dancing.

He uses mockery and smirks to hide what he's really thinking, I mused. And damn if it didn't work really, really well. Usually I was pretty good at reading people, but I had no idea what going on in his head. Well, I could hide my thoughts, too. I kept my expression bland.

"So, Arlo," he said, "I've a pocket full of tickets and, Kelly being with her friends, no one to share them with. Would you care to help me? Go on the Rota Fortunae? That means Wheel of fortune, right?" He waved to the Ferris wheel.

The Ferris wheel? Sit next to him in a small car, feel his thigh against mine, maybe his arm stretched out behind my back. In spite of the brisk night air, my cheeks flushed and my palms grew sweaty. He'd be near enough that his breath would caress my ear as he leaned in to speak. There'd be no escaping his magnetic heat, or those captivating brown eyes.

Circling up so high we'd see all of the carnival glittering below like a handful of white hot sparklers. And the operators always made sure to give each car a moment at the top. Did I want to be trapped there with the Devil? *Hell yes!* But what would I say to him? What might he say to me? Or do to me?

Scary shiver. In a good way.

I realized I'd let the silence lengthen. He was beginning to get a curious look, like he couldn't believe I was taking so long to make up my mind. From what the demoness—Kelly—had said, I don't think he was often left hanging.

That's when I came back down to Earth. "I... don't go for games of chance," I demurred. Yet even as I said it, a part of me threw up her hands in disgust. *Idiot! What are you doing?*

I'm keeping my feet on the ground, I mentally retorted. *Last thing I need is to wake up in the morning feeling like a cheap carnival prize.*

Piers eyed me sidewise and waggled his brows. "What if I predicted you'd get lucky?"

"I'd tell you that I'd rather a long term investment over short term gain," I replied. That wasn't true at all; I would have loved some short-term gain.

But I didn't think it wise to admit that. "Maybe a spin around the world, instead?" I waved desperately to the carousel.

"As my lady wishes." He agreed cheerfully enough, but I could swear there was disappointment in his voice. He rose and, like the prince of darkness he was, offered me the crook of his arm. Accepting it, I allowed him to lead us toward the hurdy-gurdy music of the merry-go-round.

I wondered if its dizzying spin would leave me even more off balance than I was already.

"You're using too much lip," I critiqued. "You'll never get hold of it that way."

"Kibitzing isn't helping," snarled Piers, hands behind his back, saliva wetting his beard. "I'm doing this my way, okay?"

"Your way sucks," I muttered, but the Devil wasn't listening. He kept nosing in, mouthing at the apple on its string. And it, predictably, kept slipping away.

The first few minutes of the carousel ride had been as awkward and uncomfortable as I'd feared, at least on my part. "Allow me," Piers had said as I'd picked out a purple horse, and lifted me by the waist with barely a grunt into its saddle. He'd then hopped on the black one next to it, sitting sideways one leg crossed over the other, to face me.

I'd gulped, still feeling his grip as the ride started. I couldn't help imagining those strong hands on my bare skin. Holding me steady as he gazed down at me, our breaths coming quick...

My horse rose up and down, and I felt myself going hot and melty again. *Shit!* What was it with this guy? I was twenty-six, not fifteen, and he wasn't my type. I went for "beautiful dreamers," as my sister would say. Free and easy skylarks who worked for non-profit organizations and always spoke from the heart.

And always leave you to save an endangered species in one hemisphere or an endangered people in another, I reminded myself. There was that drawback with skylarks.

Piers, by comparison, was an unapologetic magpie, all chatter and flash and a glimmer of greed. I ought to have been repelled, but I wasn't. Very much to the contrary, which made me wonder if I'd been lying to myself all these years about my type. It wasn't, however, his hedonism or his sexy red-and-black suit alone that enticed me. It was his energy. I could almost see it coiled up inside him, like a jack-in-the box waiting to pop. Even on this merry-go-round, silent and looking like he might take a nap there on that wooden saddle, it waited, an electrical charge itching to pounce.

I found it disturbingly exciting. What would he be like when he released all that energy? Was he ever sated and calm? Even as I contemplated him, he contemplated me in a way that seemed equally curious. Like I wasn't doing what women riding a carousel with him usually did. Which was what? Giggle? Talk? Make out?

"So, do you really believe?" he asked, over the music.

"Believe what?"

"That you're getting a message from some higher power when you lay out those cards. One that can put someone like me on the right path."

He had an apathetic expression on his face and in his voice, as if my answer didn't matter. But I had a feeling it did, and if I bungled this, we'd part. *Well, screw him,* I thought. Was that why he'd invited me to take a ride with him? Why he'd tried to casually seduce me? To ask that?

"Let me answer your question with a question," I said, "Would you ask a rabbi, minister or imam if they believed in the power of prayer?"

"Um," he scratched at his goatee. "I see what you're getting at and probably not. But it's not the same."

"They're seeking messages from a higher power, to pass on to those seeking their help. And getting paid for it. They even put up signs saying that prayer is the way to peace, healing and happily-ever-after."

"Well, yeah, but..." he glanced over at me worried now. "I've stepped into it, haven't I?"

I shrugged and smiled, a little coldly I imagined. "We're all in search of that magical something that will never change, never leave us. Nothing in this world does that. But maybe there's something beyond it that does? Belief may be a foolish rock to cling to, but if the alternative is drowning.... Can you say you've never clung to anything?"

The ride was slowing down, his horse and mine coming to a stop at the midway point. He blinked at me as if I'd sucker punched him. Good. Let him feel awkward and uncomfortable for a change.

"Um, I think I'm way out of my depth. I also think I might have offended you again. I didn't mean to. Honestly, I was just curious."

Shit. I blushed. Had I jumped the gun there? Stupid question, of course I had. I'd gone uber-defensive with a man I'd only just met, and why had I done that? Why, again, had I felt like his opinion mattered?

"Sorry," I said back, as he slipped off his horse and, hands back around my waist, helped me down. "I went overboard."

He flashed that white grin of his. "No, no. It was very enlightening. And I enjoyed traveling around the world with you." He waved at the merry-go-round. "So. What shall we spend my tickets on next?"

Which was how we'd ended up at the apple bobbing booth. However clever the Devil in other ways, he was having a hellish time sinking his teeth into the forbidden fruit. It slipped away, again and again, making him curse and chase after it.

"Maybe you should try to stab it with your horns, like a bull," I suggested.

"Goring the apple isn't how you win," he said making another futile attempt. Finally, he lunged. The apple went flying, his teeth clacked on nothing, and then...

"Ouch!" he rocked back, hands flying from behind his back to his face. "My eye!"

"Told ya," I said, even as the timer rang, putting an end to the game.

"Fine." He glared at me with his one good orb. "Show me how it's done then."

"Gonna need another ticket," the booth's plump, motherly proprietor said. "New string and apple for each contestant."

Piers, finally blinking open the bashed eye, fished out his wad of tickets and handed one over. Within a minute a fresh, red-green apple was dangling from a "branch" on the plywood and paper-leaved apple tree. I tucked my costume necklaces under my blouse, so they wouldn't get in the way, and clasped my hands behind my back.

"Ready?" The proprietor, set the timer for three minutes. "Go!"

"You gotta get your lips out of the way," I said to Piers, drawing mine as far back from my teeth as I could.

"You look like a piranha."

"Good." I opened wide and angled under the dangling apple. As it tried to slip away, I moved round to catch it. Chomp! My teeth sunk in, and tart-sweet apple juice dribbled down my chin.

"Ha!" I crowed around the captured mouthful, and, releasing my hands, took hold of it. Snapping it off its string, I completed the bite. "Gotta finesse it, not bully it."

"You've won a prize" the proprietor enthused, pointing to a shelf of small, cellophane wrapped candied apples. They were all for sale, but winners got one for free.

"Which would my little devil like?" I cooed at Piers.

He looked annoyed, but I got the feeling that he was laughing inside. "A red one, of course. But you shouldn't be robbed. Let me buy you another and keep things even."

"'All right. I'll take traditional caramel."

"I can't believe I got trounced by an apple," he said as the woman brought over the confections. "And no jokes about 'the apple of my eye.'"

"Darn."

"As for your apple bobbing 'technique...'" he added, paying for the caramel, "I don't know whether to be aroused, impressed or horrified."

I clacked my teeth at him. "Be afraid."

He laughed and split the apples between us.

"So why are games with apples the thing for Halloween?" he asked, waving his cellophaned prize. "I've always wondered."

"Because it's apple season."

"It's also turnip, pear and quince season.". The carnival was now going strong, and October's waxing half-moon was swinging over the crowded midway. We cut past hordes of children, groups of friends and couples, most in costume. A man in a top-hat and bow-tie performed little magic tricks on a card table, while, on the main stage, a trio of trumpeters played out a resounding jazz composition.

"Do you really want a caramel turnip on a stick?" I asked over the noise.

"I just want to know if there's more to this apple fetish than just it being that time of year. Like, Snow White got poisoned with one by a witch, so witches mean apples, so apples for Halloween."

"Hm. Well, there is one magical aspect to apples that might explain, as you say, the fetish for them at this time of year." I snagged a plastic knife from the corn dog booth. Stopping at a table, I unwrapped my caramel apple and pulled out the stick. Then I sawed away at its circumference.. It wasn't easy with that knife, but I divided it through the middle and held up one half for him to see. .

Piers' brows shot up and he looked genuinely surprised. "Well, whadda ya know?" He took it from me and gazed with wonder at the star shape of seeds at its center. "It's my sign," he said, lifting it, inverted, to his forehead. There, between his enamel horns, it did look a bit like an upside-down pentagram.

"No, it's not," I retorted, taking the half back and restoring the apple to wholeness by jamming both sides back on the stick. "It's a magical symbol that, up or down, wasn't considered evil until it was demonized by certain ignorant occultists."

"And put into horror films, I suppose. I wonder if Da Vinci looked inside an apple when he sketched his infinite man?"

"Maybe. It also stands for a man's path. Upright he's on his way toward the spiritual. Inverted, he's going for the material." I saw my tent up ahead. Sure enough, there was a line of people waiting. "I really have to get back to being Madam Marzanna."

"And I should find Kelly," he agreed. Was that reluctance in his tone? He was holding his candy apple in one hand. He offered his free one for a shake.

"My fingers are all tacky from the caramel."

"So are mine," he said, still waiting, but as I put my sticky hand in his, he brought it up to his lips. His goatee tickled my knuckles as he gave them a respectful kiss.

"Uh, thanks for the fun and games," I gulped, trying not to show the shiver I felt racing up and down my chakras.

"Thanks for the apple," he said, pulling off its wrapper.

Clutching my own caramel apple, I darted for my tent.

"I'm going to be in town till the second of November." His strong voice stopped me. "Maybe I'll see you around?"

Was that hope I heard? I paused and brushed back a lock of gray-pink wig. "Sure. And, ah, if you want another reading, I'll be back here tomorrow." I tried not to sound too eager. The kiss he'd planted on my hand still burned.

I saw him lift the candy apple in a salute then, and, baring his bright white teeth, he took a hearty bite and strode away.

Chapter 3
A Spot of Witchy Witches' Brew

A few days later, gazing out at the rain, I found myself still thinking about devilishly handsome Piers.

He'd not returned to my booth Sunday, nor, as I could have predicted, had he sought me out. There was no point in being blue about that; he'd fed me spun sugar promises, destined to melt away as fast as they'd been created. I'd known it as we talked, and I didn't resent him for it. But I could still feel his touch lifting me onto the merry-go-round horse. I could still feel his lips on the back of my hand, and I could still taste the rich, deep flavor of caramel and crisp apple.

I'd eaten the treat before going to bed that Saturday night. A bad idea, as the Devil had haunted my dreams. In them he'd sat across the table from me, as cards danced to trumpet music and shaped themselves into pentagrams. His tux had literally been on fire, and when he'd lifted my hand to his mouth, he lipped away at it like an apple on a string. I woke breathless with arousal, his growling laugh humming in my ears

Well, he is the sexiest man you've ever met. Are such dreams so surprising? Yes. Maybe. No?

Guys who caught my interest usually gave me very solid feelings. But with Piers, my emotions were splashing, flowing, rippling all over the place, like the rainfall outside. It was unsettling; my brother's sentiments had been like that, rising high on waves one moment, descending down into the depths in the next. It hadn't been good for him, and I didn't think it'd be good for me.

Work. *There's work to do,* I reminded myself. I had to move new deliveries from boxes to canisters, fill out online forms, ship online orders, and update accounts. I ran a teashop, you see. A pretty nifty looking one as

120

back in the 1900's it'd been a pharmacy. It still had hints of that alchemical past here and there, like in the huge, floor-to-ceiling unit of wooden nooks where jars of powders and drugs used to be stored, perfect for tea canisters.

In front of that was the original, L-Shaped pharmacy counter. It was wide enough for a PSO stand, a digital scale , jars of cookies, and, on the short, corner side, two electric urns that kept water just the right temperature. With all of that and wall shelving for knickknacks and sales items, there wasn't much floor space, but I'd managed to squeeze in three tables for sitting and sipping.

A bit tight, yes, but it was charmingly odd and welcoming. At least I thought so; especially when the fragrance of black tea and warm cream wafted about the dark wood, and sunlight streamed in through the paned bay window—which, given the rain, wasn't today. The downpour was keeping customers away, too. I'd barely had any since I'd opened two hours ago. So, I took advantage of the quiet to catch up on my chores. I'd just climbed the rolling ladder, however, and finessed an empty canister from a nook, when I heard the door open. The bell over it ting-a-linged.

"A tea shop, huh?" Piers said. I spun around, barely remembering where I was and almost dropping the canister. He was looking up, hands deep in the pockets of a pea coat, and his eyes widened a bit on seeing me.

"So that's what you look like without the wig," he murmured.

"So that's what you look like without devil's horns," I retorted. I think I was a bit wide-eyed, too. I don't know why I thought those horns were a natural part of him, but it was odd to see him without them. He didn't have an umbrella, and droplets sparkled here and there amid his wild black hair.

"Hello," I ventured, carefully returning the canister to its shelf. "Um, you can hang your jacket on the hooks there."

I came on down as he did so, surreptitiously glancing in a small mirror I'd hung in the doorway between the counter and the back room. Nothing in my teeth, but I wished I hadn't gone for my old, gray-green sweater and jeans. Not that I'd known he was coming, nor what I would have worn if I had.

I felt better as, his coat off, I saw he had on jeans as well. Also, an orange thermal topped with a faded, black, *Hellboy* tee shirt. Nothing elaborate, just the white B.P.R.D. logo.

"No, really, I'm not sure I would have recognized you," he went on, head tilting in that birdlike way of his, so very like a magpie examining something shiny. "I knew from your eyebrows that your real hair had to be brown, but I'd have never imagined all those curls. And the makeup hid the freckles. I like them."

I rolled my eyes. "I guess that means I can keep them."

"And the gray eyes." He glanced about the store. "Nice witchy tea display, by the by. Though, it might make customers leery of your tea."

"Thank you." For the bay window, Lucy, the kids, and I had created a cardboard silhouette of witches around a steaming teapot-shaped cauldron. In front of this, I'd set Halloween-themed tea cups—all for sale of course—along with scattered bottles and jars labeled "belladonna" and "eye of newt." I was rather proud of it.

"So, first question—" he started.

"Why don't I read tea leaves?" I crossed my arms on the counter. "Because they're a pain. The hot water, the mess of the leaves. Easier to carry around a deck of cards. Next?"

"Where are the charts and crystal balls?" He was peering in and behind objects on the shelves.

"I don't do readings here. Clients want readings in a private place, and as you can see, this place isn't that. So if you've come for another reading..."

"No, no. Just a look 'round."

"Also, I'd have to hop up in the middle of readings to take care of customers. So, I only do them off hours and by appointment."

"So your website said."

I felt my brows lift. He'd been checking me out, had he?

"Which brings me to my last question." He came to a stop and faced me. "Did you Google me?"

I glanced away. "Mr. Piers Tatham, son of Wayland Z. Tatham, founder and majority stock holder of WZT fitness machines. Located in Manhattan." I paused, remembering but not saying that he was an only child, and that his mother, a chemist, had passed away a few years back, about the same time Piers had been made WZT's head of design.

"Your Company provides machines for *Sunflower Fitness*," I finished up, "mini studios conceived and owned by one Kelly Dawson."

"Whom I am not romantically involved with anymore," he put in. "In case you were wondering."

"The only thing I'm curious about right now is your choice of tee shirt," I drawled, though yeah, I had wondered about his relationship with Kelly. Also about what it would be like to kiss him. I'd never dated anyone with a beard; would it caress my lips like it had my hand? I shivered.

"I honestly didn't even think about it," he said, glancing down. "Subliminal, I guess. Why shouldn't I wear it?"

"Seems a tad ironic for a skeptic like you."

"It's fiction," He tapped at the logo. "Until and unless someone tries to tell me the Bureau for Paranormal Research and Defense is real, there's nothing to be skeptical about. But I am a little surprised you know what it is."

"I read the comics in high school, and I've seen the movies. Are you a fan?"

"Bit of comic book movie nerd, yeah." He had moved in on the other side of the counter, close to me, close enough that I caught a whiff of his cologne. It had an earthy, woodsy smell, like the ruby-black tea grown near the Sun-Moon Lake in Taiwan. The sort of fragrance the god Pan himself might have worn. I swear, it warmed the air, and I leaned in towards him, wanting to nuzzle his neck.

"Do those tables mean that we can drink tea on the premises?" he asked, breaking the spell. "Because I think I'd like to continue this over a spot. If, that is, it's not against policy for you to join me."

I flushed. I'd gotten so lost in him, in fantasizing about him while holding my own with him, that I'd completely forgotten to ask him if he actually wanted anything. "Um, yeah, sure, um.... Any particular kind? We have some seasonal flavors, made up by me. A green apple spice. That's green *tea*, not green apple."

"Not sure if I want to revisit apples with you," he murmured. He was reading the labels on the tea canisters now.

"Pumpkin pie…"

"Spice," he finished and fairly sighed. "Of course." I merely shrugged. Pumpkin-spice-anything sold like gangbusters this time of year and I was a business woman.

"That one's rooibos. Oh, and there's a caramel pear black. You see? Some of us do consider pears as well as apples. If you want a recommendation, I'd go for that one. It's not sweetened, it simply has this burnt-sugar and roasted pear aroma."

"How I can say no to a sales pitch like that? A pot of caramel pear it is. And maybe some cookies? What are those?" He pointed to the little flute-cut sandwich ones.

"Pecan with maple buttercream," I said, pulling out a white pumpkin-shaped tea pot from under the counter.

"Sold again. Did you make those?"

"Bakery down the street. They're small, so you get three per order." I tossed scoops of pear tea into the pot, added hot water , and set the timer for four minutes. Piers settled at the table nearest the window.

"*Traveler's Moon Tea Garden*," he mused, gazing up at my interior logo, the one written in Nouveau lettering over the canister shelving. "Can I ask why? The name I mean."

I piled the cookies on a little plate featuring bats. I always went for thematic, seasonal serving china when I could. Customers often came in weekly just to see what kind of cup and saucer they'd get.

"It used to be *Ray's Candy Corner*," I said, setting out spoons, napkins and pumpkin-shaped cups on leaf-shaped saucers.

He frowned. "We're not on a corner."

"That didn't bother Ray." I brought over the cookies. "He and his family decided to move to New Mexico. That's how I came into possession."

The timer beeped. I carried over the pot with its strainer and a caddie that held a little pitcher of milk and a choice of sweeteners.

"Yeah, but why *Traveler's Moon Tea Garden?*" he emphasized as I settled across from him. "Why not, I dunno, *Celestial Fields Tea Shop?*"

"My mom loves to garden," I said, pouring for us. At that moment I felt myself relax, and realized that I'd been jittery. The ritual of tea, the smell of that steam, like a pear dessert fresh from the oven, settled me. He wasn't going to rattle me now. Not by being sexy, or by throwing verbal curve balls.

"She does something with plants every day of the year," I went on.

"Even in winter?" He blew on the tea, then ventured a tiny, cautious sip.

"She has a small, hydroponic solarium attached to the garage. So, yes, even in the winter." I sampled my brew in turn.

"This is terrific tea."

"Glad you like it. Anyway, when we were little, and it was time for sleep, Mom would say 'The Moon's arrived to take you to your dream gardens.'"

"Which got you into bed?" He bit into one of the cookies.

"Yep. Dream gardens were where we planted what we wanted to dream about that night. Mom would tuck us in and give us this story about following the moon, traveling through woods and over oceans. Finally we'd arrive at our silvery gardens. Then she'd ask us what we wanted to plant. We'd say things like, 'I want to dream that I'm an acrobat in Cirque du Soliel,' or 'I want to have super powers.' She'd tell us to close our eyes and imagine watering that dream with stardust and warming it with solar winds. By then we'd be drifting off."

"Did it work?" He'd finished off the cookie and was holding the cup in both hands, like a magical elixir. "Did you dream about being in Cirque du Soliel?"

"A lot of the time, yeah."

"So, the subconscious as a garden. And please have one of those," a nod to the cookie plate. I accepted, dunking mine into my tea.

"You don't think it's a good metaphor? Following the moon into dreamland?"

"It doesn't take into account the hard work and practice needed to become a Cirque du Soliel acrobat."

"Do you think customers sitting at these tables want to be reminded of all the work they still have to do? Is that why they came here for a pot of tea and cookies?"

"Ah...no. They probably came to relax and daydream. Point taken. But it is a bit long for a name. And a bit twee."

"It's a lot twee. I'm selling tea, not tequila."

He chuckled, and a brief silence descended. Not an awkward one, more like we were reassessing.

"I suppose it's time for me to fess up," he ventured. "I'm not here just to find out who was under the pink wig. Kelly wants to hire you for a party she's throwing."

Oh? That made me wary. "And she sent you? Why not email me?"

"She's going to, but she felt someone ought to explain the situation, answer any questions you had about it. As she's very busy with visiting friends and scoping out places for a new *Sunflower Fitness,* I volunteered."

"She's going to open one here?"

"That's always been her dream." Piers said this easily, casually, but I could almost see that coiled energy in him tightening up. There was some issue between them over this.

"I don't work on Halloween," I said, refilling our cups. "That's non-negotiable."

"What?" he gave me a side-wise look. "Not even if we offer you copious amounts of money?"

"Not even then," I said coolly.

"Interesting." He broke the last cookie roughly in half and handed me the larger part. "Fortunately, Kelly's party is the Tuesday before that, the twenty-ninth. She says that's when we'll get this special full moon—"

"Harvest Moon." I nodded. "Or Hunter's. Usually shows up in October, very big, close and really impressive. Either bright enough to finish the Harvest by or to hunt deer by, depending on the source of the name."

It had more names than that, of course. One in particular. But I didn't think Piers was interested in coincidence.

"If you say so. Anyway, she's holding this costumed séance party—"

"I don't do séances," I cut in tersely.

"That's the theme of the party."

"Sorry no."

He was frowning, and I realized I'd snapped at him.

"I only read tarot cards," I added and shrugged lamely. "It bugs me when people assume that means I can contact spirits or get answers from beyond the... the grave."

"I don't think Kelly wants you for that," Piers said in gentler tone, as if a house cat sitting next to him had suddenly spat and growled. "You're being hired as a reader for the guests. And her. She's a believer, into psychic power and past lives and all that. And she was really impressed by you. But she doesn't want to have a reading done at any old time. She wants it done the first night of that full moon. So it has more..."

He tapered off, his hand swirling helplessly. Clearly he wasn't sure how to say it without being snide and demeaning.

"Lunar zing?" I ventured.

"Exactly! Just readings, nothing more."

I felt a wave of relief, which was stupid, but this time of year I was always on edge. Usually I managed it, but Piers was throwing me off with his smooth prattle and his seductive brown eyes and that damn god-of-sex fragrance.

I had to get a grip.

"How many readings?" I kept my tone as business-like as possible.

" Ten to twelve guests, not counting Kelly and her mom. She'll want you from seven till eleven and she'll provide you with an appropriate costume, and transportation to and from the party. You'll get all the details in the email. She's happy to pay extra for all this."

From what I'd read on her website and in the few news articles, Kelly could more than afford it. Yes, I'd looked her up, too, and I was... jealous-not-jealous. Kelly Dawson had started off as a personal trainer for her mother's friends at the tender age of fourteen, in this very town. Two years later, with her mother's help, she'd created her signature mobile gym, driving it around nearby cities and suburbs on weekends. A customer could walk in and get a quick, tailored exercise regimen or, if the customer wanted more than that, they could buy a membership.

A membership got them the outfitted bus parked outside their residence at a given time, making sure they stayed in shape. Kelly got so many memberships that she soon had a fleet of these buses. That's when she took the next step and created her first brick-and-mortar, mini- gym on the ground floor of a Manhattan apartment building. Now, at the age of twenty-five, she was the head of a thriving empire worth several million. She was also super healthy, super energetic, and, as I'd seen with my own eyes, super pretty.

And yet I didn't want to be her. Or change places with her. I was content with my single shop, with what I was and who I was, even how I looked. No. What had me jealous—I found myself meeting Piers eyes. They seemed strangely open, like for this one moment they weren't hiding anything. Then the mocking gleam came back, and I felt my own mask of cool distance fall into place in turn.

He glanced at his watch, this one plain steel, but equally expensive looking. "I've got to get going. But I'd like to buy some of that tea."

"Sure. We start at two ounces. That should be enough for several pots."

"Give me four," he said. I got the canister back on the counter, weighed out the tea, and sealed it into one of our little brown bags. He handed me a gleaming credit card so black it might have been sliced out of the night sky.

"How's the watering hole down the street?" he asked, signing the screen I turned his way.

"Estelle's? They were running the bar at the carnival."

"Ah. So, limited high-end liquor, but some solidly good whisky." He got on his coat. "Thanks. I'll, um, see you around."

I had this annoying, sinking feeling. He was going, and I didn't want him to go. I wanted him to stay and sit across from me for the rest of the day, verbally trying to grab at me, while I dodged and wove.

Which was something to realize—that he'd been snatching at me and I'd been slipping out of his grip. I'd never imagined I had a liking for the chase. Well. No. Wait. A liking for the chase, or just a liking for *this* man to chase me?

"At the party, if not before," I agreed.

"Well before that, I think," he said, moving sidewise toward the door, his gaze still on me. Ting-a-ling! And the smell and cold of rain came in. Then the door shut, and through the window I saw him pull up his collar and dash off.

And what, I thought with a stirring deep inside, *did that mean?*

Chapter 4
Dark and Stormy Nights!

My tea shop, located at the exact center of a building containing five establishments, was the only one with a second story. This was in the form of a squat clock tower with two gabled "wings." Inside this roof-topper, walled off from the workings of the clock, was a room where various store owners—or their assistants—had lived. It'd been updated several times over the decades, the last during Ray-of-the-candy-store's watch. He'd remodeled it for his college-aged daughter. She'd left with the family, so now it was all mine.

It contained a tiny bathroom and closet at one end, a built in desk under the window at the other end, and a kitchenette along the clock-side-wall. I had barely enough room left for my twin bed under the window across from the kitchen, a nightstand, and a couple of wicker chairs. Still, I was happy with it. There was a green and brown color scheme to cushions, and bed quilt, and my collection of antique tea signs gave the place a rustic-nouveau vibe.

My one almost-complaint was that back in the 1920's the building's owner hadn't connected this room to the then-new central heating unit. To this day, it still had to be warmed by a wood-burning stove. Fortunately, Ray had installed a classy one for his daughter. I didn't much like buying, storing and hauling up tinder for it, but it kept the place toasty and didn't smoke

A second front of rain was coming in, and though the windows had good seals, the building was old. Chill air still managed to seep in. I tossed cut logs into the stove in anticipation of this, and got a good flame going. Then I kicked off my shoes and fetched out the "soup of the day" I'd bought at the General Store —tomato-bisque, yum!

Settling at the desk, I ate my dinner with crackers and, for the fourth time, went over the conversation I'd had with Piers, which had me shaking my head at myself, for the fourth time. Was I honestly trying to figure out, yet again, if he *liked me*? If he was going to come back and see me again? If more could happen between us?

Give it up, Arlo, I chided myself. *It's dangerous and stupid to even lust after him.* I knew this. That charming self he displayed wasn't the real him. Other ladies might want him badly enough to deny this, but not me. The genuine Piers Tatham likely had the heads of former girlfriends hanging in his closet.

At the very least, he had notches on his bed.

So what do you care if you're a notch? I asked myself. *You could notch your own bed. When are you going to get another chance with a man like that?*

Probably never, but I wasn't going to let that be a reason for going further. There's no way a man who could bed high-powered business babes like Kelly Dawson would view me as a notch. So either I was an amusement, or he wanted something else. Traveling down that road would only land me in hell.

I'd finished off dinner, and was washing off my make-up when lightening flashed. Distant thunder rumbled after. I hurriedly stuffed more wood into the stove and got an oil lamp out of the closet, just in case. And that's when I heard the pounding. At first I thought it was the rain, but then I noticed the regularity of it. It was coming from the door to the shop.

My heart-rate notched up as I skipped down the stairs. Could it be Lucy? Her husband Matthew? Mom? Emergency scenarios came to mind: the kids sick or hurt, mom's car broken down, something. But wouldn't they have called? I flicked on the light and peered out the bay window. There, under the dripping lantern above my sign, was Piers. He was leaning on one outstretched arm, hammering at my door with the other.

I threw open the lock. "What the hell?" I demanded, letting in the autumn storm. Piers, rocking back on his heels, gazed at me with eyes that ticked, as if he wasn't quite sober.

"Good. You're still here." And then he lurched forward. I grabbed at him, thinking he was falling, but his wet arms wrapped about me and, with a furnace whiff of bourbon, his mouth was on mine.

For a second, I lost all sense of anything but the heat of his lips, the snake of his whiskey-flavored tongue on mine, the damp tickle of his mustache. Then the cold water dripping off his goatee splashed on my cleavage, making me jump and yelp. Rain from without, along with drops from his hair, got my face and shoulders.

Wet and cold and wet and cold!

"Get out of the rain." I grabbed the lapel of his jacket, pulled him in and shut the door.

"Couldn't stop thinking of you," he said, head cocked. "You...you witch. Glad you're still here."

"I'm not still here," I snapped, trying not to lick my lips and savor the kiss he'd planted there. My breath was coming short. "It's nine o'clock. I closed hours ago. You're lucky I hadn't any readings scheduled, and that I live upstairs."

"You do?" He peered at the ceiling.

"How much have you had? You haven't been drinking since you left this afternoon?" I unbuttoned his jacket and got him out of it. His hair and goatee were drenched, the shirts under the jacket wet around the neck, and his jeans saturated to the knee.

"S'not as bad as you think," he assured me, a tad subdued. "Only had one for lunch. Did a lot of hiking after that."

"In the rain?"

He gave me a dismissive wave. "I've hiked up mountains in blizzards. Exploring the forests around here in the rain? Nothing. Did that until dark, then went back to Estelle's for three more drinks."

"Come with me," I sighed, taking hold of his cold hand. He still smashed into my bike, there in the storage room. He glared at it in offense as I pulled him upstairs. .

This is a bad idea, I thought. *Especially if you're planning on taking advantage of him.*

He's going to catch his death if I don't get him warm and dry, I argued back. *And who said I was I planning on taking advantage of him?*

"Nice," he said of my place. "Warm."

"Should I call Kelly?" I asked, pushing him down into my desk chair and toweling his hair with my one towel.

"Naw. She's got *things* she needs to do, and won't notice I'm missing any way. Why should she? I'm not even staying with her at her mother's big old house. S'got seven guest rooms, and instead of putting me in one she booked me into a bed & breakfast. Proof that we're no longer involved that way."

Was he angry about that? I wondered, lifting a booted foot and pulling. Off the boot popped with a squishy sound, revealing a very wet black sock.

"Now there's a pleasure I don't understand," he added. "Staying at a Bed & Breakfast. What's with that? All the frills and ruffles and stairs up and down to these itty-bitty rooms. I mean, the breakfast is good, but you have to share it with meatheads so boring zombies would spit out their brains. Why would anyone *want* to do that?"

"Do you ever shut up?" I got off his other boot, and both socks, then took the towel and dried his icy feet.

"If I run out of breath, yeah. Let's see how fast we can get to that point." He reached down and before I knew it he'd woven his hands into my hair and was drawing me in for another kiss.

Fuck! I barely had a chance to suck in air before his tongue was caressing mine in a way that had me tingling. This time I felt both mustache and goatee brushing past, felt his cool hand leaving my curls to stroke my cheek. He nipped at my lower lip as he finished, and yeah, I was warm and damp down there. The towel fell from my hand.

"Been wanting to do that since I saw you this afternoon," he murmured. "You were on that ladder, and I gazed up at your round ass, which I so wanted to squeeze. But then I saw all those ringlets and I thought, hmmmmm. What would it feel like to run my fingers through those curls, or have them brushing over my stomach…"

I gulped. "How drunk are you?"

"I'm not. Tipsy maybe. I didn't have any dinner. Like I said, couldn't stop thinking about you. So I downed some liquid courage and marched up to your door." His face was inches from mine, his brown eyes dilated. Not sober, no, but he was at least half in his right mind. I could see it in the way he looked at me, straight on as if he were deadly serious.

"Stand up."

He did so, with a little help from the back of the chair, and I pulled at his tee. He brushed me off, crossed his arms and got the thermal and the tee off in one. Well, almost off; they caught on his arms. I helped to free him, and then had to take a moment as my heart sped up.

Oh. My. He was one of those furry men, soft hair covering chest and belly on down. But under this down were sleek muscles, firm and taut. A smirk flitted across his lips as he noted my admiration. And then he tugged at my sweater.

I mimicked what he'd done and got it off. His eyes fairly glowed on their way up and down my curves—and then, he pounced. His sensual lips, combined with that beard ran up and down my neck, leaving behind a trail of fire. The straps of my bra fell, and his thumbs slipped under the cups to my nipples. I gasped and jerked against him as they went pebbly. My crotch bumped into the hard-on under his jeans, and I fumbled to break open his belt.

I also sank my teeth in his neck; one whiff of that spicy-dark fragrance of his and I couldn't resist. Intoxicated by it, I nipped away at his shoulders and upper arms. He responded by gasping and working to unhook my bra. It came off even as his belt buckle flapped free and he paused just long enough to break open his jeans. Then he pushed them down along with black underwear.

Holy shit. I took a step back in awe as I got the whole of that fallen angel body. Tight ass, powerful legs, and a narrow cock—alert, bright red and dripping pearls of excitement. And then a flash of lightning washed through the room, followed by a rumble of thunder that shook the walls. The lights went off, leaving only the glow of my wood-burning stove and the sound of rain storming down on my roof and windows.

The dark didn't stop Piers from laying hands on me again, this time to push down my jeans along with my underwear. Hopping on one foot then the other, I got them off. His strong arms snaked around my waist and he pulled us onto the floor.

Fuck it, fuck it, fuck it. And why the hell not?

He was tweaking my nipples, little pinches and twists that had me squeaking with each delicious flicker of pleasure, which would have been embarrassing, except I was milking his slick hot wand and he was grunting and thrusting.

"Wait, wait, wait," I gasped as he started to knee his way between my thighs.

"Can't, can't, can't!" He gasped back.

"Damn it," I shoved myself up on an arm and reached for my nightstand. Piers took the opportunity to start nuzzling his way south from my navel.

No, no, no, I thought, as slippery drips trickled down my inner thighs. He was almost at my crotch and my pussy was clenching in anticipation. I had to fight the desire to lay back and spread my legs wide. Trying to concentrate, I got the drawer open and felt around blind. Piers reached my mound and started licking. I bucked as he got to my slit, each whip of that tongue tip a punishing sizzle.

My trembling fingers found the little foil package. I tore it open with my teeth.

"On!" I said, giving him a rap on the head. He was trying to burrow between my legs, and my control was nearly gone. I smacked him again. By the glow of the fire, I saw his face come up, his eyes reflecting red in that low light. In them I saw pure animal lust. I could almost hear him snarl at being commanded to wait.

I answered that by swatting him on the nose with the condom.

"Huh!" he huffed and the light from the stove was just enough for me to see him roll onto his back. "Help yourself."

I felt my way over his sweat damp muscles to that nest and, hands shaking with desire, got the top of the rubber over his swollen crown. Holding him firmly, I put my mouth over it. He seemed to suck in a cry as I rolled the condom over his rod with lips and tongue. His dick was so stiff I took him down easy, which made me want to start sucking, but I didn't think Piers would last and I wasn't sure I had any more condoms.

He thrust up as I shifted over him, right into me, deep into me, and I fucking exploded. Next I knew, he'd taken hold of my "round" ass, as he'd put it, and was kneading it as he pounded. I couldn't help thinking of the merry-go-round as I bounced up and down. Sweat dripped over my body and I yelled every time his cock glided past my clit.

My pussy clenched and orgasmic fireworks went off, again and again, and now he was yelling. Finally, with a loud, wolfish howl, he stiffened and shot. And I went off, yet again, with him.

It felt like that moment went on forever, with the two of us heating the room, blazing within. When I came back to my steamy, quivering self, I was collapsed over Piers, my nose in his sweaty chest hair.

"You Devil," I growled.

"Wow," Piers lay in my bed, lost in exhaustion. "You can ride my carousel pony any time."

I laughed. I'd lit the lantern, and by its flickering I was getting an eyeful of every sinful inch of him.

"That a compass or a star?" I asked, tapping the tattoo marking his right shoulder. It was minimalist and uncolored, four long points with four short points between those. .

"Both," he said, playing with my curls. He really seemed to like tugging and releasing them as if they were little springs. "It's a logo I came up with for products I'd like to someday make. It stands for guiding insight, the magnetic pull of ideas. Finding your way, getting where you're going."

"True north, true inspiration?" I reflected. "Works for me. Is that your only ink? I would have thought you'd have an inverted pentagram somewhere."

"Too obvious. What about you? No tarot card tattoos?"

"Too obvious," I smiled, and played with his chest hair.

"So, Kelly says there's this pumpkin-patch-thing this Saturday? Out in a cow pasture? She's going and wants me to be there, of course."

"Pumpkin festival, and it's at the *Pasture Farms Market.*"

"Which I'm guessing is near a pasture?"

I nodded. "One where cows still graze in the spring and summer. Creating, I should add, very expensive grass-fed milk for the market."

"And expensive fertilizer?"

"Yep. And, thanks to that fertilizer, expensive organic produce. The market's one of those old, sprawling, barn-like places. Been around for, like, sixty years."

"The kind that sells seeds, lumber, and shovels outside, and heirloom vegetables inside?"

"Yep, again. The festival is where they off-load all the remaining pumpkins and gourds before Halloween. There's a carving contest, a guess-the-weight-of-the-biggest-squash contest..."

He rolled his eyes. "Sounds like a blast."

"Tsk. You don't want any of what we have to offer here, do you? Not our quaint bed-and-breakfasts, not our innocent carnival, not our venerated country market..."

"New Yorker," he tapped his furry chest. "I don't get this pace of life. No Broadway plays, no midnight pizza places, no crazy street fashions. No nightclubs! I like the chatter, the buzz, the lights. I'm going nuts here."

"Maybe," I said thoughtfully. Seemed to me he was protesting too much. I had a feeling that he wasn't quite the happy rake he pretended to be.

"Still," he added. "There is *one* thing this place has to offer that I like a whole lot." His voice went down to a throaty growls and his arm tightened about me. "Want to offer me more?"

I looked into his eyes; they were on the edge of wild again. "Let me see if I've another condom..."

Chapter 5
Tightening Ghostly Chains

As it turned out, I did have another condom. This time, we exhausted ourselves on the bed. It was even faster and shorter, but there were no complaints.

"Family?" Piers said, when we were finally settled comfortably under the quilts. My twin bed was a bit tight, but I certainly didn't mind having my leg over his, feeling his damp and flaccid cock against my thigh. And he didn't seem to mind my breasts pushing into his ribs, or my head pillowed on his arm. His fingers aimlessly stroked my curls.

His question was aimed at the framed photos on my nightstand, the lantern light reflecting off them. "That's your mom right? The gardener?"

"How could you tell?" I grinned. The pic had been taken over eleven years ago. Mom in her gardening clothes, big soiled gloves on her hands, big floppy hat shading her eyes. Over her arm was a basket overflowing with tomatoes, herbs, flowers and summer squash. Her other arm was lifted to triumphantly display the dirty bunch of carrots she'd just pulled from the ground. It'd been our first summer here, and her first harvest in her new, fertile backyard.

"She's a nurse practitioner," I went on. "Now-a-days she works from home, diagnosing patients on the phone or online."

Piers reached across me to pick up the second of the three pictures, and I felt myself stiffen a little. It showed me and my brother at age fourteen, cross-legged on the floor. Lucy, aged twenty at that time, knelt behind us, her head above and between ours, her hands on our shoulders.

Lucy had run around a lot as a teen, and then been away at college. Getting a picture of the three of us together was a rare thing. In fact, we'd been lucky to get that one, as she'd left home almost immediately after to take a teaching job on the East Coast. Eight months later she'd announced she found her soulmate and was getting married. Our mom, deciding she didn't want to live that far from her first born and possible grandkids, moved us all here.

Best decision she'd ever made, my brother and I agreed at the time. We loved Lucy's husband-to-be, and more, that she was finally in our lives as a big sister. We loved the town. We loved our new house, with tons of yard for mom. My brother and I even liked our new school. We were happy—for that first, amazing year.

"Brother and sister," I said to Piers. He lifted a brow at me, and I swear I heard his question in my mind.

"Dad was... What was that old term? An 'itinerant musician.' Back-up guitarist for different bands. He came and went, and left for good when my brother and I were still in diapers. Never heard from him again. Mom raised us, all on her own. She has pictures of him, but since I don't remember anything about him, I figure why bother?"

He nodded and set the photo back in place. He pointed to the last picture, about a year old, with Lucy, Matt and the kids, all grinning almost identical grins.

"Niece and nephew, I presume. Will they be going to the pumpkin festival?"

"I think they're slated to go to the *Haunted Woods* that day."

"How stimulating," Piers said flatly, and then added, hopefully, "Will you be going to the pumpkin festival?"

"What? That dull old thing?" I joked. Then, "Maybe. If I have time. We'll see."

He smirked. "Now I'm looking forward to it," he murmured, his eyelids starting to sink. I was feeling like I was slipping away, as well. Using the very last of my strength, I turned the lantern knob. The flame vanished and the room went dark, but for the red glow of the stove.

"Siblings..." Piers murmured, as I rested my ear against his chest.. "I'd say I wished I had some, but I'd have been a rotten brother..."

That, and his heartbeat, was the last thing I heard as I drifted off.

Clicking and clanking sounds woke me, along with rain pattering on the roof. Another front, I thought muzzily, as I remembered the storm ending last night, and the quiet it had left behind. I came up slowly, feeling heavy and a bit sore. Why would I be...?

Oh. I blushed furiously into my pillow, which smelled of Piers, and ended up grinning so hard my cheeks hurt. I probably would have giggled if I'd had the energy, but I was sapped. Totally, wonderfully sapped.

Damn. That had been fun. And delicious. And hmmmm. And no, I did not regret it. And no, I did not care if Piers was gone and that was all there was between us. At that sleepy moment all I wanted was to put a notch on my bedpost and point it out to, well, someone, anyone. *I bagged* the *Piers Tatham. Yes. I had sex with him. Right here. Twice.*

I felt like I finally understood why hunters mounted heads on their walls.

Clink. Clank.

What the hell? Was there some chain-banging ghost in residence? I blinked open my gummy eyes to watery morning light.

Clank. Whirl.

The room was warm, suggesting someone had added more wood to the stove, but I still didn't want to leave the quilts. So instead of sitting up, I rolled towards the sound.

Piers, dressed, hair wet and slicked back from a shower, had brought up my bike and was working on it. He had all the tools out from the repair kit I kept on hand and was currently tightening the pedals. And there it was. What I'd been looking for since I'd met him. Inner stillness. His brown eyes still ticked, but with intent and the gears whirling in his head clearly had a purpose.

This was why he was always restless. Because nothing else streamlined his energy like working on some device. Tinkering was like a wire to flow down, leaving him with no reason to chatter, no reason to play games. No reason to be other than quiet and serious. I'd had my doubts about his position as head designer at WZT. No more. I was absolutely sure he'd earned that title fair and square.

For what seemed like a long while, I watched him spin wheels, and squeeze the handlebar breaks, then—

"I used your towel. Your one and only towel," he grumbled. "Why do you have only one?"

"Because I'm the only one who usually showers here. And that towel usually dries between showers."

"Would it kill you to have two?" he asked

"On behalf of *Chez Symons*, I apologize for the lack towels. And for not having a monogrammed bathrobe and complementary slippers waiting for you. I'll notify housekeeping and send a severe reprimand."

"You do that." He glowered down at my bike and heaved a sigh. "I'd tighten your chain, but you don't have the tool for that. It's a pain without it. You could also use new brakes and brake lines, but I wouldn't bother. This piece of junk is way old and wasn't worth fixing when it was new. Why'd you buy this model, anyway?"

"It was what my mother could afford at the time," I said. "She didn't know much about bikes, and she had to get two. One for me, and one for my brother."

"Well, you should toss it. Let me pick one out for you. Or design it. This... *thing* is making you work twice as hard to get anywhere."

Having huffed and puffed up many a hill while other bikers seemed to race by me, I couldn't argue that, and it did seem to slip gears every other day—hence the kit. But I didn't use it to ride far, so I'd always figured it did the job well enough.

Or maybe I didn't want to get a new bike, because our first year here, my brother and I had ridden them all over the place. This bike held those memories.

"So...you design bikes?" I ventured.

"Bikes." He nodded, going back to work. "Also hiking and mountain climbing equipment, since I was kid." He tapped his shoulder indicating the star hidden under his sleeve.. "S'what I designed the logo for. To put on the outdoor equipment I was going to create."

"So, where can I buy a WZT bike?"

He snorted and I saw a shadow darken his expression. "WZT only makes stationary and spin bikes."

That took me aback. "You don't make any regular old bikes?" "

" Nope. My father built our company around fitness machines, and that's our one and only mission. To keep innovating those machines and make them the best in the world. Taking detours into recreational equipment doesn't do that."

Safe bet that was his father talking. Still, it was evident he felt that arguing would be disloyal , which was unexpected. So far as I'd seen, Piers wasn't into self-denial. Flat-out was not. So why abstain from this, which mattered so much to him? Not that I was likely to find out before he was gone from my life in — what? Nine days from now?

There was a depressing thought.

I should cook breakfast, I decided, finally getting out of bed. I wrapped my robe about me and got my feet into slippers. While Piers made his final fixes to my wheels, I soaked bread in a mix of eggs, milk and spices and fried up French toast. On the other burner, I got the kettle going, then readied a teapot with scoops of another seasonal tea I'd created: English Breakfast with dried orange and clove.

"One pot, one pan." My bike done at last, Piers had come over to critique. "How can you cook with so little?"

"I'm the only one I cook for," I reminded him. "But if I do get the urge to bake a pie or something, I head over to my mother's or sister's and use their kitchens."

"What if you have guests?"

"I get take out. Or we go to the General Store down the street. They have really good soups and sandwiches."

"You've got a grocery called the 'the General Store?' This place is unreal! The tree-shaded streets, the quaint shops, the bay windows. Is there a little red school house? A white church with a tall steeple?"

"There was, but it went out business." Boiling water went into the pot, and I plated breakfast. Piers brought cups and my two forks to the desk, which also served as my dining table. "You're in a part of the country where almost every structure is historical. This is how it looked two or three hundred years ago and this is how it's going to keep on looking. But the shops use computers, and the General Store delivers through an app. We've a sushi and an Indonesian restaurant."

"How very modern of you," he drolled.

"And on the other side of the coin, the streets can be dirty and not smell nice." I delivered the tea and French Toast. "We deal with drunks and crime and political corruption. Yes, mostly it's pretty and quiet. But it's also a real place. Real people live here. Maple syrup? Powdered sugar?"

"Sugar."

I shook out some atop both our plates, and we dove in unsurprisingly ravenous.

"I still don't trust it." Pier said in between bites. "Carnivals and hay rides. Who does that anymore? Though I will admit, staying here has given me penetrating new insights into our national holiday."

"Fourth of July?"

He sneered. "Halloween."

"I wouldn't say Halloween is all that American. At least, not like Thanksgiving or the Fourth of July."

"Hah," he barked, and waved his fork, "One's a big meal and the other is a firework display. A proper holiday should have more to it than that. Halloween has all these moving parts, and they're pure Americana."

"Like candy?" I threw back.

"Like your caramel apples, grown by Johnny Appleseed. Like headless horsemen and misty bridges where people get hanged. There was some American story about that, wasn't there?"

"Yeah, but don't ask me the title or who wrote it. I fell asleep in my early American literature class."

"So did I. Also; Pumpkin carving. Pumpkins are very American, so long as they're carved or in a pie. Not in bath soaps, lotions, or beverages. Speaking of which, what's with the pumpkin spice shower gel? It's bad enough my B&B sprays the air with pumpkin spice freshener, offers pumpkin spice coffee creamer and even has complimentary pumpkin spice lip balm! Does everything this time of year have to smell like pumpkin pie? Even me?"

Leaning in towards him I inhaled deeply of that fragrance, and took a nip at his neck. He caught a breath.

"I'd love a slice of pumpkin pie for breakfast," I murmured.

"Don't do that," he growled, his hand slipping under my robe to squeeze my bare thigh, high enough to quicken my pulse. "I've got to get back to the B&B in about ten minutes for conference calls. Much as I'd like, I don't dare blow them off for more… pie."

With an effort, I pulled back from him, thigh included; which, in spite of what he'd just said, got me a frown.

"You were saying that Halloween is as American as pumpkin pie?" I said sweetly, and went back to my breakfast.

"And trick-or-treating," he asserted, with a little clearing of his throat. "That's American. So is toilet papering houses."

"You've got powdered sugar on your beard. And I really think England had trick-or-treating first."

"Not like here," he insisted, wiping at his goatee with a paper napkin. "And I mean here, in the land of pilgrims and Jamestown and Quakers and Philadelphians."

"I don't think any of them trick-or-treated."

"But they lived in the spooky woods with the old barns. With the bats and owls and scarecrows. And they traveled those scary old dirt roads at night. The ones that pass by all those little graveyards filled with old headstones and crosses." He swabbed his last bite of toast through the sugar on his plate. "Every Halloween cliché can be linked to colonial and revolutionary New England, and is, therefore, quintessentially American."

"If you say so."

"I do." Finished, he rested back, sipping his tea in silence. I joined him, and it felt strangely, wonderfully comfortable. Like we'd been doing this forever.

More mornings like this would be nice, I thought, gazing out the window at the falling rain. The glass, protected from too many splatters by a jutting gable, offered a fairly clear view of a shady crossroads where kids waited for the school bus.

The storm had torn down brown leaves and turned them mushy in the gutters, and the children, dry in their slickers, were stomping on those piles with their duck boots. I noticed that one golden leaf had escaped. It wasn't actually in the gutter, but rather folded up on the corner of the sidewalk, dripping down a stream of rainwater.

"What're you looking at?" Piers asked, and I realized that I'd gone away for several minutes.

"Sorry. The kids."

They were a riot of color against the brown landscape. Patterned backpacks and colorful umbrellas, which when they huddled together, made them look like a cartoon mushroom patch. Some had now picked up handfuls of the wet leaves and were throwing them at each other.

"I spent the first fifteen years of my life on the west coast," I said, trying to explain my preoccupation. "In places with Mediterranean-type climates."

"No rain or school buses?"

"Not rain like this, no, and we took public transport."

He grinned. "Stranger in a strange land, huh?"

"Oh, yeah. Our first winter here was a revelation, and one hell of a steep learning curve. Scary-embarrassing. Also the humid summer. I'm a pro at handling both, now, I'm happy to say."

"You became a New Englander?"

"Not possible. I've been reliably informed that, as I wasn't born here, I'll always be an outsider. And you know what? I think that's true, because even after eleven years, there are times when I still feel like tourist. Like now—I look out at all those yellow leaves carpeting the sidewalk and street and I want to snap pictures."

"A decided advantage not to take it all for granted. So how did you like it when you first rode in one of those old fashioned buses? In the rain past autumn leaves?"

"I thought I'd died and gone to heaven," I laughed. Silly, but I really had found it magical. Even the hard seats, the motor oil smell, and the gossip ping-ponging from one side of the aisle to the other. Probably I wouldn't have liked it so much if I'd been hazed or pranked, but my brother was a natural at making friends. By the end of the week we were one of the gang.

Outside at the stop, the bus appeared. Even as it pulled up I noticed a girl approach a slightly older boy, one standing a bit apart. She offered him something. A candy bar from the look of it. Her head tilted onto one shoulder coyly.

"Heartbreaker," Piers chuckled.

The bus, wheels sending up a whoosh of water, opened its doors. The kids jostled to get their umbrellas folded and push up the stairs. That's when the boy snatched the candy from the girl, laughed in her face, and darted in. The girl's hopeful expression collapsed. The doors of the bus stayed open and I could almost hear the bus driver shouting at her, the only remaining kid out there, to get on.

Head bent, she climbed aboard.

"Nasty devil," I said through gritted teeth. The morning suddenly didn't seem so lazy and carefree.

Piers was grimly silent. Then, "He's going to regret that someday. And really regret that he's never going to be able to forget it or make up for it." He sounded very different from his usual self. Like he had lot of those regrets, and was trapped in a mnemonic purgatory with them.

"I hope you won't judge all us devils by him," he added.

"Piers, why did you really come in person to tell me about Kelly's party?" I asked then.

"I told you. I wanted to meet the woman behind Madame Marzanna."

"You didn't need an errand to do that. You could have dropped by anytime. That makes me think there's something more to all this. Something you're not telling me."

He eyed me with that flicker of fire, the one that said the mask was back on, and he was playing Lucifer. "Why don't you ask the cards? Right here, right now," he challenged.

I heaved a loud sigh and shook my head, but, nevertheless, opened the lower desk drawer and drew out the deck I'd used at the carnival. I quickly shuffled and flipped one card off the top. The Devil. Of course.

"You came yourself because you're ambitious and you like being in control. That's in control over everything, no matter how minor. You also can't resist temptation."

"As you saw last night, I don't resist." He smirked. "Is that all?"

I flipped one more card. The two of cups. My heart rate kicked up. "I'm not sure how this relates to you giving me Kelly's message, but, obviously, you wanted to revisit having a drink with me. And you wanted to see if you could get us to go where you wanted us to go this time." I said coolly as I possible. "Either that, or I haven't been shuffling this deck very well."

He laughed. "You know, if I didn't have a lot to do, I'd ask to have yet another drink with you. But I've put off these calls too many times. So, I'll do my best to resist temptation... at least till Saturday. You will be at the pumpkin festival, won't you?"

He said it playfully, but there was an earnest tone underneath, something that reminded me of the little girl offering the candy bar. She'd acted arch, but she'd been sincere.

"You'll have to wait and see," I said.

A little "touché" smile flushed in his goatee, then. "Show me out?"

Chapter 6
A Hoard of Ghoulish Gourds

"Madame Marzanna!" I was greeted at the Pumpkin Festival by none other than Kelly. It wasn't a chance encounter. I'd gotten email from her the same morning as I'd made breakfast for Piers, and she'd asked if I'd be coming to the festival and if she might meet me there.

"Ms. Dawson! Good to see you." I finished locking up my bike and shook her hand.

"Call me Kelly," she brushed back a lock of her beautifully coifed fiery blond hair. This was the first time I'd seen her since the carnival and I had to say, without the frilly costume and theatrical makeup, she was even more intimidating. Her flawless cream and rosy complexion, including pouty, petal lips, were perfectly complimented by a cashmere cream sweater and dusty pink jacket. Tight, fawn trousers and stylish riding boots finished the picture. She screamed *royalty*!

All she lacked was a polo pony and riding crop.

As for me, knowing that Piers would be here, I'd gone for a plum turtleneck that flattered my shape and black jeans that flattered my ass. Atop this I wore my brother's soft, green-and-brown plaid coat. It didn't really go, but Piers or no Piers, from the moment the weather went crisp till Thanksgiving, that was the jacket I wore.

Of course, seeing Kelly, I was now wondering why I'd bothered.

"I'm excited about having you at my party." Kelly took me by the arm as if we were old girlfriends. "Did you get the costume?"

"I did." I'd sent her my measurements as soon as we'd finalized the deal, and by nightfall the costume had arrived, express delivery from Manhattan. "It's beautiful and it fits amazingly well. Do I return it to you, or to the shop?"

Said costume was a rental and came with a long list of instructions on what it would cost if I spilled, burned, or otherwise damaged it. I hadn't bothered reading them. I planned on being careful, but I figured that if anything did get stained or singed, paying for it would be on Kelly.

"Return to me," she said as we left the back lot and headed forward. There was a line of food booths in this area, ones selling pumpkin pie, others selling pumpkin candy, pumpkin cakes, pumpkin cookies, and pumpkin flavored drinks.

I smirked. Piers wasn't going to find any relief from pumpkin spice today.

We got past these to the front of the market and its equally busy parking lot It was full of people instead of cars—also banners, scarecrows, the ubiquitous petting zoo, and the all important, for-sale-squash. Crates of squash, raised wooden pallets of squash, pyramids of squash. Arranged in three long rows, they stretched from one end to the other and around the corner.

Eleven years I'd been coming to see this annual display of Autumnal abundance, and it still wowed me. Kids climbed on pumpkins big as truck tires while their mothers picked through baskets of pumpkins small as golf balls. And the colors! There were swamp green pumpkins, mystic blue pumpkins, haunted gray, creepy black, and ghostly white pumpkins. There were pumpkins pale gold and pale pink. There were pumpkins bumpy and smooth, spotted and grooved.

It was like looking at a rainbow of muted, earthy colors. I could have stayed there gazing at them all day, but Kelly wanted me to meet her friends. She directed me to a mind-boggling display of carved pumpkins. Hundreds of them atop rows of hay bales ranging from the usual one-tooth-grins-and-triangle-eyes to those etched with scenes so amazing they could have hung in the Louvre. Some already had blue ribbons pinned beneath them.

"Isabelle, Teal, Yasmine, this is Madame Marzanna."

Three ladies, all about the same age as Kelly, turned from examining an orange pumpkin carved with the OZ character, Pumpkinhead. They were all, like Kelly, wearing form-fitting slacks, high boots, Uber-soft sweaters, and expensive jackets. Had they coordinated, or did they simply think alike? I didn't have time to wonder as, after a heartbeat to process what their friend had said, they descended on me like hungry birds.

"You're the fortune teller?" Isabelle had high cheekbones and a high voice. "You're so young!"

"Kelly says you're truly prescient." Teal, pale and auburn haired, was a little shy. "I hope that means I don't have to say my questions aloud."

"Which deck do you use? I had a reader tell me Marseilles is the only accurate one." Tawny Yasmine met my gaze with sharp, dark eyes.

For a moment I was thrown off balance. My usual clients weren't so well informed about the cards and readings.

"Um, I'm twenty-six," I started with Isabelle, "and no, you never have to say your question aloud." That was for Teal. "I have a lot of decks and will use which ever you like," to Yasmine.

"Good to know," Yasmine said. "Now, what spreads—"

"Oh, there's Gabe," Kelly—fortunately—interrupted, and her friends went curiously quiet, glancing in the direction she was pointing. They looked for all the world like female deer sensing a buck.

"You have to meet Gabe!" Kelly was excited again. She waved. "Gabe, over here!"

I saw a blond man from the back, wide shoulders straining a plaid shirt and a mouthwateringly muscled ass cradled by brown slacks. When he turned around, Kelly's three friends heaved a united sigh that lifted and dropped pert breasts.

My not so pert breasts rose and fell as well. *Oh my gosh,* I thought, as a very fine hunk of manhood strolled our way. This wasn't mere eye-candy. This was eye-cake, pie, and strudel.

"Gabe, this is the tarot reader I was telling you about," Kelly said as he arrived in our midst.

I looked up, and up some more, as the man before me swallowed up my outstretched hand in a gentle-giant grip. His rock hard pecs and washboard stomach could be made out under the white thermal he wore under that open plaid shirt. Wow. He was impressive, though oddly not all that handsome. Not that anyone was likely to notice his face.

"Very pleased to meet you." His blue eyes were kind, and his smile genuine. "It's really amazing that Kelly met you right at this time."

"I know," Kelly gushed. "Talk about a gift from the universe."

"Ladies and gentlemen," a loud speaker came to life atop a pole. "The pig races will be starting in fifteen minutes. Will all contestants..."

"Oh, no, I lost track of time!!" Isabelle cried out. "Come on!" She pulled at Teal and Yasmine's hands and they dashed off.

"Gotta go. Be right back. Gabe, keep Arlo company." Kelly ran after.

I was stupefied. What the hell? "They're going to the pig races?"

"Isabelle breeds pet pigs," Gabe explained. "Tradition is, she always has an entry in the race, and her friends always have to be there to cheer the pig on. They have a lot of traditions actually, and they think it's unlucky to skip any."

"Oh. I see." I guess that meant I shouldn't take their sudden departure personally. "Um, so, you're a friend of Kelly's?" I not so subtly probed. Boyfriend, paramour or bodyguard? And did this mean that Piers was telling the truth about him and Kelly no longer being together.

"I'm trying to get her to work with me," he corrected, hands slipping into his pockets. His trousers were already so tight around his powerful thighs, I feared the seams might split.

"Are you a personal trainer?"

"Well, yes, but what I want to do is help her create a new model for her gyms. She's aiming to expand to residential areas, and I don't think what worked in Manhattan will work so well in those places."

"Oh?"

"She's reluctant to break off with Piers, however." He paused to brood on that. "Which she's going to have to do to move forward with this new model. You read for Piers at the carnival, right?"

"Yeah, but I don't understand. Why does partnering with you mean she has to break with Piers? Do you make exercise equipment, too?"

He snorted. "God, no. Just the opposite. I'm trying to get Kelly to do away with the machines. Don't get me wrong, Piers has been very clever. The equipment he's designed is super compact and well suited for Kelly's 'boutique' gyms. But that's not the future of fitness. Yoga's the most popular exercise in the world, and it only requires a mat. And then there's Pilates and barre and jumping rope. Modern fitness is forgoing machines, which, let's face it, are expensive, old fashioned, and usually end up in landfills."

I was blinking up at him now, taken aback by his intensity, and uncertain what to say or feel. What had I gotten myself into? Was I in it?

"Also…" he looked a tad uncomfortable and glanced side to side to make sure no one was listening. "Again, nothing against Piers, but he's a rich man's son. Went to private schools, traveled first class, never had to work for a living. What matters to men like that is making more money, not making people fit and happy."

"Um…" Piers was no angel, but I seriously doubted he only wanted to make money. Given what he'd said about my bike, what he'd looked like working on it, he at least wanted his devices to do what they were supposed to do. Gabe, however, was on a roll.

"Gyms with high tech equipment, like WZT machines, have to have high membership prices to buy and maintain them. But those who most need fitness can't afford those memberships. I know. I was raised in a suburb. Lower middle class. That woman in St. Paul who's bundling up her kids for school, trying to get to work herself, get in the shopping and do the laundry, she hasn't the money for a gym membership. And that clever, WZT home elliptical she paid for in installments, the one she hoped would melt away those pounds, it's stored in the guest room gathering dust. Because she hasn't the time to pull it out and use it every morning, she wasted her money."

I found myself nodding, and it worried me that I couldn't refute that. I knew plenty of people around town who'd spent their hard-earned cash on such devices, intending to use them during the winter months. The machines usually ended up in the basement, forgotten.

"What that woman needs is a nearby gym that gives her a fitness program she can continue, anytime, anywhere. Like yoga and barre. My program does that. If they can't make it to the gym, they can exercise in the office, or at the grocery store or even in the car. A few minutes here and there of cardio and fat burn and muscle toning."

"But if they can do these exercises anywhere, why go to the gym at all?" I ventured.

"Why go if you have a fitness machine at home?" He countered. "You go to learn the exercises, to get motivated and stay motivated, to try new things and take part in classes. The appeal of Kelly's gyms, in that way, remains the same, but now at a cost that more people can afford."

Piers is in trouble, I was thinking now. *This is serious competition. Real serious. Super serious.* I was surprised, in fact, that Kelly hadn't already dumped Piers for Gabe.

"You sound very passionate about your program."

He nodded. "I am. It's a holistic experience—which is another problem with machines. Even composite ones tend to strengthen only one or two parts. Arms or legs or stomach. My set up strengthens arms and legs and stomach together. The mind, too. That's the way fitness should be."

"Like sex..." I murmured a little too softly for him to hear, even if he'd been paying attention. He was, in fact, gazing off, lost in his holy vision of unified health.

"And," he added, as if he couldn't resist putting a cherry on top, "my program allows Kelly to go for even smaller places. Which means more little gyms close to average people, easy to get to, even in bad weather. Bright and cheerful places."

"It's a really compelling argument," I sighed. Poor Piers! "But you're saying you haven't sold Kelly on it yet? Why not?"

"Well, she's got some high powered investors behind this expansion, and she's going to need to convince them. They think she's going to keep the original business model, and changing it might lose them. But she's very interested in my ideas and that's why I'm here. She's agreed to use this time with her mother and friends to get back to her roots, to where it all began, and consider. She's going to make her final decision after the party."

He looked significantly at me, and *ding-ding-ding-ding-ding!* So THAT was the ulterior motive behind Piers' personal visit to me the other day... and the other night.

"You mean, after she's had a tarot reading," I said.

He nodded. "Which I totally get. It's not just what you want to do, it's doing what the universe says is best for you, right?" The way he said it left me with no doubt that he believed this.

"Right," I said. "Well, um, I think I see Kelly coming back, and I actually have to shop for a pumpkin or two. But I'll be thinking on what you said. Thanks for the company."

"Very nice meeting you. And I have every faith that you'll give Kelly true insight. She's lucky to have found you." He made it sound like some higher power had given me to her. More, that it'd given me to her for the express purpose of guiding her to his superior fitness theories. I almost blurted out a retort to that, but his gaze had gone back to being distant and thoughtful. This was a man completely in love with his philosophy and no earthly entertainment could possibly compete with that.

I left him to it, and went back to the piles of pumpkins. I was at the half-way point of the lot when I finally saw Piers, leaning against the next bin. Clearly he'd been standing there for a while. He was wearing a black turtleneck under the pea coat today, which made him look like he'd come off a freighter.

His expression, as he met my gaze, was unusually wary. "How did you like Thor?" he asked, mildly enough.

"Seemed more Captain America to me. I found him a bit much."

"Kelly booked him into this hunting-themed inn," he added with disgust. "I get the B&B with tea and cookies; he gets the lodge with beer and beef jerky. Think Kelly's sending me a message?"

"Yes. That she can joke around with you, but doesn't feel she can with Gabe. Also that she wants to be even-handed. Neither of you get to stay in one of her mother's guest rooms."

He made a face. "I suppose it could be read that way," he grudged. He knew I was right, but didn't want to admit he might have misjudged Kelly.

"Speaking of messages, Gabe told I me what you didn't. That Kelly is thinking of dropping you for him, and my reading is going to be a deciding factor," I heard my own ire. "Maybe *the* deciding factor. That would have been useful to know before I agreed to it."

Which was why Piers had weaseled his way into playing messenger boy. He wanted to control the flow of information. If keeping me in the dark benefited him, he'd keep me in the dark.

"Harsh way of putting it, but yes." He sounded uncomfortable. Was he feeling contrite? Hesitantly, he slipped his arm around me. I allowed it, but I kept my posture stiff. He got us walking.

"I admit to having impure motives for withholding that information at first," he ventured. "But I could have told you later. I withheld it from you later because I didn't want you doubting my interest in you."

"You're not trying to get me to favor you in my reading?" My tone was more than a little sarcastic.

"I'd like you to." He pulled me in tighter. It was hard not to soften into that embrace. "But no, I'm not trying to seduce you into it. I'd rather seduce you back into bed with me."

"So you say," I murmured, not quite convinced. And yet, not quite doubting it, either. "Gabe's going to be tough to beat, you know. He's got one hell of a pitch."

"He's got a sermon," Piers corrected me. "I'm a salesman, he's an evangelist. Actually he's more than that; he's the archangel Michael with a fiery sword. And where are we?"

We'd wandered from the pumpkins into one of the roped off fields. There were tents, fenced rings and squares. On one platform men were gobbling down pies, spectators loudly cheering them on.

"This is where they're holding contests," I said.

"The fun never stops around here. Hold up. Kelly and posse ahead," he warned, arm dropping away. It hurt more than it should. I would have said it was telling, but, sex or no sex, we'd only had two, um, "dates." We weren't a real couple.

Isabelle, Teal and Yasmine were milling with other spectators on the sidelines of an empty stretch of dead grass. There were several teams lining one end of that stretch, Kelly and Gabe included. At the moment, a man was tying Kelly's left ankle to Gabe's right with a ribbon.

"Piers!" Kelly waved. "Grab a partner and see if you can beat us."

"A three legged race," Piers groaned. "Really?" He sighed, then glanced at me. "Would you care to…?"

"Are you sure? I think one of the other ladies would be faster. I'm not a runner."

He gave me an exasperated look. Yeah. Duh. We were going up against Supergirl and Captain America. My ability or lack thereof wasn't going to change the outcome.

"Right," I said. "Let's run a race."

Chapter 7
Three-Legged Monsters

Entering was easy enough. You hung up your jacket in the nearby coat booth, joined the couples at the starting line, decided how you wanted to orient yourself, and let the guy with the cloth strips tie ankles together. Within minutes, I was hip to thigh with Piers—he had a few inches on me — his arm snaking about me possessively, mine about him. God, I loved the firmness of him. We pretty much had to stand like that, arms about each other, yet I found myself blushing, as if we were being intimate.

"You're going to have to be careful there of the height difference," Piers said to Kelly. Gabe was way taller than her.

"We have to give you some advantage," she laughed. Gabe smiled, but his eyes were on the finish line.

The rest of the contestants, kids-and-parents, kids-and-kids, teen couples, didn't seem to care that they were so outclassed. They were in the race for the fun of it. So were we, presumably, except Gabe and Piers were looking very determined. Probably because they were in it for Kelly, to get her attention.

That's the real prize here, I thought, and Piers hadn't much chance of winning it hitched to me. Unless...unless we did something that got more attention than being the fastest? *Hm. Okay, Arlo. Like what?*

"What am I doing here, again?" Piers murmured to me.

"Taking in the local color," I said.

"Is that what we're calling it? At least I get a chance to feel you up," he added, his hand slipping into my back pocket and giving my ass a small but promising squeeze.

"Contestants ready!" The man in charge shouted, and we all set our free legs back. That's when it came to me.

"Take eight steps," I said in Piers ear. "On the ninth, grab me tight and stop."

"Huh?"

"On your mark!" The man bellowed, and we all leaned forward.

152

"Do it!" I hissed, as a raised cap gun fired.

BANG! Our rivals were off, Gabe shortening his steps, Kelly lengthened hers. Within seconds they'd left everyone in the dust. Piers pulled us after them, and I did my best to match his run-hop.

Five, six, seven...

"Ouch!" I shouted, on the eighth, and Piers, belatedly remembering my instructions, barely caught me as I faked an ankle twist. I still nearly sent us tumbling.

"Are you hurt" he cried, even as Gabe and Kelly crossed the finish line to a roaring cheer.

I bent and quickly got us free of the tie. "Pick me up!"

He scooped and lifted me into his arms, cradling me so hard against his chest I could feel the thump of his heart. I clutched at his shoulders and leaned into his sweaty neck. There was that intoxicating fragrance again, earth and woodland spice. I barely resisted kissing him.

"Carry me to the finish line," I whispered. "Be very concerned, and however heavy I am, try to make it look easy."

"Um...okay. It's okay, I've got you," he said, all solicitous, and strode with seeming ease the rest of the way. "I'm in good shape, and you're not that heavy," he added under his breath. I guess I'd tweaked his pride suggesting this might be an effort.

The spectators, especially Kelly's shrieking friends, were still congratulating the couple. Less for winning, I think, than for being impressively coordinated. But sure enough, as Piers and I got close, eyes turned our way.

"Are you all right?" Kelly sounded so concerned that I felt guilty.

"Should I get some ice?" Gabe asked, equally worried.

"Doctor?" Isabelle ventured and other spectators drew near in curiosity.

"No, no. Really. I'm fine except for feeling dumb," I said as Piers gently deposited me on a straw bale and, kneeling, reached for the wrong foot. I quickly lifted the other one. "It's the tied up foot that's supposed to get you into trouble. Trust me to mess up with the free foot."

Bystanders laughed and, seeing that there was no more to see, started to disperse.

"Are you sure?" Teal asked.

"It twisted a little and I thought I'd sprained it, but I didn't. I told you that," I mock chided Piers. "You didn't have to carry me!"

"Your 'ouch' convinced me I did," he said, pressing at my "injured" ankle. Also reaching up under my jeans to stroke my bare leg. I gritted my teeth and tried not to smack him as his eyes twinkled innocently. "It was in our three-legged race contract. One side shall get the other to the finish line."

Which was laying it on a bit thick, but neither Gabe nor Kelly seemed to notice. "Thank goodness for your quick reflexes. He kept me from falling and taking us both down," I added to Kelly.

"Doesn't look swollen," Piers got to his feet.

The fellow with the cap gun came over to Kelly and Gabe. "That was one heck of a run," he complimented them. "The prize is two free pumpkins. Just exchange these for your choice, medium size." He handed them a pair of tickets. Kelly beamed, but I noticed that her pleased look at Gabe switched to a thoughtful look at Piers. In fact, Isabelle, Teal and Yasmine were eyeing him, too. Which, with Gabe right there, was significant.

Score!

Gabe offered me a hand up and I made a show of carefully putting weight on the foot. "See?" I sighed with relief. "Not sprained. Well, that was embarrassing. Sorry for messing up the race for you," I turned to say to Piers, only to find that Kelly was chatting with him. My heart went cold. Scoring, I belatedly remembered, meant restoring Kelly and Piers' partnership. Maybe even their former romance.

Damn.

"You should tighten the laces on your boots," Gabe suggested, not seeming to notice or maybe care about the Kelly-Piers reunion. He was probably too confident in his vision to think it mattered.

"Good idea," I thanked him.

At around nine that night, there was knocking—rather than pounding—at the shop door. Sure enough, there was Piers, leaning on one arm, backlit by hazy lamplight. Cold, misty night air drifted in, and his breath puffed out with each husky word.

"You are a very naughty girl." He was eyeing me as if I were a caramel glazed dessert. And then he was kissing me with cold lips, touching my cheeks with chilled hands. I snaked arms about his neck, intent on heating him up. As our tongues caressed, I tasted only coffee. This time we were going at it cold sober.

He tangoed in, directing me back, and somehow the door got kicked closed. His goatee swept sensuously over my lips with every kiss. He couldn't seem to stop, nor did I want him to stop—which got awkward when he decided to shed his outerwear. So, long kiss while he shook off jacket. Kiss-with-hand-against-the-wall as he unlaced a boot and got it off. Lingering-tongue-kiss for the other one.

By then, we had reached the back room. Parting for a breath, we gave each other an excited look and raced up the stairs. And then we were at it again, only this time we were nipping earlobes between kisses, nuzzling jaws and necks. Pier's hands, now very warm, had slipped under my sweater to stroke my sides, my belly, my back with feathery caresses.

Sparks trailed every touch, and now I was the one feeling in a hurry. I got his belt unbuckled, his zipper down. His jeans dropped even as he dragged my sweater off. My bra snapped free, and before I knew it we were naked but for our socks.

I took the opportunity to rub against him, my bare breasts loving the feel of his furry chest, my vulnerable crotch pressing against this stiff, dripping hard-on and swinging balls.

"Wait, wait," it was Piers who said it, and I almost cried out as his hands left me. Bending to his jeans, he pulled out a foil packet from the pocket.

Ripping it open, he gloved his alert rod, then grabbed me about the waist and rolled us onto the mattress. And almost off it; we grunted and tumbled back to the center with me on top, at which point I went back to rubbing against him. He was hard with muscle, yet almost downy with hair, and I felt that if I kept moving skin-over-skin, I'd spark a fire. He put a stop to this by flipping our positions.

Now I was on my back, which made me wet with anticipation. Looming above me, Piers grinned wickedly, and started to slip downward. "Naughty girls deserve a reward," he murmured, as his head vanished. I felt his fingers digging into my thighs parting them and spreading them wide. His nose was at my pussy, his breath tickling my pubic hair so softly and erotically that I gasped and eagerly lifted my hips.

And then I felt torturous little licks at the creases between thigh and pussy lips. I groaned, and squirmed. But he was strong and wouldn't let me scoot down any closer to his mouth. My clit was pulsing, desperate for that stoke. But he continued to deliberately and methodically tongue one side, then the other.

That's when I grabbed a double handful of his hair and tried to pull him to my clit. He stubbornly resisted, feasting on his dessert and intent on relishing every last drop. My tender pussy lips got laved next, and then that hot, hot, tormenting tongue circled round, making me cry out and writhe and swear that I'd get him for this!

Devil indeed! I could almost feel him laughing. Or maybe he was humming. And then, just as I was sure I couldn't stand any more, he gave my clit a slow, lingering lick. I let out a shout, and spasms took me. I arched and shook.

Piers rose above me and his cock entered my tight, pulsing interior. I was still jerking and exploding, as he pumped and huffed and raced toward consummation. We were going at it so hard we shifted the bed over the floor.

Finally, Piers let lose, sending me into another paroxysm of orgasms. We held tight to each other as they quieted and our flesh went from fiery to damp with perspiration. Our ribs heaved, panting. God. I felt like I'd been heated white hot and dumped in a bucket of icy water. I could almost feel the steam rising up from me.

"Can I buy you instead of one of your workout machines," I huffed.

He chuckled, and, very reluctantly it seemed, pulled out. He appeared as sore and tired as I was, which was gratifying. I had wondered—and secretly worried—if I was up to par with his other lovers. Women more athletic and, likely, flexible than me. More experienced and sophisticated. Well, but he wasn't with any of them tonight, was he?

"Believe me, I've thought about sex machines," he was saying. "If I could pull them off they'd beat out elliptical in sales and there'd be no question of needing extra bells and whistles to motivate people to use them. The whole of North America would be fit and healthy in no time."

"Or having very strange accidents and injuries."

He laughed. "True. And thank you, that was just what I needed."

"Three-legged race didn't give you enough exercise?"

"No more than lifting and carrying you. Which, by the way, was an unexpected treat." A pause then, "Though I do have to ask, didn't you want to even try and win the race?"

"As the saying goes, it's how you play the game. I'm not into winning, and I don't think you are either."

He came up on an elbow. "Excuse me! I'm all about winning! I'll cheat to win."

"I've no doubt," I smirked. "But did you see Gabe? All he wanted was to rush to the finish line. You, on the other hand, wanted to feel-up your partner."

"Which means what?"

"Your goal is to enjoy the steps you take to the finish line, not just to get there fast as you can."

He frowned uncertainly. "Maybe. So that dirty trick was part of enjoying the steps?"

"And to reach a more important goal. Did it work?" I rolled on my side, the better to admire his sexy profile. I had only the little light over the kitchen on, and that, along with the red glow of the stove, gave his bearded face an unearthly handsomeness.

"Kelly is certainly paying more attention to me than she has since Mr. Olympia arrived. So, yes, it worked. Thank you." He sounded pleased, but something was bothering him. "Not to dwell on it, but you've got me curious. What do you think Gabe's finish-line hyper-focus means for Kelly? If she partners up with him instead of me, I mean?"

I was regretting bringing up Kelly, as I really didn't want to talk about her in my bed after making love to him. The question however, suggested he now valued my opinion. Quite a change from his original skepticism. Happy with that, at least, I considered for a moment, then, "I think if Kelly partners up with Gabe, they'll end up opening fitness center after fitness center, but never pausing to smell the roses."

"So it *would* be a stupid move on her part," he said under his breath. "I wish she'd listen to me."

That had me frowning. "I understand that you wouldn't want to lose her business, but are sales of fitness equipment really going down? Like Mr. Olympia says? Would parting with her be that devastating to WZT?" *Or to you personally?* I thought but didn't say.

"Yes and no. It'd certainly be a blow to our pride, to our stockholders, and to our market value. Also, Kelly's centers are being seen as the up-and-coming new thing in fitness. So, if she foregoes equipment, we lose the chance to make money off her new places *and* those copying her."

He was looking very serious now, and not in that good way, like when he was fixing my bike. This was a cold, hard, almost mean look. He might be all jokes and cheerful confidence about this competition, but in him was seething resentment that he had to compete at all.

From what I'd read on Kelly's website, Piers had seen the potential of her centers right away, and created uniquely small and portable equipment for them. They'd helped each other out, and Piers clearly thought he'd more than proved himself over the years. He shouldn't have to jump through hoops to keep her. As for Kelly... Maybe success had gone to her head, as Piers seemed to think, or maybe she really felt it was time to move on. Either way, I'm not sure she knew how personally Piers was taking this.

"That does sound bad," I said gently. "But you said 'no,' too."

He blinked, and, moving his hands behind his head, relaxed.

"Well, if she breaks with us, she loses exclusive rights to all those compact machines we made for her gyms, and then we can mass produce them and sell 'em for home use. And they'll sell really well, believe me. Fitness equipment isn't going extinct, whatever Gabe-the-holy preaches. So, WZT will lose points, if Kelly drops us, but we won't go bankrupt. That's far more likely to happen if we can't keep up in the marketplace. It's fierce out there. My whole job is creating new innovations to entice cruise lines and resorts and hotels to update their gym equipment."

"Sounds exhausting."

He blinked. "It wasn't when I started out in the design department, before dad made me head of it. It was invigorating. Now..." He shrugged. "It is what it is."

"You could get out of the indoor business and into the outdoor business," I offered. "As you said, biking, hiking, climbing."

He shook his head. I wanted to argue, but as much as I felt like I knew him, I really didn't. And it certainly wasn't my place, anyway. So I simply dragged the quilts higher and, like our first time together, nested my head on his chest. I felt his fingers stroking at my hair, tugging at the curls, and I fell asleep with a smile.

The next morning he was gone, which didn't bother me because he'd left not only his impression on the pillow, but a tiny pumpkin. He must have had it in his coat pocket. A prize for "losing" the race?

I grinned and burrowed my nose into where he'd slept. My whole body felt hyper-sensual, and I rubbed against the sheets as I had against him, inhaling his fragrance, remembering the sex. I shivered, and flushed and nearly orgasmed with the memory. Damn, I wanted him. Wanted to kiss him, and lick him, and suck his cock, which I hadn't gotten a chance to do yet. I wanted him to do what he'd done to me last night, all over again. And I wanted to hold onto him tight as he entered me, and we rocked and moaned in unison.

I wanted him *now*, and for the whole week. Not just an evening here and there. I sighed with want. And then I winced. Fuck me. Oh, fuck me. I had it bad for him. And when the hell had that happened?

Maybe after he went down on you so exquisitely? I mentally rolled my eyes. *And did you forget that he's only here till November 2nd?* Yes. Yes I had. Would I even get more time with him before that? And if I didn't, would I go into withdrawal?

Forcing myself to get up, I noticed a cluster of small post-it notes stuck to my bathroom door. *Wish I could have stayed...* One said in neat, block print. Then *for breakfast,* the next finished. *Super busy.* The third continued on. *Used your towel again.* Onto the fourth note: *you really need two.* Fifth: *Maple-apple soap? For me?* With a heart around it.

He'd noticed! I blushed. And indeed I had changed it for him. Changed it without knowing if he'd even be back. Which was more than little embarrassing.

The final note was set low, making me bend to read it. *See you at the party.*

At the party. That was two days away! My heart sunk and so did my stomach. *I wasn't going to see him till then? No fair!* And, again, *Shit! I had it* real *bad.*

Maybe that's exactly what he's after, some part of me observed, and I tripped, emotionally, like I'd missed a step down. That first night he'd arrived drunk. *Liquid Courage*, he'd called it, implying that he'd been uncertain about propositioning me, and fought off his hesitation with liquor.

But was that the truth? Hard to believe that Piers would have doubts about seducing, well, any woman with a pulse. Thinking about it now, as I hadn't before, I could almost imagine him at *Estelle's*, brooding over Gabe and how tough it was going to be to win, if he played fair. Which, he'd said himself, he didn't.

Fortunately, Kelly wanted to hire the fortune teller Piers had flirted with at the carnival. Hire her to help pick that winner. This fortune teller was attracted to him, very. How not? He was handsome and rich and sexy. He'd tell her exactly what she wanted to hear. That he couldn't stop thinking about her. Then he'd give her a night like she'd never had before, and she'd be in his pocket.

A few belts of liquid courage and he could do it. He might not actually be lusting for her, but it wouldn't be too arduous a chore. Maybe it'd even be pleasant. Maybe she'd even feed him breakfast.

Shit. Yet even as considered this, I questioned it. Whatever else, his desire for me, his affection, seemed genuine. *And what would you know about that, Arlo? You said it yourself; you've never met or fallen for anyone like him. How would you know if this consummate liar was telling the truth?* I wouldn't, and he'd already admitted that he'd manipulated Kelly, me, and the situation.

Damn.

I showered and dried myself best as I could with the still damp towel. After dressing, I put the tiny pumpkin he'd left on the nightstand among the photos. I'd see Piers at the party, and sometime that night, I'd do a reading for Kelly. Whatever the answer, Piers would probably leave as soon as he could rather than waiting till November second.

And that would be that; the last I'd see of Piers Tatham. I'd better find a way to come to terms with that. Fast.

Chapter 8
A Séance of Mediums

It was October 29th, and as the sun went down, it became clear that Kelly had gotten lucky. Really lucky. The weather was mildly cool, a little breezy, and incredibly clear. Clear enough that Kelly's wished-for full moon, hidden all this week by rain, mist or clouds, rose unobscured.

It was a sight to behold. A vast, deeply golden orb, close enough to touch. Leaving the horizon, it floated like a lantern among the stars and treetops. Magical. Fifteen minutes later, when the horse drawn carriage arrived to pick me up, I barely blinked in surprise. With that moon, it seemed almost natural that this was my ride to the party.

Still, "This is crazy," I blurted to the driver as she opened the door and let down stairs into that cushioned interior. She laughed, and her pale horse blew out a wicker of agreement. Gathering up the skirts of my costume, I got myself in, and self-consciously pulled my shawl close. Very soon, however, I fell into the rhythmic clop of hooves and started to enjoy the spin of wooden wheels. As we traveled down familiar streets, I began to see the town in a different light almost as if I was touring the ghostly streets of a prior century. Weird to think that a lot of these shops and taverns had been here when there were only horse-drawn carriages.

The vision gave way as digital music from bars and restaurants and the glow of smart phones reasserted themselves. Pedestrians crossing and crisscrossing with the stoplights paused to gawk at me as if I were the one who'd appeared from another time. This was how Cinderella must have felt.

Escaping the center of town at last, the driver took us off the main road, onto one covered in brown leaves, possibly a bridle path. We were on it for some while, rolling past groves of maples, elms and oaks. Then, finally, it met up with a paved drive. At the end of this was a house. A big one.

It was a nineteenth century Greek revival, arrestingly symmetrical with four stout, white columns under the portico, and four double-hung windows on each side. They glowed with candle and lamplight. The only electrics were the porch lights, which allowed me to see the house's gold-pumpkin color, eerily and coincidentally like that of the full moon. The contrasting window shutters were a deep, vine green.

I'd read on Kelly's website that the first thing she'd done with her newfound wealth was buy her mother a house. Her mother's dream house to be exact, which apparently meant this restored beauty.

The carriage stopped before the front steps, bordered to either side with carved pumpkins. Each had a different, glowing face: Happy, sad, angry, scared. Like emoji. *Interesting welcome,* I thought as the driver gave me a hand down, which I needed given the full skirts of my costume. "Thanks," I told her, and, lifting her top hat, she jumped back up and drove away.

I took a moment to nervously straighten my bodice and pat my hair, making sure the pins weren't going to give way. Then I checked that the purse at my waist, the one holding three of my decks and my very un-period phone, was still attached to the belt. Usually, I wasn't so nervous before a reading, not even readings for parties. But this time, I had butterflies in my stomach because Piers would be there, and I both couldn't wait to see him, and dreaded seeing him. Would he say anything to me about the reading I was to do for Kelly? Would he eye me expectantly? What would I say? Or do?

The front door opened, and a man dressed as a butler frowned at me. He must have seen the carriage arrive and been waiting for me to knock. I lifted my skirts and went up the stairs, careful of the pumpkins. The butler gave way and I entered a world of dim lighting, chatter, and wood smoke.

Lights might have been on outside to help guests see the house, but inside there were only those candles and lanterns. It made for strange shadows down the narrow entry hall. Peering that way, I saw stairs to the second floor and, at the very back, a dining room. I was able to make out a red velvet cloth on the table and a crystal ball. It was good guess that's where I'd be doing my readings.

"Welcome," the butler said, shutting the door and relieving me of my shawl. "To the Séance House. We have here gathered the greatest mediums and psychics in America. If you would take a name tag?"

On a silver tray were filled-in "Hello I'm..." tags. Kelly had a sense of humor. I found "Madame Marzanna," peeled off the back and stuck it right over my heart.

"Be aware that the house is full of spirits which may appear or speak at any moment," the butler continued with his script. "Also that a daguerreotypist is taking candid portraits. If you wish to take your own images with your own device, please do so only in the sitting room. If you have any questions, or want for anything, don't hesitate to ask me, the maids, or footmen. Food is being served in the parlor and drinks in the sitting room."

He waved left, then right, and then, with a final bow, walked away. I peeked into the airy, squash yellow parlor, which was dominated by a white fireplace, hurricane lanterns, ghoulish black pumpkins and stuffed ravens. Guests in gowns and suits sat on spindly chairs and couches. Finger food was arrayed on side tables, and two footmen were circling with laden trays.

On the opposite side of the hall, was the smaller, hunter-green "sitting room." It had a card table at its center, where three costumed gents and a lady played by candlelight. The aforementioned maids hustled past these guests, with quick curtsies, to refill wine pitchers on a sideboard and spiced cider steaming in a copper pot near the hearth. There was enough verisimilitude to the scene that I felt like I was gazing through a time portal rather than a doorway.

I noted that the maids also tended to a pair of teapots, one filled with a rare Gu Zhang Mao Jian from China, the other a Kyoto Sencha. I knew this because I'd provided both. Contrary to popular belief, America did keep on drinking tea after the revolution, green in particular. Which I'd explained to Kelly when she'd asked me to send her a couple of teas for the party, the best and most historically accurate I had. These fit the bill.

Food or tea? I was trying to make up my mind when Piers, as usual, appeared out of nowhere. "I thought that was you."

My heart leapt and damn if I didn't blush like a kid with a crush on a teacher. "Hi." I patted at my hair again, which I'd parted in the middle and, with a lot of product, slicked back into a bun, as close to late 1840's style as I could manage.

He tilted his head, then swirled a finger. "Spin."

I performed a twirl. My autumn brown skirt was simple but satiny. The matching bodice, on the other hand, was a "fan bodice," or so said the notes that had come with the costume. It had complex folds from shoulder to waist forming a wide V over the lacy white blouse I wore beneath. I had to admit, the way the bodice (and the spine straightening corset) hourglassed my figure was very flattering.

"You look like you stepped out of *Little Women,*" said Piers, but his eyes were glowing.

"About fifteen years too soon for that," I retorted, giving him a quick once over. He had on period style black trousers, a black waistcoat, a black jacket and a thin black cravat wrapped sloppily about the high collar of his white shirt. One look at the way his hair was combed back from his forehead and I didn't need check the name tag.

"You're *Edgar Allen Poe?*"

"You sound shocked. Don't I look the part?" he posed with hand slipped in between the buttons of his vest.

This time I was who tilted my head. "You're not scrawny enough. Your eyes aren't crazed enough. And he didn't have a goatee."

He made a face, which twisted said goatee. "Yes, well, there's only so far I'm willing to go for a one night of dress up. I love my beard, and even if I didn't, Poe had a crummy mustache."

"He did that. But why Poe? I'd have thought you'd gone for Houdini. So you could debunk the séance."

"I wish! But Houdini debunked Roaring 20's séances. Talk about too late for this shin-dig."

"I thought the theme was famous American spiritualists." I frowned. "That's what Kelly told me."

"Kelly wanted the theme to go with the house, so she went for the first big spiritualist wave which was between 1840 and 1870. The renown cynic back then was Ralph Waldo Emerson. He called séances 'rat revelations;' gospel being tapped through the walls." He grinned in approval. "A kindred spirit for certain."

"But?"

Piers wrinkled has nose. "Ever seen a picture of Ralph? What a hayseed! I told Kelly that if I was going to be cast as a 19th century American poet, I'd rather be the alcoholic, laudanum-imbibing, womanizer. Not Mr. chicken-neck."

"Also the American saint of Halloween?" I ventured.

He bowed with a flourish. "Poe thought highly of himself. I figure we're kindred souls in that way. And why are we standing out here?" He leaned in close and whispered into my ear. "There's got to be an empty room where we can engage in a little bodice ripping. Don't worry; I'll pay for all repairs to the costume."

His goatee brushed my earlobe and I shivered. Tempting. Especially with his hand at my waist pressing through bodice, corset and chemise.

"If I were a guest, I'd take you up on it," I said, regretfully. "But I'm here to do a job."

"Ah, yes." He sighed. "I forgot. Shall we step into the sitting room and fortify you with some pomegranate sangria?"

I maneuvered my rustling skirts and petticoats through the door and lifted a hand in hello as the card players glanced up.

"Do you like Poe?" Piers asked not-so-nonchalantly, as he handed me a goblet filled with the blood red drink.

"Haven't read him since my early American literature class. I remember liking that his stories were short, and didn't put me to sleep." I took a sip of the drink. It had a tart, earthy flavor that I liked a lot. "Wasn't Poe a skeptic? Said something about there being no afterlife?"

" *'No man who ever lived knows more about the hereafter than you or I,'* is the precise quote." He paused, glanced side to side then leaned in confidentially. "Only Poe never said it. Internet meme."

"You seem to know a lot about him."

"If I'm going to play a part, I do my research."

"That's why you were so convincing as the Devil," I grinned. "How far did this research go? A visit to Baltimore to get falling down drunk? Or did you take up a quill and write poems about ravens?"

"There's method acting, and method acting. Though I could have probably used that trip to Baltimore, given the ups and down I've had this week."

"Speaking of getting into character," I said, enjoying another draught of sangria, "I'm blown away by all this. The house, the decorations, the costumes, and that carriage ride!"

"The moon," he laughed. "I'm almost convinced that Kelly ordered it special, it goes so perfectly. Hunter's Moon didn't you say?"

"Or Harvest. And a few others names. My favorite," I added, shyly, "Is Traveler's Moon."

"What? Wait, like—"

I nodded. "Bright enough to travel by."

"So. The tea garden of this particular moon," he said wonderingly. "The moon of travelers. I take back the twee comment. That's genuinely mystical."

"Thank you."

"Bright enough to travel by, huh? Now I'm picturing a bike ride under that moon outside." His tone went dreamy. "I sure would love to be doing that right now."

"So would I," I said, catching his gaze. It had gone dark and still, and I almost blurted that we ought to leave and do just that. Instead, I cleared my throat and took a gulp of sangria. "Plenty of lunar zing for Kelly's party. I guess she really did think of everything."

"Does she know you're here?"

"I don't think so."

"Well, we'd better tell her." He offered his elbow and escorted me across the hall to where piano music was now playing behind the chatter. Either my eyes had adjusted or someone had turned up the lantern light, because it seemed brighter and more lively. And, sure enough, there was a man with a fake-old camera on a tripod, posing guests in one extra-illuminated corner.

"So, everyone here is playing a famous spiritualist?"

"Sorta," Piers said. "Didn't you get the cheat sheet? No? I'll give you the historical highlights, starting with our three ladies getting their picture taken." Meaning, of course, Kelly's friends. They were all in short-sleeved, plaid gowns. I was amazed at how vibrant the colors were. To me, the nineteenth century was funeral wear and sepia toned photographs. I'd assumed the attire would be drab. These dresses were anything but, and the women looked lovely in them. Green-black for Isabelle, lavender-blue for Teal, and red-gold for Yasmine. Talk about *Little Women*.

"They're playing the most infamous mediums of this age, the Fox sisters," Piers finished.

"The Fox sisters...the Fox sisters," I repeated. I had heard of them, and remembered something. "Didn't they start the whole rapping-the-table-for-answers thing?"

"Yes they did. But decades later, one of the sisters confessed it was all an elaborate prank. They were pre-teens, see, with no Snapchat or instagram. Bored out of their minds, they decided to scare their mom. They practiced snapping their toes and cracking their knuckles, so the sounds seemed to come out of thin air. Mom thought the noises were a ghost. So did the neighbors. When they asked questions of the ghost, it rapped out yes and no answers."

Piers paused as a tray-bearing footman passed by. He grabbed a couple of shrimp canapés, handing one to me. "The girls' big sister got the truth out of them, but instead of lecturing them about lying, she bullied them into rapping out ghostly answers in front of a paying audience, which resulted in fame and fortune. Ghostly rapping became their life-long career."

"They were stuck performing that stupid prank over and over again." I was disturbed. "That's terrible!"

"Hellish," he agreed, popping the shrimp into his mouth. "But what's important here is that their prank got the whole ball of wax rolling. Before them, only the cool goth kids like yours truly," he jerked a thumb at his E.A. Poe self, "were wearing black and going into trances. Once the Fox sisters made national news, séances became the hip new thing. Everyone wanted to be a medium. Or at least to hold a séance. Which brings us to our next historical highlight..."

He nodded to the older woman in black velvet playing the piano. There was a brown Chihuahua wearing a doggy frock-coat costume sitting beside her. It gazed at her hopeful of attention.

"Kelly's mom?" I guessed. She bore a strong if plainer resemblance to our hostess.

"That's Mrs. Mary Todd Lincoln to you!" Piers said haughtily.

"She wasn't a medium."

"No, but she became an avid spiritualist after her favorite son died and held séances in the White House."

"I didn't know that."

"President Lincoln went along with it, but probably didn't believe." Piers dipped his fingers into a basket sitting on one of the tables and handed me a small, puff-pastry tart.

"Baked Brie and fig," he said, even as I bit in. The crunch of the warm shell gave way to melty cheese and delicious fig. It went perfectly with my sangria.

"And, um, what about Gabe?" The big man was standing—more like looming—over Mrs. Lincoln, flipping the sheet music for her. He had on a nice suit, with a prim white shirt and a red cravat. Also, a fake Amish-type beard.

"Andrew Jackson Davis. Every website touts him as the John-the-Baptist of American spiritualism." Piers sounded like he had a bad taste in his mouth. I wondered if his distaste was for Gabe or Davis, or maybe for Gabe being cast as Davis? Kelly, I presumed, had made the assignments.

"He wrote this manifesto that became the medium's bible." Piers went on. "Basically, it said that in the beginning, everything was one, then it stopped being one, but having been one, it was all still connected."

"That...sounds scientifically accurate," I pointed out, setting aside my empty sangria glass. It was immediately whisked away by a footman.

"Not when you get down to the details," Piers countered, "but, on the vague-general-surface-level...yeah."

'You're here!" That was Kelly, and she was wearing, of course, the most beautiful gown of all. Made of pearl gray silk-brocade, it was short sleeved and form fitting. Embroidered purple grapes, small red apples and green pears dotted it like jewels. Her bodice, pleated far more elaborately than mine, formed a scooped neck that hugged her bare shoulders.

And her hair! It was parted in the middle, the same as all the women here, but from there it fell into shiny blond ringlets—all pinned on hair pieces, but the effect was still stunning. The demoness had become a saint. All she needed was a heavenly light shining down on her.

"Kelly, hi," I fumbled. "Wow. You look incredible. Who are you?" She was, I noted, the only one not wearing a name tag.

"The queen of mid-nineteenth century mediums, of course." Piers flashed his most alluring grin and bowed over her gloved hand. "Cora Hutch nè Scott."

"Her picture is there on the mantle," Kelly said, waving a folded fan to the fireplace.

"She was a renowned beauty," Piers half-whispered to me, as if in confidence. "Spirits supposedly spoke through her, and audiences were smitten."

"We'll see if I can live up to her tonight." Kelly said. Then, "Are you ready to start, Arlo?"

"Whenever you like," I said, and Piers frowned, as if, for a second time, he'd forgotten that I'd been hired to be here, like the butler and maids.

"Attention, attention everyone!" Kelly barked in her best fitness-teacher-voice, and the piano music petered out. "This is Madame Marzanna, our tarot reader," The room was quiet now, and the card players from the sitting room appeared in the doorway. "I'll be passing around a bag with numbered tiles. If you want a reading, pull out one from the bag and we'll go in order. Ten minutes per reading."

"Aw!" Yasmine wasn't happy about that.

"Meanwhile," Kelly went on, "we'll be serving a light supper, then dancing here in the parlor and, after that, as the midnight hour nears—our séance!"

Nervous laughter and a patter of applause.

"Carry on!" Kelly finished, then, once again, linked her arm though mine. As she dragged me off, I saw Piers watching us, looking as if he'd lost control of something. Or someone.

Of Kelly or me?

Chapter 9
Reading by Paranormal Moonlight

"I knew that dress would be perfect for you," Kelly gushed as we strolled down the hall. "You look like you belong in the past, yet might have come from some distant land."

"I love it," I said. "Everyone's costume is amazing, and so right for them. Especially yours."

She flushed with pleasure, and held out a bit of skirt, delighted. We reached the dining room and she waved me in, like a director presenting a finished stage set.

I'd been worried about reading in near darkness, but there was a big candelabrum in the center of the table. The area it illuminated wasn't large, but it was bright enough to see the cards and the old clock ticking away on the mantle of yet another fireplace. There was the crystal ball I'd noticed, and, pinned to the walls, the palmistry and phrenology charts I'd loaned Kelly to help with the ambience.

There were also some foggy old mirrors which, again, helped with the light. The thematic pumpkins that seemed to be a part of every room were, in this one, spooky gray, but nestled among red and yellow flowers, like ashes among flames.

"This is great!"

"It is, isn't it? So, what will happen is the butler will get the, um—"

"Sitter," I provided.

"Sitter, yes. He'll bring them here, and shut the door so you'll have privacy. You do the reading, and when ten minutes are up," she pointed to the clock, "he'll come back, knock and take them away."

"Repeat as necessary," I smiled. "And you'll be last? With no time limit?"

"Well, yes, but I don't think I'm going to need a very long reading. Oh, and you won't have to read for Piers again, or for Gabe. They both told me they didn't want to take up your time."

"They want you to get to your reading faster?" I guessed.

She laughed uneasily. "I'm sure they'd rather I went first. Anyway, does that work for you?"

"Perfectly. I have to tell you, I'm beyond amazed by all this. You really thought of everything, and it's all so beautiful."

"Mom was a huge help," Kelly said all bashful.

"You bought this house for her, right?"

"She gave up so much so that I could succeed." Kelly's cheeks had gone rosy. "I am where I am today, thanks to her. I was so glad when I could buy her this place and pay her back, a little. Piers feels the same about his father," she added thoughtfully. "It's what first drew us together, and made us connect. We both wanted to make our parents proud."

A worry line appeared between her brows. Was she maybe realizing that if she picked Gabe, Piers would have to tell his dad that he'd lost her lucrative business and deal with disappointing his father, rather than making him proud?

"I figured you'd want a room with a window," Kelly said then, a forced change of subject. "So you could absorb the moonlight. When it rose this evening, the energy was incredible. Being psychic, you must have really felt it.. Are you sure you won't stay for the séance? I haven't told anyone yet, but I'm planning on trying to summon *them*—the mediums and psychics they're playing!"

Her pretty eyes gleamed and she actually shivered with the idea. "Won't it be exiting if we can get in touch with one? And could there be a more perfect night for doing it?"

"Wow. I... would love to join you for that, but I really can't chance it after performing readings." I wasn't actually lying there, but it wasn't the whole truth either. "There can't be any, um, open windows, clairvoyantly speaking, at a séance. Otherwise you get unwanted spirits. You have to make sure there's only that one door you've opened to the invited soul."

"That never occurred to me. You must be extra-sensorially exhausted after reading at parties," she offered sympathetically, reminding me how canny I could sometimes be in manipulating others. I was beginning to think there was a lot more Devil in me than I'd thought.

"But between the magic of the moon and all you've done to make the spirits of these mediums feel at home," I told her, "I've no doubt you'll succeed in speaking to at least one of them. Maybe even your alter ego."

"Cora! Oh, that would be awesome!"

"I imagine everyone who wants a reading has pulled a number," I said, seating myself near the candelabrum. "I guess you should send in my first sitter."

She actually clapped her gloved hands together—well, one gloved hand and the folded fan, and skipped out. I sighed. I wasn't looking forward to that last reading, and it was going to be hard to do right by each guest as I waited, in dread, for Kelly, with her fateful question.

Yasmine was my first sitter. Which would have had me rolling my eyes, but I was ready for her.

"I hope you're not going to use a Crowley deck," she said, as the butler shut the door. I'd offered her the chair catty-corner from me, which would allow her to see the cards upright, but not be right next to me. "Everything I've heard about that deck has me scared of it. There's evil in it."

I didn't even bother arguing. "Actually," I said, reaching into my pouch, "I brought my Marseilles deck, just for you."

"Oh?" She blinked with surprise. Apparently she didn't remember what she'd said to me at the pumpkin festival. Or maybe she hadn't expected me to remember.

"This deck is very old," I went on. "And very special. I don't use it for many sitters. But knowing how you feel about the Marseilles, I think it will give you a very good reading."

"How old is it?" she breathed.

I smiled and shuffled, allowing her to imagine what she liked. I figured that she'd probably end up telling her friends I'd used one of the original seventeenth century decks, never mind that most of those were incomplete and too fragile to even touch.

"Your question?"

Yasmine gave me no further instructions on how I should read for her. In fact, it all went very smoothly and the ten minutes were up quickly.

The rotation of sitters blurred after that. They asked about love lives and businesses, travel and getting past whatever was in the way to happiness. Half-way through, the butler appeared with a pot of tea —the Gu Zhang Mao Jian, happily!—and a plate of canapés, which was very welcome.

Kelly's mom arrived soon after for her reading, carrying the dog, which was fairly lost in her costume's wide puffy sleeves. I assured her that I was fine with the pup staying, so long as it didn't bark or get in the way. She was a very sweet lady, but her question was troubling.

"My daughter's going to be making a big decision. I want to know if it will be the right one. She drives herself so hard, and has such grand ambitions." A rueful smile. "She's a little too much like me, I guess. Never quite able to slow down. I just want her to be happy."

"I'm afraid the cards can't tell you that," I said carefully, "Because being happy with her decisions and her life is up to her. What I mean is, there are people who do everything right, like slowing down, but aren't happy. And people who do a lot wrong, but still end up happy. Do you see?"

Mrs. Faux Mary Todd Lincoln seemed taken by that observation. "I do. Yes. That's true. I know a lot of people who have no reason to be miserable, but are."

"I could, however, find out how you can nudge your daughter in the right direction. To, um, decide to be happier."

She sat up straighter at that. Which caused her dog, curled up in her lap to jerk in alarm, sure they were under attack. He stood for a moment on his tiny legs, checked out the room, then, finding all was well, settled back down. I, in the meantime, laid out a quick reading and told Ma Dawson, quite honestly, that according to the cards she was already doing all she could for her daughter. Which seemed to relieve and please her.

Vexing, I thought as she left, Chihuahua in arms. Now I really didn't know how to feel about Kelly's reading. Having heard her talk about her mom, and her mom talk about her, I knew she was good hearted. It'd be wrong to lie to her if the cards told me she ought to stay with Piers. But if I told her that, the two of them would go off into the Lovers card. I'd lose him in every possible way!

Please! I sneered at myself; *You can't lose what isn't yours. His staying with you isn't in the cards; that's been clear from the start. His father matters to him. The company matters to him. Living in Manhattan matters to him. You might as well throw him Kelly's way.*

No! My heart rejected that categorically. *I want him!*

Fuck. Piers hadn't merely rubbed off on me, he'd entered my bloodstream. I was no selfless martyr, but I'd never been this covetous. Not of anyone or anything.

So what was I going to say to Kelly?

It was ten o'clock when she finally showed up, all the guests who'd wanted readings having gotten them.

"My turn," she said, shutting the door behind her and smiling nervously. Her dress rustled as she sat down, and she tapped the fan against her skirts. She wasn't the only anxious one. I had out my regular deck, and was shuffling, trying to "cleanse" it from the other readings. Most especially, I didn't want it to tap into my ambivalent feelings.

"Okay," Kelly breathed. "So, as you might know, I've had this partnership with Piers since before I opened my first *Sunflower* studio. And it's been great. Even when we... When it didn't work out between us personally, Piers still came up with the best equipment for my gyms."

She paused, chewed on her full lower lip and tapped the fan against the chair. "But this year I met Gabe and he's had me thinking in a whole new way. It's my dream to expand into places like here, quiet towns and suburbs. But my studios were created for high rises and urban centers. I'm not sure that model will work for people like my mother. On the other hand, why tamper with success? I just don't know. There are so many pros and cons..."

She trailed off and looked at me in a way that was so desperate my heart hurt for her.

"Piers is super smart, and he's always been right," she added. "But Gabe's a visionary, too. I can feel that he's also right. I've been trying to think of ways to incorporate both of their ideas, but that won't work. My studios are small. And they work best when they have a central fitness philosophy. One that can guide every workout, every class."

Okay, this was no dim ingénue. This woman knew her business, and knew what she was about. I could see that now. I could also see, quite unexpectedly, that what she thought was her problem, what Gabe, Piers, and even I'd been thinking was her dilemma...wasn't.

And wasn't that a flip in perspective?

"You know," I ventured, "I'm getting the feeling that this isn't really about whether you should change the studios."

"It's not?" She blinked. Which I understood, as she'd just explained at length that it *was* about that. But my instincts were saying different.

"I think what you really want to know is what will happen if you work with Gabe rather than Piers. Or Piers rather than Gabe. That, I think, is at the heart of this. I mean, it doesn't matter if Gabe's vision is the most brilliant ever, if you can't work with him. Same with Piers."

Her mouth dropped open and she gawked at me. "Oh, my God! You're right! You're absolutely right! The idea doesn't matter. What matters is being able to work with the man behind it!" She shook her head, utterly astonished—which was pretty darn flattering. *Yay me.* Did it again, and why couldn't I bring my own conundrum into focus so easily?

"I knew it!" she went on. "I knew it from the carnival. On the way home, Piers kept going on about your silly costume—"

Oh, he did, did he?

"—and how he didn't believe any of it, but I told him. 'She's the real deal. You're lucky to have gotten a reading from her.'" She was gazing at me with hero worship now. That was embarrassing. "So, what does this mean for the reading?"

"It means it's a lot simpler. We pull cards for what you can expect from each guy, and you decide which is best."

She nodded, all eyes and ears. I felt the change as well, as if we finally had a direction. I shuffled the cards vigorously, then set them down. "You're right handed? Cut them with your left." She did. I gathered them up and put down the first two cards, one to the right, one to the left.

Kelly leaned forward.

"This first set is what each man will see as their goal in this partnership." I touched on the left-hand card, which I'd instinctively assigned to Piers. "Devil. Piers' goal will be make your brand the fitness leader and controller, and he won't stop till he's achieved that. He also wants customers addicted to your studios. They should never want to leave."

"That sounds like Piers," she admitted. "He's always coming up with little extras for the equipment, so if a customer goes elsewhere, she misses them and comes right back. What about Gabe?"

"Temperance." The card featured an angel pouring fluid between two cups. "He's wants those who come to your studios to feel like they're in this together."

"Huh?" Kelly was confused.

"Think about those exercise classes you've taken where everyone knows what they're doing and they're completely into it. You look around, and you see them all sweating like you are, and all in step with you and you with them, and the energy is through the roof. Synergy. That's what Gabe wants."

"That's…that's a pretty high bar."

I shrugged and flipped out the next pair, right to left this time. "Gabe's negative. Strength." This card had a lady in white, gentling a lion. "He's going to require a close partnership. I think you already know that he can be over enthusiastic and ready to rush forward. You'll need to check that, keep him under control. Which could get annoying."

"And Piers?"

"Hermit." A man in a hooded robe with a lantern. "He's the opposite. His negative is that he's hyper-focused and competent. Which might not sound bad, but it means he wants to do his thing, his way, with no oversight. I don't know how it was before, but he won't want you involved in his process. He'll assert that he knows what he's about, leave him alone to do it. I'm guessing that's not good for you."

"He wasn't like that when we first got together," Kelly sounded perplexed. "He asked for my help and advice and encouraged my ideas. But, for the last two years he's been closing me out when I offer suggestions. Like I don't know enough."

Quelle surprise! I thought, remembering the Piers I'd seen working on my bike.

"Positives," I went on, snapping down the cards. "Ah. The Magician for Piers." A red-and-white robed man lifted a wand over a table with cup, staff, pentacle and sword. "I couldn't hold back a grin. "He can really sell your brand. He's full of ideas and customers won't tire of hearing him talk."

173

Kelly laughed. "As Piers would say, I didn't need a tarot reader to tell me that."

"And for Gabe, the Sun." A boy on a horse, surrounded by sunflowers and watched over by a rising sun. "He's youthful and optimistic, clear-sighted and full of energy. He makes others feel that way, too."

"I knew that too," Kelly smiled.

"Outcome card." I hope I didn't sound as worried as I felt as I placed the next card in the right hand position. The ten of pentacles, which featured a rich old man out in the gardens, gazing at his family as they strolled about his castle. I frowned.

"Something wrong?" Kelly asked, noticing my confusion.

"No. Just not what I expected. I thought I'd see this card for Piers. It indicates that Gabe will bring you a lot of money. Actually, maybe it's not such an odd card for him. Pentacles can stand for health, too. So, health that creates wealth, Enough to continue on into the future..As for Piers..."

I flipped that final card off the deck. *The World.* On that card a woman danced within an oval of laurel leaves.

Kelly's brows shot up. "He'll give me the world?"

"In a way. He can spread your brand around the world."

"How's that different from Gabe's outcome?"

And there it was. Did I say what I saw and maybe ruin it for Piers, or did I tell her what Piers wanted her to hear, even if that wasn't what I was seeing in the card? The answer came back to me, as if it had floated up from a deep well.

"Gabe's card says you could have money and fame," I said, before I could reconsider. "The World card isn't about that. It's about gaining wisdom, traveling and becoming a master of your profession. A worldwide fitness guru. That's what you'll become with Piers."

"I see," Kelly said then, but I could tell from her tone that she either didn't see the value in that, or didn't want to surrender what she'd need to surrender to gain it.

I'd already guessed, of course, but that's when I knew for sure that she was going to dump Piers.

Chapter 10
The Poe and the Pendulum

The carriage ride had been a one-way treat. To get me home, Kelly summoned a car. She warned me it might take a while to arrive, as it actually took automobiles longer to get to the house than horses. She offered to have one of the footmen keep an eye out for it so I could stay warm by the parlor fire, but the séance was about to start, and I didn't want to be in the house while it was going on.

Which had me pacing the drive when Piers came storming out, his cravat undone, his eyes wild enough to be Edgar Allan Poe's. I braced myself.

"Kelly just broke the news." His breath was puffing out like that of an angry dragon. "Said she didn't want to keep me hanging. What the hell happened? I thought you were on my side? That you were going to put in a good word for me."

That tweaked me. "Is that why we had sex?" I snipped. "So that I'd be on your side?"

His face went still and hard. "We had sex because I offered and you accepted. Don't change the subject. This isn't about us. It's about you guiding Kelly down a really stupid path."

"I didn't guide her anywhere."

"The fuck you didn't!"

"The fuck I did," I barked back and heard our voices echoing among the surrounding trees. "There's no way I could have guided her anywhere because she'd already made up her mind. Before I entered the picture, maybe before she even invited you both here."

"You can't know that," he snarled.

"Say I strongly suspect it. How old was she when you two partnered up?"

"Twenty-one. So what? Dad argued she was too young, but I could tell she was this fitness prodigy and we'd better partner with her before someone else did. I convinced him."

175

"And she's how old now?" I folded my arms. In part because I was cold, and in part because I wanted to hide that I was trembling.

"Twenty-five. Almost twenty-six."

"Almost my age."

He shook his head. "You're not...that is, she's emotionally younger...I mean..."

"You're putting your foot in it again." I almost smiled. "But you're right. As far as Kelly's ahead of me in business acumen, she'd behind me in emotional maturity. But that doesn't change the fact that she's no longer a newbie. She knows what she wants."

"But not necessarily what's smart." He was getting frustrated with me, like he didn't think I was hearing him.

"You'd be surprised."

"What does that mean?"

"You're a wild card, Piers," I said, "one she's never been able to influence or direct, and that was fine when she was twenty-one and starting out. But now she's older and way more experienced. She's after a partner who will, now and then, do what she says and what she wants." I thought about the lady and the lion card. "That's Gabe, and I'm betting she saw that from the moment she met him."

"So all your reading did was hold her hand and tell her to follow her heart?" he mocked.

I sighed. This kept swinging back and forth between us, and every time it cut deeper. Where the fuck was that car? "My reading went over the facts, one being that Gabe can do a lot for her, like make her richer and super popular. Don't." I lifted a finger, forestalling more protests. "You know he can. But my reading also said you see her true potential and can develop it. Like one of your machines. That's the real mission in staying with her isn't it? You're not finished making her into the fitness guru you know she could be. But she'd rather be free of the leash."

"Get all that from your psychic powers?" Piers was moving from angry to bitter.

"My powers of observation were enough. And don't tell me you were entirely blindsided. Why else were you so desperate for my help? You saw it coming, too."

He threw me a seething glare. "Well at least I don't have to go on being desperate. Playing dress-up with her and her friends, going to children's festivals, getting my fortune told." It was a petty sting, but it did hurt. "I'm out of that dumb-assed B&B tonight, and if I'm lucky, I will never have to even pass through this New England tourist trap again. From now on, I stay in Manhattan."

He was circling round now, like a wolf looking for a place to lick his wounds. Yet another way to avoid facing the truth. *Jesus, Arlo, let it be! Why force him to throw away the mask?*

Because just as he knew Kelly could be so much more, I knew he could be so much more, that's why. Still, I hesitated, listening for tires on the road, hoping my car would arrive before I did this. Silence but for crickets and the caw of a crow. Ah well, in for a penny...

"Not that I doubt your anger," I said slowly and carefully, "But aren't you also relieved? A part of you might have wanted to finish your work with her, but another part of you wanted this."

I saw his jaw clench. "No. No part of me wanted this." His tone held a warning.

I shook my head. Maybe it was the Traveler's Moon. It was far higher and more distant now, but its lunar zing was still shining down on us, and I couldn't seem to keep from saying what I was seeing.

"There you were, at my age, twenty-six. Working for your dad. Which you wanted to do. Badly. But you also had this dream to create the best outdoor equipment ever. Biking, hiking, climbing. Dad said no, so you buried that. Then you found Kelly, with her ambitions and potential. Dad was happy to let you grow those in WZT's dream garden."

His expression was like stone now. "Do go on, Madame Marzanna."

"That's pretty much it. Except that, maybe, Kelly subconsciously figured it out and didn't think the partnership was doing either of you any good. She'd always be a substitute, a stand-in, not what you really wanted to work on. Maybe this decision isn't entirely selfish on her part. This break means you can finally live your life."

"*Stop it!*" he shouted, so loud I jumped back. "Just stop it! Stop pretending you understand. *You. Don't. Understand.* Hear? You've no idea how hard I worked to get this far with Kelly, how much of myself I put into her studios. Four years of my life, gone. You can't how that feels, or what it means to me and my dreams. However... intimate we've been, I've known you all of five days, tops, and you do not know me!"

Oh. He was going to play that game, was he? I straightened up. He thought he'd met Madame Marzanna? He thought my laying down cards in a carnival tent was it? He was the one who didn't understand. Not at all. I met his flaming eyes with pure ice and let Madame Marzanna rise up. And out.

"What the fuck does that matter?" I demanded, and his head went back, as if the spider he'd swiped at had jabbed him with venom.

"I don't have to understand shit," I went on. "Not about you, your situation, your relationships, nothing. You are not living your life. You want to deny it, deny it. You want to excuse it, excuse it. You want to argue that

177

working for your father makes you useful and gives you real purpose? Fine. But you're not being you. You're lying to yourself if you think you are, and to everyone else. Your father included. Would he be proud of you for that?"

I expected Piers to snarl and retort, but instead he stared at me, shocked. Then he got this odd, crushed expression on his face. He'd accused me of betraying him, but I don't think he'd believed it till now.

"I don't expect you to care, of course, what I think." I went on, finally hearing car tires rolling up the road. "But the truth isn't going away. You've been holding yourself back, Piers. You can have the world if you want it."

Headlights appeared and the vehicle turned into the drive. Piers wasn't saying anything. He was simply standing there in the dark, half-lit by the soft light from the house. His rumpled costume made him seem a phantom of himself.

"A. Symons?" The driver called, coming to a stop. "Sorry for the wait."

"Coming," I said and, swirling my skirts around, got into the car. Alas, my big exit was ruined when I had to fumble to fit in all the rustling petticoats. Sure that nothing was going to be caught in the door, I shut it and buckled up.

"Safe travels," I ventured to Piers as we started away. He didn't even lift his hand good-bye. Unable to help myself, I turned to gaze at him through the defogged rear window. My ire was dropping and my heart plummeting with it.

I'd never seen Piers like that, the confidence drained out of him. It was like... like my naming him a liar had wounded him to the quick. I found that hard to believe. Even if he refused to admit that he was deceiving himself, he had to admit he'd been deceiving others. Me included.

Even so, I still felt like I'd broken something rare and special; something I'd always wanted, without even knowing it. If I had, well, there was nothing to be done about it. Whatever I should have done to keep it whole and mine, I hadn't done it.

Tired and hallow, I turned around and gazed unseeing out the front window all the way back to town.

My sister's home was a modest Cape Cod style, built after World War II for returning service men. It had the classic, cedar shingled walls of faded oyster gray, and a steep, black slated roof. Inside, it was more modern. Unlike Kelly's mother, my sister was not interested in period restoration. The white kitchen had marble countertops, as big an island as possible, and a huge refrigerator able to send reminders to her phone when it was out of milk.

If, at the time my brother and I had taken that picture with her, someone had told me she'd end up living in a home like this with a husband and kids, I'd have said they were crazy. Freewheeling Lucy? But here she was, rooted, content and more mom-ish than our mom.

"Can we go now?" Ardie was whining.

"Ten minutes," Lucy said. She had on her flowy green Enchantress costume, but the zipper was stuck. Mom, reading glasses low on her narrow nose, was trying to finesse it.

"It's after six!" Eden cried from the living room. She was peering out the window, in agony that other kids might have already snatched up all the good candy. She darted back to the kitchen.

"Got it!" Mom said as the zipper went up.

Lucy sighed with relief. "Okay, out we go."

"YAY!" The kids bounced and cheered and grabbed their pillowcases. Even after all these years, that seemed a strange tradition to me. In the west-coast towns were we'd grown up, kids carried glow-in-the-dark plastic buckets. A pillowcase didn't seem nearly so festive, and very much like overkill. Who got that much candy? Yet every year, to my continued amazement, I saw kids hauling bulging sacks over their shoulders.

Had Piers spent Halloween night like that as a kid? Running around with a pillowcase? I flinched inside, something I'd been doing since the party.

"Did you light the pumpkins?" Lucy asked husband Matt as we crossed through the living room.

"Pumpkins lit," he said, without looking up from the tablet he was reading. "Dancing skeletons on the lawn glowing. Big bowl filled with candy on the entrance hall table. And yes, I know, there's extra in the pantry." He leaned back his head as she bent to kiss him.

"Moooom!" The kids had the door open.

"Coats," Lucy snapped, grabbing her enchantress cloak.

I nabbed Eden's tapestry cloth bolero, the one that kinda matched Beauty's in the movie, and helped her with it. Mom did the same with a fur vest for Ardie.

"Have fun," Matt called.

"Good night for this," Mom remarked as we stepped out. "Clear, and that full moon."

"Yeah," I said, buttoning up my plaid jacket. The full moon didn't have the gravitas it'd had that first evening, but it still could have come right off a Halloween greeting card. By its light, scores of costumed children careened from house to house like blind bats.

179

The twins, of course, had already darted off to join the fun. Lucy shouted at them not to cross the street without her. I kept pace with my mother, listening to the laughter, the ring of door bells, and the shouts of "trick-or-treat!" Three years ago, without consciously deciding to do it or discussing it, Mom and I had shown up at Lucy's house and joined her in shepherding the kids. Now it was a Halloween tradition. Likely we'd keep on doing it till Eden and Ardie were old enough to reject adult supervision.

Not a bad way to deal with October 31st, I mused. Maybe not the best way, but good enough. It got us outside, walking, talking to the neighbors and enjoying the twins' happy shrieks, whenever a cartoon ghost or wicked witch popped up from behind the shrubs.

"Lucy said you did readings at a really amazing party," Mom said, hands deep in her coat pockets.

I hid another inward flinch. "Its theme was 19th century psychics," I said, trying to sound casual. "Everyone was dressed up in these really stunning gowns and frock coats."

"Did you have to wear one, too?"

"Oh yes. A really nice one, with a period corset and several petticoats. I'll show you pictures when we get back." Before leaving, I'd given the "butler" my phone and he'd taken a few photos of me in the sitting room.

"Oh, look at that!" Mom pointed at a home with web silhouettes in the window, and an impressive, giant spider on the roof.

On we went. One house had a haunted maze that the kids had to go through to get to the door. We listened to the twins giggle and shout as they encountered its scares. Another place had a bouncy castle, and we held the kids pillowcases while they jumped and rolled around. We also passed several yards where the owners had dragged out their summer grills and, by that firelight, sat watching the parade of costumes go by.

At almost every corner, the twins encountered friends, which required they stop, check out each other's loot, and exchange inside information on must-visit houses before rushing off again.. Lucy stayed just near enough to make sure her kids didn't deviate from the route she'd set, didn't grab more than their share, and said "thank you.".

And always above us was that Traveler's Moon, steadily rising to its apex, making me remember, even see and feel what wasn't there. Piers' hands at my waist, helping me down from a carousel horse. Piers' arm about me as we tried to run a three-legged race. Piers holding me close.

Gone. I flinched. Fuck. I had to stop doing that.

By eight-thirty, the kids were flagging. Luckily, we were almost back home. We passed neighbor kids leaving the front door as we came up, whatever they'd nabbed out of Matt's candy bowl now in their pillowcases.

"There's a carafe of Irish coffee in the kitchen," Matt said helping Lucy off with her cloak. "Hey, hey, hang those up," he added to the kids as they shed their jackets onto the floor. They rushed to do so, then, dragging their plunder behind them, hurried up the stairs.

Watching them tugged at my heart. I remembered how my brother and I would dash to our bedroom when we got home from trick-or-treating. We'd dump all the candy in one pile, and start going through it. The twins were doing the exact same thing now. Eden, who loved peanuts, would claim all the chocolate-peanut bars, while Ardie went for the caramel ones. Being good kids, they'd also set aside some plain chocolate bars for their mother, a few white chocolate ones for grandma and sour-tart gummies for their dad.

Auntie Arlo, they'd been told, wasn't into candy, which wasn't true. It was just that by the end of the October, I was usually sick of sweets.

Matt checked on the kids, making sure they washed up and put away their costumes and their stash. Meanwhile, Lucy, Mom, and I drank coffee and talked, Lucy getting up now and then to answer the ring of a doorbell. I gave them the highlights of the party, and showed them pictures of myself in fan bodice and skirt.

"Wow!" they enthused, which encouraged me to go to Kelly's Facebook page and show them pics of the other guests. Most had been taken in the parlor before and after the dance. I showed them the "Fox Sisters" in their matching plaid gowns, and "Mrs. Lincoln" with her dog at the piano. Of course, there were plenty of Kelly.

"Incredible," Lucy cooed over the dress. "I'd say I want one, but I don't have the body to wear it."

Mom and Lucy went off on the idea of having their own themed costume party, perhaps for the holidays, while I glanced over a few more images. I came across one of Piers, of course. Had I been looking for it? Stupid question. The professional photographer had posed him with one of the stuffed ravens under his arm. He was flashing his white grin and his eyes were gleaming.

Glutton for punishment, I scrolled down looking for more. There was the three-legged race. The photos, taken by Kelly's friends, were all of her and Gabe, but I saw Piers and myself in the background. There was one with him carrying me over the finish line. Expanding the image, I made out his expression. Very serious, his eyes gazing down on my curly head as if to say, *"She's mine."*

Probably, I was reading too much into that. Down the page a little more —Shit. There was a picture of Piers in a canopy bed; a white, frothy frilly one, with white frothy frilly covers. I couldn't say how naked he was, but he was bare from the waist up and I could almost feel his furry chest under my cheek. He was waving hands before his face. The caption below read: *"Caught luxuriating in a B&B, Piers fears for his reputation."*

A good guess that Kelly had taken that picture. Probably she hadn't been in bed with him before she took it. Probably she'd just showed up that morning with the camera to catch him amid the frills.

Are you going to keep torturing yourself this way? I demanded of myself. *Probably.*

"Arlo?" my mom said for the fourth time and I blinked up, realizing she'd been trying to get my attention.

"Sorry. I didn't get much sleep last night."

"It's almost ten," she said gently. "Do you want to go?"

Lucy was looking away. There was no need for anything to be said aloud. We all knew what we were thinking and feeling at that moment. I sucked in a breath and stood. "Sure."

Lucy and mom were rinsing out the cups and carafe, and I was fetching our coats when the kids appeared on the stairs. They were in PJs and slippers and robes, looking sheepish because they knew it was past their bedtime.

"Arlo?" Ardie whispered.

I slipped on over. "Eden, Dee! Why aren't you asleep?"

"We know you don't like candy. But we thought you ought to have a treat, too," Eden whispered. Ardie nodded and held out his hand. On it was a small, green-and-red apple.

"The woman next door has an apple tree. She had a late crop this year. So she handed out apples," Eden explained. "They're really good."

Well. Damn. I felt my eyes well and had to swallow a few times. "Thank you. I love it." I gave them quick hugs. They were small and warm in my arms, and for a moment, the grief pinching my heart went away.

Chapter 11
The Haunt and the Hunted

My mom lived in a white washed cottage behind a white picket fence off the main road. Piers would have rolled his eyes; it was as quaint and charming as a B&B. Exiting out of the attached garage, we stopped in the back mudroom, where Mom shed her coat. "You want something?" She asked.

"No. I'll be fine."

She looked worried, sensing I wasn't telling her everything. But Mom wasn't a talker. She took a moment to wrap her arms around me and hold me close. I rested my head on her shoulder, felt her heart beat against mine, and, once again, blinked back tears.

"I'm off to bed," she said, patting my arm as she stepped away. "Wake me if you need anything."

I wished her good night before going to the kitchen, where I cut the apple in half, put the pieces into a plastic bag and into my jacket pocket, next to my other "gift." Then I returned to the mudroom, grabbed one of Mom's battery powered lanterns and a wool blanket. Finally, I put my phone on "Do Not Disturb." *Ready,* I thought, heading out into the backyard.

Mom had set up some solar lights, but they were dim things, and the third-acre of garden was pretty much illuminated only by star- and moonlight. There were trellises bare of roses, trees bare of leaves and fruit. The garden beds where mom grew summer carrots and corn and tomatoes were fallow.

But far back, almost at the border between her land and the neighbor's, was the squash patch. Here grew a bumper crop of butternuts for soup, acorn for roasting, and delicata for cakes. Pumpkins also, but only the small sugar ones. My lantern illuminated them, resting among their vines, patient and heavy as a pregnant women.

Here also was the empty, carefully tended corner where my brother's ashes were buried. A plaque with his name marked it. Mom and Lucy had paid their respects that morning, placing a wreath of dried oak leaves on top. I found a spot for the lantern, shook out the blanket, and sat on the cold ground.

That was the tradition. Mom and Lucy visited together during the day; I came at night, alone.

"That time again," I sighed. "Ten years. That's hard to wrap my head around. It still feels like it happened yesterday."

Maybe I shouldn't have said that, because as I did the wind rustled through the bare branches like a sigh and it was yesterday, at least in my mind. "We came here," I said softly, remembering. "And we were more of a family than we'd ever been. And we all seemed to have found our dreams. Mom had her prefect garden, Lucy her teaching career and man who loved her. I was going to a school I liked, making friends. We were happy. *You* seemed happy."

My gaze dropped to the plaque. "And then you put a crack in the glass."

Maybe that family unity was what I'd been waiting for, I heard him say, there at the back of my head. Not a new notion, but if it was true... How messed up was that?

I shifted my legs to get more comfortable and resettled. The one thing I didn't want to do tonight was run around in circles chasing *those* elusive thoughts.

You, Mom and Lucy did all find your way back, that voice in my mind, his voice, pointed out, as he always did. *And isn't it time you stopped having mental conversations with a dead teenager? You're twenty-six. Find someone older. Alive would be good, too.*

I snorted. That was my brother's sense of humor, all right. Mild but sharp. "I did just that, actually. It's quite the story. This guy...he wasn't my usual; you know, nice, pretty smart, has a good job. This guy was really different. Off the charts different."

The night was settling around me now. I heard the hoot of owls. From my left pocket I brought out the tiny pumpkin Piers had gotten me and set it in the center of the wreath.

"That's from him. He's rich and handsome. Not billionaire rich, but up there. And not men's-cologne-ad handsome, but...up there. Sexy. He has a goatee." Even as I said it I could feel it brushing over my lips..

For a moment, it was as if he really was there, heat from his kiss radiating down to my core, and out from there to every limb. It drove the chill from my fingers and toes, and even kicked out the thoughts in my head. For a moment, there was only that one memory: being loved by him.

And then it was over, and I sat there stone shocked. Here, at this time of year, nothing should have been able to bounce my brother from my mind. Nothing in ten years ever had. Not even for a second.

"Wow," I said aloud, my fingers and toes still tingling. "Did you see that?"

Some powerful mojo, came the agreement.

"Mojo, yeah. That's the right word. The whole affair seems like some kind of Halloween spell. I mean, how else can you explain that *I* ended up with the whole package? That he wanted *me*."

Trouble? I could almost see my brother now, phantom-transparent, seated in his usual cross-legged pose. His elbows would be on his knees; hands bent at the wrists so he could press his knuckles together and rest his chin on them. Like some kind of forgotten yoga position. A bundle of lanky arms and legs, that's how I remembered him. Not yet seventeen, and with a few more growth spurts to go.

"Of course," I went on, "Rich, handsome, smart *and* into me. That's fruit right out of our Dream Garden. Too good to be true. So it couldn't be true, right?"

I could make out my brother's eyes now, the same gray I saw in the mirror each morning. The same freckles across the nose, too. His brown hair, like mine, was all curls; shorter in cut, and highlighted with polished brass like Lucy and our mom. I was the only one who'd gotten hints of our father's coppery mane.

Which of those 'too goods' were illusions? he asked.

"None. They were all real. Even him wanting me. What wasn't real was that I could keep him. I knew I couldn't, but I wanted to believe I could. Fooled myself."

That's okay, he said. *We all do that. We need to do it. I wish you weren't taking it so hard.*

"I'm more haunted by it than I am by you right now," I laughed. "Which is really disturbing. I barely knew the guy! I'd say it was fucked up, but maybe it was simply time for another lost soul to take your place in my subconscious. I don't think about you so much anymore. And I almost never dream about you."

You sound disappointed. Do you want to be Mary Todd Lincoln? Obsessed with the dead?

I pursed my lips. "That isn't you talking," I chided him. "That's me. I'm the one went to the séance party and learned all about Mrs. Lincoln."

I could see him shyly grin, glad I'd caught that. In my mind's eye, his ghostly hair drifted up and down as if underwater. It's why I came at night. In the day, I couldn't imagine him, but at night I could stare out into the dark and reconstruct him. His shape, his coloring, his expressions—even the corduroy slacks he liked to wear, and his favorite plaid jacket, the one I wore every Autumn. The one I was wearing now. The one he'd taken off and set aside before leaving us.

185

You could just look at pictures and videos of me, he said.

I shook my head at that. There were hundreds of family memories, on the computer and in leather albums. Photos of our life before we came here. I couldn't speak for Mom or Lucy, but I hadn't revisited any of them. Not in ten years.

Crunch. I blinked and looked around. *Crunch, crunch.* Were those footsteps? Mom didn't usually come out to check on me, but she had been concerned. I glanced around a tree trunk toward the house and saw another electric lantern coming my way. Behind it was Piers' goateed face.

Wow. This illusion looks really real, I thought, almost dazzled by the way phantasm-Pier's inky beard and hair seemed to disappear into the night, and how the lantern made his eyes glow as if they were bright with ideas. I was absorbing the vivid details of this mirage, from the mud on his boots up to the buttons on his hooded wool jacket when I realized he *was* real!

What the hell? He was supposed to be in Manhattan. How could he be here? Why? And how did he find me? And why?

He strode toward me as purposefully as he could, while looking down to be sure he didn't stumble over a rock or step into a hole. Some five paces away, he came to a stop.

"I know I shouldn't be here," he blurted. "I shouldn't have gone to your sister's to find you, and please apologize to her that I wasn't the late night trick-or-treater she expected. Do you want a *Snickers* bar? I took two from the bowl. Anyway, after I convinced her I wasn't a crazy stalker, and she told me where you were and why, I knew I ought to wait till morning. But, obviously, I didn't."

I blinked. "Does my mother know you're out here?"

"Uh, yeah, I—I'm afraid I woke her. And I shouldn't have, but I didn't want to be stumbling around in a stranger's yard. She gave me the light, and was really understanding, and this is all wrong. The thing is, I went back to Manhattan, but every time I tried to return to work, I remembered what you'd said. And I wanted, *needed* to talk to you. I thought of texting or phoning but, what I have to say—it has to be face to face." He heaved a frustrated sigh. "Once I realized that, there was no slowing down. Or stopping. Not till I got to you."

I didn't know what to say, so I shifted to one side of the blanket. "Would you like to sit down?"

"Thank you." He did, placing his lantern opposite mine. He crossed his legs, wrapped his arms about his knees, either to stay warmer or... Was he trying to keep from touching me? Pulling me into his arms and ravishing me?

"I'm sorry about your brother." He sounded honestly mortified to have interrupted my very private grief. "Your sister said you were twins? She, um, explained things, and told me this year was particularly hard."

"It's the tenth since he took his life," I said flatly. "I don't know why that should matter so much, but it does." *Ten. The Wheel of Fortune card in the tarot was number ten, spinning round and round.*

"The quick rundown," I went on, "is this: He had lots of friends and a loving, accepting family. He wasn't being bullied and he wasn't on drugs. But something made him want to leave us. He did it on Halloween night. Eleven weeks and three days short of our seventeenth birthday. He did it out in the woods, where no one would see and stop him. He used a gun. He didn't leave a note."

"Shit," Piers muttered.

"There were some teens not too far away, getting secretly drunk, they heard the shot, followed it and found him. Otherwise, it might have been a long time before we knew."

I hadn't meant to sound so terse, so angry, but during those first few years well-intentioned friends and neighbors had asked the same well-intentioned questions, over and over again. I'd learned how to checkmate them by front-loading the answers and firing them off.

'His name was Arden," I finished. Lucy had named her son after him. I hadn't liked it, but I hadn't objected because I knew that was her way of holding onto her little brother. Still, I was glad that everyone called my nephew Ardie. I couldn't manage even that aloud. "Dee," I called him. Because my brother, and only my brother, was *Arden*.

"Oh, Arlo," Piers said, with such hurt for me that it brought a sting to my eyes. His gloved hand found mine and held it. "What was he like?"

"Odd. Kind of the peacekeeper, you know? Always easy, never in hurry. Never ambitious or greedy or petty. I remember this one time, aged nine, he and his friends planned to go to this movie, but one of them had spent his allowance. The others wanted to go without him, but Arden convinced them to hang at the skate park instead. He said it was more important they all have fun together. The next weekend the kid had the money and off to the movie they went."

"So he was the shaman of the tribe?" Piers offered.

"That's it. Yeah. The one who listens and figures things out. He seemed to absorb all he heard, so when he finally did say something…"

"It changed the world," Piers put in, and he almost sounded envious. He probably was. Piers sold his position to others with a lot of concentrated charm and chatter; Arden had been able to do that with a single, effortless word.

"Would you like some apple?" I ventured.

"Apple?" he repeated. "Sure."

I got out the plastic bag and split the pieces between us. Biting in, I found it crisp and juicy. "My niece and nephew got it trick-or-treating. I was going to share with Arden. But I think he'd want his portion to go to you."

"I see you gave him the pumpkin." He sunk his teeth into his own half and the crunch sounded oddly pleasant in the silent garden. "I'm honored."

"Halloween was Arden's favorite holiday. Especially when we were little. Carving the pumpkin, creating costumes for us. And sharing the caramel apple, as mom would only let us have one between us." I finished off a last bite and tossed the core. Piers did the same, wiping his gloved hands on his jeans.

"He used to say that October, was like a month long journey to mom's Dream Garden. Arriving there being Halloween night with everyone dressed up as someone they wished to be. He never wanted it to end." I reflected. "I was the one, by the way, who planted dreams of being a Cirque du Soliel acrobat.. Arden dreamed of being a super-farmer who could feed everyone on the planet.. Or a scientist who could bring back extinct animals.. He was always wanting to make things better."

"Sounds like he was hard to live up to," Piers said. "Maybe hard to compete with?"

I shook my head. "It wasn't like that. Arden and I shared every step of almost seventeen years. When people liked him, I felt that they liked me. When he dreamed big, I dreamed big. We weren't competitors, we were a team. Lately, though, I've started thinking that maybe his altruism wasn't such a good thing. What if he left us because he thought staying would be selfish?"

"Off the top of my head, I'd say that's messed up and it's probably better not to brood on it.""

"True that. You know what else really twists me in knots this time of year? His end taints every memory I have of us. I flash back on him as a kid, laughing and playing, and the image goes gray, because I know what's coming. He leaves, and I don't get to share any more with him. I didn't even get to see the finished product. The man he would have become."

I paused, listening to the rattle of brown leaves, like the dying breath of those skeletal trees.

"Would it be dumb to say I get why you don't like séances?" Piers broke the silence.

That made me laugh, which was a welcome surprise. "Actually, this *is* a séance. A personal, yearly one, here in my mother's pumpkin patch. I avoid the other kind because I don't want some spiritualist playing messenger for my brother."

"If he can't talk directly to you, you don't want to hear it?" Piers said wryly.

I laughed again. "Yeah. And I don't have any questions for him anyway. Except maybe, '*Could I have stopped you?*'"

"You wouldn't ask why he did it?"

I drew in a breath and, as I released it, only then did I realize tears were trickling down my cheeks. Piers pulled out a pack of tissues from a pocket and handed it over. I dabbed at my eyes and sniffled.

"'*Why*' doesn't keep me up at night. He didn't want to stay in the world. That's why." *And,* I thought to myself, *he'd been desperate to leave for a while.* . I'd never told anyone else that, but in my heart of hearts, I'd knew it. He'd wanted to leave, but had waited till he knew for sure that Mom and Lucy and I would be okay. "What eats away at me is not knowing whether I could have changed his mind."

"Totally understandable."

I wiped at my nose again, which was feeling red and swollen.

Piers cleared his throat. "Also totally understandable that you yelled at me. In your place, I would have shouted at me to live my life, too."

"That, oh, ouch." I winced. "That was so wrong of me. I'm sorry."

"Super sensitive time for you and, as usual, I stepped in it. I still can't believe I said what I said to you about not understanding loss." He winced in turn. "Big ouch. I don't blame you for sticking it to me."

"It still wasn't fair. I do understand your side of the argument; that we can't always live life like we want, when we want. Sometimes we can't ever do it. And sometimes, that's good. Maybe it's even for the best."

"Like a college student obediently studying for exams, rather than getting roaring drunk with friends."

I gave him a sidewise look. "This example comes from experience? What happened?"

His lips quirked, his goatee with it. "I suffered through exams with one hell of a hangover. Somehow, I didn't die and I didn't throw up. I did not do as well as I would have, but I passed."

"So, lesson not learned?"

"Half-way learned." He was rubbing his gloved hands over his legs, and I realized that the temp had gone down. Way down. His muscles had to be frozen and cramped. Mine were.

"Let's go inside. I'm pretty much done here, and we might as well talk where it's warm."

He glanced uncomfortably toward the cottage. "Could we go to your place instead? You mother seems like a very nice lady, but—"

"She's my mom and there are things you don't want to say in her kitchen even if you're sure she won't eavesdrop?" I grinned. "We'll go to my place. Let me tell her I'm leaving.."

Mom, as it turned out, was up and watching a gardening show on her extra-large phone. She eyed us both with such avaricious curiosity that I had no doubt Piers was right. We couldn't trust her not to listen in.

"Piers is giving me a ride home. I'll talk to you in the morning," I said as he, gloved hands behind his back, pretended with all his might to be interested in her potted herbs.

"All right, dear," she said, then mouthed, *"who is he?"* and pointed.

Piers having noticed that, answered before I could. "*He* is a man of wealth and taste," he flashed his best evil grin. "Hoping to earn your daughter's sympathy. It's a fascinating story and, once she tells you about it, you'll be the toast of your social media page."

Mom's expression said she couldn't quite believe he'd said that. Then Piers winked at her. She giggled. Actually giggled. "Well, I guess that's okay, then."

Sheesh! Even my mom couldn't resist him!

Chapter 12
Going to the Holy Devil

Piers had parked his large, black vehicle not-quite in the drive. It was some kind of gleaming, expensive hybrid. He opened the door for me, and I slipped into a leather-luxurious interior, all lights and digital instrumentation. Shit.

The hush of that opulence made me feel odd, especially when he got us on the road. *His territory*, I thought of the car. His world. Which, I realized, I hadn't experienced 'til that moment. I'd known he had money, but I'd only seen Kelly's material riches, not his—excepting the Devil's costume, of course, but that hadn't felt real. Not like this car.

For the first time, I was uncertain. Like he was right, and I didn't know him at all. As he slowed to a stop at a turn and checked his GPS, I gave him a sidewise look, hoping to see the Piers in the Hellboy tee, the one who'd gotten tipsy, and the one who'd carried me to a finish line.

I found his eyes locked on me. Next thing I knew, he'd set the parking brake and his gloved hands were cupping my cheeks, and my cold hands were gripping the lapels of his jacket, and our lips were glued together, his smooth whiskers stroking above and below. Our panting breaths came through our nostrils as tongues met and tangled and demanded more.

When we broke, it was like we'd been forced apart by unseen hands. Gasping, we stared at each other, and his expression reflected every bewildered, lost, desperate feeling thumping in my heart.

"Where can we park?" he asked.

"Remember when you asked about white steepled churches?"

"Huh?" He frowned.

"The closed down one I told you about is five minutes that way," I rushed on. "It's got a big empty lot."

He'd already released the brake and slammed his foot on the accelerator. Even with my seatbelt on, his tight turns threw me against the door and then into him. He got us there in three minutes. The place was almost completely dark, but for one light by the church's double doors. The white steeple could just be made out against the starry sky.

Piers drove across the lot, and pretty much buried us behind a hedge. Before he even had the engine button off, I was unbuckled and out of the car. I threw open the back door and waved at the backseats. "Do they go down?"

The seats went down by themselves. Of course a car like this would have a button for that. My breath was fogging on the air, but my body felt on fire. I got a booted foot up, unlaced, pulled it off and went for the other. Piers, out now and at the opposite side, did the same. We threw jackets, and shirts into the front seats, shoved down pants and underwear together, tossed them forward as well, then made a dive into the vehicle.

Slam-Slam went the doors, and Piers had his arms around me, and I had my arms around him, and we were rolling around stark naked. Or nearly so; I still had my bra on. Piers' mouth found mine, and my tongue found his, even as his hands unhooked the bra.

As soon as it was free he went for my breasts. I grabbed at his cock, which was hard and slick, and milked it as he sucked my tit. His goatee tickled my tightening areola while the tip of his tongue played over my nipple, making me writhe and bark out yelps of helpless pleasure. Fire rolled down to my clit with each flick.

"OhGodohGod—" I scratched at his back and bit into his shoulder. We rolled and knocked into the sides of the car. Every time he lipped at my nipples, my skin burned with a delicious agony. I jerked and bucked under him, and gave myself rug burns as I wiggled over the carpeted back area. I both loved and hated that torturous tongue of his.

Eventually he left my breasts and tried to lick and kiss and explore more, leaving searing trails. I don't know how, but at some point in my squirming, I got my face near to his dripping dick and took my first taste. I got a smokey-sweet lick, and his mouth vanished as he jerked in surprise and cursed me.

Too late, I was on him and tonguing his slit. Now he was the one thrashing. Pre-come came trickling out as I found the under-seam of his crown and gave it some attention. He gasped and gasped like a landed fish. Very soon, his fingers were tangled in my hair, guiding me, and I was going down on him.

His rod was beautiful. A flared cherry head that was a joy to explore, pulsing veins and smooth heat that I loved sucking. He grunted as I got most of him down, and I smelled his sweat. I took a moment to lap at his nuts, wetting down their hairy, crinkly, tightening skin.

"G-get up here!" He pulled at my hair in a way that dragged me away from his cock. I didn't want to give him up, but he was insistent. Off I came and made my way, with licks and nips, from the nest at his crotch, over his salty-sweaty treasure trail to his navel, to his lean abdomen, ribs expanding with gasps, to his furry chest. His heart pounded there like his fist knocking at my door.

He was already ripping open a condom packet. Where it had come from, I don't know. Likely he'd had it on him in case, or just as likely he kept a supply in the car. Maybe he'd pushed another button, and it'd popped up from somewhere.

He got it on in record time, and I bumped my head on the ceiling as I straddled him. Trickster that he was, he got an arm around my waist as I tried to push down on his dick, and kept me ass up. Almost I yelled at him, but then I felt his fingers, slick with my wetness, stroking my pussy lips.

He tickled my clit, and I lost the ability to breathe. Tingles and flickers and sparks followed those fingers, and his damn arm kept me where I was, my hips rocking. I could feel his dick head, gloved and swaying just out of reach. His fingertips found and rolled my clit, and I chirped out begging noises, sweat dripping off me.

And then it all exploded. As I jerked over him he released me and his hips came up. His cock entered me. I bumped my head again, as we both bounced. He pumped and I rocked, my body throbbing until he stiffened and shot, and then I was flying away, twirling and twirling in space.

When I came off that soaring high it was to steamed up windows and the humid fragrance of sex. I was lying limp across Piers, feeling his belly rise under mine as he got his breath back.

"That was a damn dirty trick," I huffed, "holding me off."

"It was," he chucked tiredly. "I've got lots of them and I want to play them on you all night long."

"Ha! You haven't any more energy than I do. I'm not even sure you have the strength to drive us back to my place."

"I'm not sure I have the strength to get dressed," he admitted.

We rested unmoving for several minutes more, then, slowly and with a lot of groans, we went for our clothes. We'd tossed everything into the front so willy-nilly, we ended up exchanging shoes and pants. Getting things on was a comedy act, with more bumping around.

Finally, coatless and in our stocking feet, we dashed out and around. I swept our jackets off the seats on onto my half-frozen feet. Piers got the engine running, and the heat streaming from the vents. As we left, his headlights passed over the door to the church.

"Think we'll end up in hell for doing it in a church lot?" he asked.

"I thought what we did was heavenly," I murmured. I was grinning. Couldn't stop. Couldn't stop blushing smugly either. "And I think a church should be witness to what an angelic lover the Devil can be."

He laughed out loud, and he was the Piers I knew. Hair tousled, face still flushed, his clothes a wrinkled mess. His brown eyes danced. And I no longer had any problem with the car. In fact, I rather liked it.

As we headed toward town, I caught Piers glancing at me again and again. "That was okay, right?" he asked. He sounded suddenly uncertain. "I mean, given what tonight means to you and all..."

"Um, yeah," I laughed. "It's all right, Piers. There wasn't any sacrilege. I wanted it as badly as you."

He relaxed back against the leather. "I wish I could make Halloween, well, fun for you again."

"It is fun!"

"You don't hate it?" he ventured.

"God, no. I love it. The bats and owls and scarecrows. The string spiderwebs on store windows, and carved pumpkins glowing on doorsteps. I love the carnivals and spooky hayrides. I'm even fond of that day when dog owners put their pets in costume and parade them around town. And, yeah, I love seeing children all dressed up, pillowcases full of candy over their shoulders. Everyone is wearing a mask, but no one is a stranger. What's not to love?"

"Something," he murmured.

"Well. I don't care for the ghost stories," I admitted. We'd finally reached my place and he kept solemnly quiet till he'd set the break and shut off the car.

Then he turned, very tenderly brushed my cheek, and said, "Understandable."

"This is damn good omelets," Piers said, as we breakfasted at the General Store. "I thought all this place would have would be greasy fried eggs and those stupid little sausages. And burnt toast. Who knew?"

"Amazing isn't it? Next thing you know they'll be serving almond milk cappuccinos like in the big city. Oh. Wait. They do." I smirked. Piers had whined about coming here, his main complaint being that he wanted to spend the morning in bed with me. But I hadn't restocked the refrigerator, and we had things to discuss—which wasn't going to happen unless we were clothed, and seated on opposite sides of a table.

Or wooden booth, in this case. The General Store's café had been added on to the actual grocery sometime in the 1950's, and, like that grocery, was all white washed walls, including the exposed beams. Most of the seating was in the form of u-shaped booths with a few free-standing tables here and there.

On one side of the café picture windows looked into the market, where shoppers checked over heaps of fall produce. On the other side, matching windows looked out on the tree-lined street and its shops, mine included. It was a nice day to gaze out those windows. Gone were the mists and gray of October. It was a clear day, with drifting clouds. A breeze blew fallen leaves down the sidewalks.

"Happy All Saints Day," I said to Piers, between bites of my frittata. "Or Dia de los Muertos, if you prefer."

"Happy November." He nodded to my mug. "Is that your tea? I'd imagine you have a deal with the eateries around here. Also the B&B's."

"Not so much, actually. Most B&B's need tea bags. Easier for guests to brew their own cups. A lot of restaurants here feel the same. But I do provide tea to the sushi and Indonesian restaurants."

"And this place?"

I raised my mug. "Lipton."

"Lipton," he repeated flatly.

"It's what they've been brewing since they opened, and I wouldn't have it any other way."

He shook his head at the hokey-ness.

"So," I ventured, "Last night, you said you had things to tell me. But then we literally took a detour. And then fell asleep."

"I tried to stay awake," he protested.

"Well, we're both up now and, no, we can't detour back to my place. You went back to Manhattan, then some forty hours later, you drove all the way back on Halloween night. You hunted me down—my sister sent me texts and left a very worried voice mail, by the way, about you turning up at her door. Flattered as I am to think I'm that good a lay, I'm assuming there's more to this visit?"

"I'm not altogether sure of that," he murmured into his orange juice.

"Let's start with this. How did the news go over with your dad? About *Sunflower Fitness*?"

Piers went back to picking at his cottage fries topped, I'd noted, with lots of hot sauce. "My father wasn't pleased. No one was. He swore a lot. Then... then he told me not to take it personally. That I'd given us nearly five years of Kelly's business. He said it was what it was, and time to move

195

on. He's like that. Very 'Get back on the horse.' I'm not. I kick myself for falling off and brood."

"I know the feeling."

"Yeah, well, there was a big difference this time." He cleared his throat. "I wasn't kicking myself about losing Kelly. I was kicking myself for going off on you. For messing up with you."

My heart did a little flutter. I told it, firmly as I could, to settle down. "You keep saying that you can't stop thinking of me. Why not?"

"Because, because you *get* me." He said it intently, as if he found that astonishing. "I wear this mask—"

"The debonair suave one?"

"Yes! See! You laugh, but it fools everyone. Not you. Right from the start, you saw past it. You knew the real me, but you still talked to me. You even invited me into your bed, for God's sake."

"Onto my floor," I said, around a bite of muffin. "We ended up on the floor that first time."

"Quiet, I'm ranting. You took my side against Gabe, who is exactly as he seems and totally trustworthy. Why would you do that?"

"Because you're rich and handsome."

He frowned. "Oh. Yeah. I am, aren't I? Well, I guess you're not so special. Kidding! Seriously. I don't have to tell you that I've done some not nice things."

"Like made a girl cry?"

"Made a few girls cry," he said ruefully. "And helped my father play some dirty business tricks."

"Any war crimes?"

"Not that I can remember. Point is, you may not know much about me, but you know who I am. And you *still* like me. I can't get over that. But that's not all there is to it. I mean, frankly, you're not my type. I go for driven, dressed and styled-to-the-nines women with cut cheekbones."

"Like Kelly."

"Like Kelly. But you," he faltered as I lifted a brow, "I mean, you're super cute with all the—" he waved a hand over his head. "Ringlets and the freckles and your ass...um."

He puttered to a stop, noticing a few glances from neighboring booths.

"My ass?" I said, leaning in.

His voice went down to a whisper. "You've got these soft places, and you smell so... delectable. It's like I've been eating raw veggies all this time, and finally got a bite of a cinnamon bun!"

"Um...thanks?" I took a sip of my Lipton's. "And for the record, you're not my type either."

"What? What are you talking about? I'm rich and handsome. I'm everyone's type."

"So, you came back because I like your dastardly self and you're addicted to cinnamon buns."

"And because of the pull! Can't you feel it? It's magnetic. I really can't stop thinking of you. I don't even want to look at anyone else."

Some would call that love, I thought.

Reaching across the table, he took hold of my hand, as if afraid he'd scared me. "I know you think I only took an interest in you because I thought you could sway Kelly. I know me, and I'd've thought the same."

I kept my eyes on his. "I did suspect it. Was I right?"

He smiled a little. "Yes and no. Kelly didn't decide to hire you till the day after the carnival. So, I hadn't any such incentive when I waved my tickets at you, hoping to get you alone and beside me on the Ferris Wheel. I did that because you'd argued with me, and most women don't do that."

"They try to please or woo you? Simper, maybe."

"You met Kelly. Not the simpering type. But they rarely, um, play verbal chess with me."

"The Devil doesn't play chess," I pointed out. "You're thinking of Death."

"Verbal checkers then." His eyes laughed. "I found you intriguing, and I certainly had impure motives towards you. Then, a couple of days later, Kelly told me what she had in mind: to get a reading from you before deciding."

His expression grew uncomfortable. "That's when my impure motives become ignoble. And, yes, my reason for delivering Kelly's message in person was to see if I could influence you with my charms."

I sucked in a breath. "And when you pounded on my door that evening?"

"That..." He scratched at his goatee, and I held my breath. "That wasn't part of the plan." His brown eyes were serious, honest, and more vulnerable than I'd have ever imagined seeing them. "Like I said, yes and no. You'd gotten under my skin. I needed to scratch that itch. I thought if I did, I'd be free of you, but just like at the carnival, you turned things upside down. By morning I was under your spell."

He rested back, looking as if he still couldn't believe it. "I wanted to keep that partnership with Kelly. To beat out Gabe. I wanted to make my dad proud, and please the stockholders. That's what I came here to do. But every time I talked to you, made love to you, it ceased to matter. Do you understand how fucking wrong that is? When I was with you, I didn't give a damn about anything else."

Having finished his omelet and potatoes, he pushed aside the empty plate. "I thought a lot about what you said to me, that night, by the light of the Traveler's Moon." He paused, then, "At first I thought you'd shot me in the back. I'd been more genuine with you than with anyone else in my life except, well, probably my mother, and you still accused me of being a fraud. That hurt—" He held up a hand as I opened my mouth to apologize. "But you weren't wrong. Going over all the stupid things I said to you that night, I realized that. So, after giving the *Sunflower Fitness* news to my dad, I told him that I had a new investment idea. Outdoor equipment."

My mouth dropped open. "Bikes? Hiking and climbing gear?"

Piers nodded. "He dismissed it, as always. I pointed out that Kelly's concept for small fitness places had seemed a gamble at the time. That we'd risked a lot on creating new items to suit her centers and it had paid off. He said 'That's different.'"

He paused to sip at his coffee. I was on the edge of my seat now, afraid to interrupt him.

"I conceded that it was different," he went on, "but I still wanted to give outdoor equipment a try. He told me to put in a pin in it, come back to it later, like all I needed was time to get over losing the *Sunflower* account and I'd realize how bad an idea it was. I told him I'd left this on the back burner long enough. It was going to happen. If he wasn't willing to invest in it, I'd quit as design director, sell my stock, and use the capital to create my own company."

"Piers!" I gasped. *Holy Dream Garden! What had I created?* "Are you sure?"

He gave me a one shouldered shrug and a tweaked smile through the goatee. "That's what dad said. Yes, I'm sure. I'm very, very sure. And I have to wonder if you were right when you said that Kelly, consciously or not, knew that going for Gabe would release us to be...us."

"So, you've quit your father's company?" I didn't know whether to be scared or happy for him.

"Well, when dad realized I was serious, he changed tactics and negotiated. I'll remain part-time as WZT's head designer, and WZT will provide some of the backing. Most importantly, I can use WZT's manufactures for parts. Putting the bikes and such together, that'll be up to me. As will setting up the actual store for sales. Which I guess means I should start looking for a small factory-cum-warehouse. Is that closed down church for sale?"

Chapter 13
A Lovers Carnival

I don't know which shocked me more: that the Devil wanted to build bikes in former church, or that he wanted to build them here.

"I thought you hated hokey towns like this," I blurted, "with their B&B's and pumpkin festivals."

"Meh. The place has grown on me. And while I'll happily market to Manhattan hikers and bikers, space for making and selling outdoor equipment is cheaper here.. This place also has a better customer base: all those tourists wanting to hike or bike through scary New England woods."

"I'm speechless," I managed.

"Well, I also want to be near you and here is where you are." He'd drunk the last of his coffee, and was turning and turning the empty mug. "This should be obvious at this point, but I guess I'd better say it. I want to be with you. Hopefully for a long time. If that's not what you want, better let me know so I can find another hokey town for my business."

Now I was beyond speechless. *Yes! Say yes!* But...

"Half the time you're going to be in Manhattan. Are you expecting me to live there with you?" It occurred to me that if I didn't, he might return to cut-cheekboned and styled-to-the-nines women. Then again, if he was going to lose his taste for me, maybe I'd better know? "And what about Kelly? She and Gabe will be opening a *Sunflower Fitness* here."

He tilted his head this way and that. "As to the latter, I'm actually okay with it, now that I know keeping Kelly's business didn't matter as much to me as I thought. Funny, that. Anyway, I can deal with them... Unless they put that gym next to my new bike shop, or your tea store Then all bets are off."

"Maybe my prediction will come true," I said, "and after they open this salon they'll be off to open another. And another."

"Your predictions have been right so far." Piers grinned. "Here's hoping,"

"And what about the former?" I was nervous now, wiping sweaty palms on my knees. "You spending half the time in Manhattan. I've got my own business to run. And I'm not sure about fitting into that city life of yours. The plays and nightclubs."

He rested his head on his fist, looking at me as if I'd said something silly. "In case you haven't noticed, I'm handsome, and rich. Well, maybe not so rich, once I invest in this new venture, but I should have enough to hire some assistants to run both our businesses. When we need to be in Manhattan that is. Worth a try, don't you think? You selling tea and doing readings here and there, me selling bikes and doing design work, here and there. Sharing our lives?"

The waiter appeared at our table to refresh Pier's coffee and my tea. As the man left and the steam rose from the hot brew, I met Piers' eyes.

"Yes. It's worth a try," I said and I heard him release a huge sigh of relief. "I don't suppose you and your father would like to join my family for Thanksgiving?" I added.

He laughed. "You mean a classic New England Thanksgiving, with a long table, horns-of-plenty decorations and a big glistening turkey?"

"Of course. Apple and pumpkin pie for dessert."

He flashed his grin, bright as that of an angel. "Dad might go for it. Would you do me one favor though?"

"So long as it's a clothes-on favor. I have to open my store soon."

"Pull a card for us. To see what our future will be."

Seriously? Did he really want to know what the tarot thought, or was he testing me? Seeing if I'd defy the cards if they gave me an ominous message? I got out the small travel deck that was always in my purse, and give it a shuffle.

"Cut it," I told him, which he quickly did with his right hand.

For a moment I just held the cards between my palms, silently asking the deck for its blessing. Then I flipped over the top card. I didn't immediately look down, but Piers did. He burst out in a laugh that had everyone staring.

It was the two of cups. I started to laugh, too.

"Hah!" he said,. "Spot on. Here we are, sharing a drink on either side of a table. Again."

"It does seem to be our card," I said ruefully, and didn't bother to mention that this reminded me of my original reading for him. It had come true, hadn't it? For both of us.

"If I recall," he said, "this says we're going to have to make up our own minds, right? Create our own future."

"That is how I'd read it."

"I like it. And it's what I want. To always have you seated across from me."

"Cheers to that," I said, and we clicked mugs over that card, our card.

Eleven and a half months later....

Piers had insisted I give Madame Marzanna a face lift for this year's carnival. No more mysterious old lady. He wanted her youthful and seductive. So, with Lucy's help, I adjusted the costume to give it a waist and colorful skirts that showed some leg. I kept the lavender contacts, but exchanged the wrinkle lines for rouge, lipstick and mascara. The result, Lucy assured me, was sultry.

A bit of sparkle gel and my ringlets, held back by a bejeweled headband, threw out fire as they fell about my shoulders. Madame Marzanna was reborn! And wouldn't you know it? I had more customers than ever. Piers really was the consummate salesman.

I did lots of readings that afternoon, and, as evening fell, was gearing up to do more when I heard a familiar voice outside my tent.

"Madame Marzanna is about to go on break" Piers announced to the line, which got him a chorus of objections. "She'll be back in a half an hour; here, take a number. That's your place in line. Come back in thirty minutes. That's enough time for a funnel cake and ride."

I saw him through the opening, putting up the "Back in thirty minutes" sign as my final sitter left. He strode in, wearing his own boyfriend-to-the-fortune-teller-costume: Head scarf and blousy shirt, pantaloons, boots and sash. Very sexy.

"Marzanna! My darling!" He opened his arms.

"Zorba! My dearest!" I returned, and leapt into those arms. He gave me a sizzling kiss. "And what," I said, getting my breath back, "Am I doing on my break?"

"I can think of a lot we can do in thirty minutes, but the tent fabric is thin and this *is* a children's carnival. So..." He brought out a pair of tickets. "Ferris wheel ride!"

And then he was pulling me by the hand out into the crowds.

"Ferris wheel?" I tried not to bump into people as he cut between booths. "We've gone on every Ferris wheel at every fair since spring!" *And traveled to all of them riding Tatham "Light Flyer" bikes*, I thought with a grin. Test models, but the final models had gone on sale in July and were selling quite well. In fact, a small tour company had bought twelve for their autumn biking excursions. I'd seen them, helmeted and pedaling through the woods last week.

"But this is the Ferris wheel you refused to go on with me," Piers threw over his shoulder. "That makes it special."

I laughed and kept pace with him. If I'd learned anything in our almost year together, it was that I'd better be ready to move. Not an hour after we made our deal at the Country Store, he'd arranged for my mom to watch my shop, and, with barely time for me to pack an overnight bag, had us on the road to Manhattan. He wanted to introduce me to his city, and to his Dad. Not in a week or tomorrow, but that very day.

"Arlo!" young voices cried from the merry-go-round line. "Piers!"

"Hey, Eden! Hey, Arden!" I called to my niece and nephew. Eden, having read a children's book on ancient myths, had insisted that she and her brother go as the fraternal twins Apollo and Diana this year. Ardie had balked against wearing a toga, so Lucy had cut and glued together craft foam sun "armor." This made Ardie happy, especially when Piers gave him the golden bow and non-lethal arrows he'd devised. Eden was equally pleased with her silver, skirted "moon" armor, and matching bow and arrows. She and her brother waved as we passed. Lucy, standing over them as mythic mom, Leto, smiled.

Perhaps I should have gone mythic, too? I mused. Hecate, goddess of witches, would work. As for Piers, all he needed was a pair of winged sandals and a stick with snakes. I didn't think I'd ever gotten across the carnival so fast.

We reached the Ferris wheel, but as I started for the line Piers pulled me past it, right up to the front gate.

"Hey!" I said, as those in line frowned at us. But the man letting people in held back the next couple, and took our tickets instead. And then we were seated in the carriage, the safety bar down over our laps and the wheel moving.

"Did you bribe someone," I demanded.

"What, me cheat? Never!" His arms locked around me and I gave up the idea of resisting as his goatee brushed over my lips, and his hot tongue found mine. His heat melted me through three turns of the wheel.

Round and Round, I thought with a happy, inner laugh. That was my life now. I'd been terrified that day, when I'd seen that familiar Manhattan skyline approaching. I'd visited as a tourist, but live here? Work here? This wasn't my world. But Piers knew what he was about. After dropping off my bag at his apartment, we'd gone to an off Broadway show and then to his favorite pizza place. That helped a lot.

Making love that night in his bed helped, too. A California King. I could get used to that. And in the morning, sharing the shower with him and a choice of towels, well, I was almost sanguine. After a deli breakfast, he'd taken me to several Manhattan tea shops. That's when I had my "duh" moment. I could order so many teas in this city that I couldn't get anywhere else. Come here every few months? Hell yes! Why hadn't I considered it before?

Make that very "duh!" So we traveled, to and fro, round and round from hokey town to international metropolis—and Piers had plans to travel farther than that, next year, to Europe and India and China. For his business and mine. All around the world.

"I told the kids we'd join them on the haunted hayride tomorrow," Piers said as we paused for a breath on our fourth go-round. "And we should make time for the pumpkin festival next week, get squash to carve and put in the store windows."

"Come again?" I raised a suspicious brow. "Haunted hayrides and pumpkin festivals? Who are you? And what have you done with the real Piers? The one who hated Halloween?"

"Don't know what you're talking about. I love Halloween. Always have. It's all American."

The Ferris wheel slowed to a stop about then, with us at the top, and my lover met my eyes, his own brown no longer full of trickery, but deep and warm and true. "This has been the best year of my life," he breathed, as we hung there, the carnival dancing below us, the stars twinkling overhead.

"Of our life," I corrected. The ribbon cutting for the new *WZT Outdoor Adventures* store had been my favorite moment—especially when Pier's dad, resistant the whole time, had gotten teary-eyed and gripped his son's hand.

"You earned it," I said now to Piers.

He shook his head. "Rota Fortunae. I spun the wheel," he patted our seat, "and got lucky. After all, if I hadn't lost that silly bet to Kelly last year, and hadn't gotten a reading from you, we wouldn't be here now, right? ."

"I will concede that some luck was involved. But that luck simply showed you where you wanted to go. Like the reading I did. Getting there was your doing."

"Our doing," he corrected, pulling me close. "We're going to have a full moon in a few days. Go on a bike ride with me?"

"By the light of the Traveler's Moon? Of course. I wouldn't miss it. But aren't you scared," I asked as the wheel started up again, swinging us downward, "to go on a moonlit ride this close to Halloween? Past graveyards and scarecrows and hooting owls? With," I added, breathing into his ear, "a witchy woman like me?"

I felt him shiver. "Oh, yes," he breathed back. "Very scared. In a good way. In fact, I'd like it if you could scare me some more."

The wheel went around several times after that. We hardly noticed, as we were kissing again. Gazing into each other's eyes, too and laughing with delight.

Fin

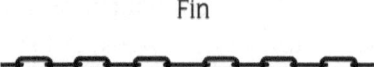

About the Author

Julian Keys is an award winning writer of erotic short stories and novels currently being published by Forbidden Fiction. Her works include *The Keys to Romance* anthology, a compilation of her most popular, romantic, heterosexual short stories like "Till Dawn" and "Pretty as a Picture." She has also written several gay male romantic tales like "Designated Driver," (recently reprinted in Forbidden Fiction's *Bring the Lover* anthology), and is also known for her *Fancy Man* short stories (gay male BDSM erotica), which were gathered together in the *Leather Wishes* anthology. She was the 2016 Rainbow Award winner for best LGBT Anthology.

Other Works by Julian Keys

'Till Dawn
A Fancy Man Holiday
A Special Occasion
Designated Driver
Down to the Bone
Exchange of Heart
Executive Benefits
Fancy Man and the Black Lion's Mark
Fancy Man and the Lipstick Lesbian
Fancy Man and the Southern Gentleman
Fancy Man and the Three Princes
Full Disclosure
Pretty as a Picture
Savory and Sweet
Valentine Prayers
Wicked Dreams

About the Publisher

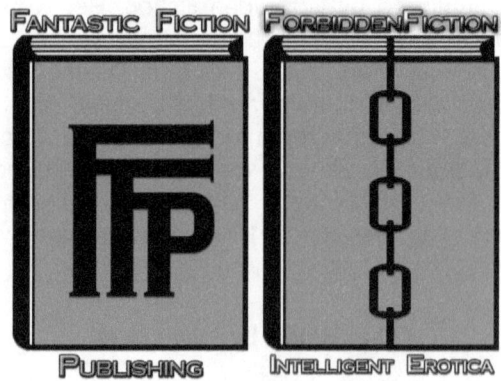

ForbiddenFiction.com is a publisher devoted to writing that breaks the boundaries of original erotic fiction. Our stories combine intense sexuality with quality writing. Stories at Forbidden Fiction.com not only arouse readers through sensations, but also engage them emotionally and mentally through storytelling as well-crafted as the sex is hot.

ForbiddenFiction.com is also designed to be a social reading environment. You'll have fun even if just reading the latest post each day, yet you will have the chance for so much more. Readers and authors can be part of ongoing discussions of specific works and individual authors as well as more general topics.

Sign up for a FREE Membership today at <u>ForbiddenFiction.com</u>

www.ingramcontent.com/pod-product-compliance
Lightning Source LLC
Chambersburg PA
CBHW020320260626
47156CB00004B/1312